# THE HEMLOCK FALLS MYSTERIES

1 pretty little tow...
1 picturesque inn o...
2 talented sisters...
than they a...
1 (or ...

## A WINNING RECIPE FOR MYSTERY LOVERS

*Don't miss these Hemlock Falls Mysteries . . .*

### GROUND TO A HALT . . .

Murder doesn't stop the Inn's pet food conventioneers from fighting like cats and dogs—but it does bring business to a grinding halt.

### A DINNER TO DIE FOR . . .

Less-than-friendly professional competition. A serious case of cold feet. And, oh yes, a local murder. Could things go worse on Meg's wedding day?

### BURIED BY BREAKFAST . . .

The leader of a raucous group of protestors turns up dead—and the Quilliams must quell fears and catch a killer before another local V.I.P. is greeted with an untimely R.I.P.

### A PUREE OF POISON . . .

While residents celebrate the 133rd anniversary of the Battle of Hemlock Falls, the Quilliam sisters investigate the deaths of three people who dined at the Inn before checking out.

### FRIED BY JURY . . .

Two rival fried chicken restaurants are about to set up shop in Hemlock Falls—and the Quilliams have to turn up the heat when the competition turns deadly.

*continued . . .*

### JUST DESSERTS ...
There's a meteorologist convention coming to the Inn, and it's up to Quill and Meg to make sure an elusive killer doesn't make murder part of the forecast.

### MARINADE FOR MURDER ...
The Quilliams' plans for the future of the Inn may end up on the cutting-room floor when a group of TV cartoon writers checks in—and the producer checks out.

### A STEAK IN MURDER ...
While trying to sell the locals on the idea of raising their own herds, a visiting Texas cattleman gets sent to that big trail drive in the sky. The Quilliams set out to catch the culprit and reclaim their precious Inn ... without getting stampeded themselves!

### A TOUCH OF THE GRAPE ...
Five women jewelry makers are a welcome change from the tourist slump the Inn is having. All that changes when two of the ladies end up dead, and the Quilliams are on the hunt for a crafty killer.

### DEATH DINES OUT ...
While working for a charity in Palm Beach, the Quilliam sisters uncover a vengeful plot that has a wealthy socialite out to humiliate her husband. Now the sleuths must convince the couple to bury the hatchet—before they bury each other.

## MURDER WELL-DONE...
When the Inn hosts the wedding rehearsal dinner for an ex-senator, someone begins cutting down the guest list in a deadly way. And Quill and Meg have to catch a killer before the rehearsal dinner ends up being someone's last meal.

## A PINCH OF POISON...
Hendrick Conway is a nosy newsman who thinks something funny is going on at a local development project. But when two of his relatives are killed, the Quilliam sisters race against a deadline of their own.

## A DASH OF DEATH...
Quill and Meg are on the trail of the murderer of two local women who won a design contest. Helena Houndswood, a noted expert on stylish living, was furious when she lost. But mad enough to kill?

## A TASTE FOR MURDER...
The annual History Days festival takes a deadly turn when a reenactment of a seventeenth-century witch trial leads to twentieth-century murder. Since the victim is a paying guest, the least Quill and Meg could do is investigate.

**Don't miss Claudia Bishop's
new veterinarian mystery series,
the Casebooks of Dr. McKenzie, including
*The Case of the Roasted Onion* and
*The Case of the Tough-Talking Turkey*!**

# A CAROL
# FOR A
# CORPSE

## CLAUDIA
## BISHOP

BERKLEY PRIME CRIME, NEW YORK

**THE BERKLEY PUBLISHING GROUP**
**Published by the Penguin Group**
**Penguin Group (USA) Inc.**
**375 Hudson Street, New York, New York 10014, USA**
Penguin Group (Canada), 90 Eglinton Avenue East, Suite 700, Toronto, Ontario M4P 2Y3, Canada
(a division of Pearson Penguin Canada Inc.)
Penguin Books Ltd., 80 Strand, London WC2R 0RL, England
Penguin Group Ireland, 25 St. Stephen's Green, Dublin 2, Ireland (a division of Penguin Books Ltd.)
Penguin Group (Australia), 250 Camberwell Road, Camberwell, Victoria 3124, Australia
(a division of Pearson Australia Group Pty. Ltd.)
Penguin Books India Pvt. Ltd., 11 Community Centre, Panchsheel Park, New Delhi—110 017, India
Penguin Group (NZ), 67 Apollo Drive, Rosedale, North Shore 0632, New Zealand
(a division of Pearson New Zealand Ltd.)
Penguin Books (South Africa) (Pty.) Ltd., 24 Sturdee Avenue, Rosebank, Johannesburg 2196,
South Africa

Penguin Books Ltd., Registered Offices: 80 Strand, London WC2R 0RL, England

This is a work of fiction. Names, characters, places, and incidents either are the product of the author's imagination or are used fictitiously, and any resemblance to actual persons, living or dead, business establishments, events, or locales is entirely coincidental. The publisher does not have any control over and does not assume any responsibility for author or third-party websites or their content.

PUBLISHER'S NOTE: The recipes contained in this book are to be followed exactly as written. The publisher is not responsible for your specific health or allergy needs that may require medical supervision. The publisher is not responsible for any adverse reactions to the recipes contained in this book.

A CAROL FOR A CORPSE

A Berkley Prime Crime Book / published by arrangement with the author

PRINTING HISTORY
Berkley Prime Crime mass-market edition / November 2007

Copyright © 2007 by Mary Stanton.
Cover art by Mary Ann Lasher.
Cover design by George Long.

ISBN: 978-0-425-21834-1

BERKLEY® PRIME CRIME
Berkley Prime Crime Books are published by The Berkley Publishing Group,
a division of Penguin Group (USA) Inc.,
375 Hudson Street, New York, New York 10014.
The name BERKLEY PRIME CRIME and the BERKLEY PRIME CRIME design are trademarks of
Penguin Group (USA) Inc.

PRINTED IN THE UNITED STATES OF AMERICA

10  9  8  7  6  5  4  3  2  1

For Julie

# CAST OF CHARACTERS

## AT THE INN AT HEMLOCK FALLS

| | |
|---|---|
| Sarah Quilliam-McHale | owner and manager |
| Margaret "Meg" Quilliam | her sister, owner, and master chef |
| Doreen Muxworthy-Stoker | head housekeeper |
| Dina Muir | receptionist |
| Mike Santini | head groundskeeper |
| Kathleen Kiddermeister | head waitress |
| Peter Hairston | sommelier |
| Elizabeth Chou | sous-chef |
| Mikhail Sulaiman | sous-chef |
| Melissa Smith | dishwasher, a GoodJobs! recruit |
| Zeke "the Hammer" Kingsfield | real estate mogul |
| Lydia Kingsfield | his wife, editor of *L'Aperitif* gourmet magazine |
| Albert "Scrooge" McWhirter | business consultant |
| Ajit Hadad | director of the TV show *Good Taste* |
| Bernie Armisted | makeup, costume design for *Good Taste* |
| Benny Pitt | set design for *Good Taste* |
| LaToya Franklin | assistant for *Good Taste* |
| Fred Sims | guest |
| Max | dog |

# RESIDENTS OF HEMLOCK FALLS

| | |
|---|---|
| Myles McHale | government investigator, former sheriff of Hemlock Falls |
| Davy Kiddermeister | sheriff |
| Jerry Grimsby | owner, master chef of Elise's restaurant |
| Elmer Henry | mayor |
| Adela Henry | mayor's wife |
| Dookie Shuttleworth | pastor, Hemlock Falls Church of the Word of God |
| Wendy Shuttleworth | pastor's wife |
| Marge Schmidt | businesswoman and board member of the bank |
| Carol Ann Spinoza | village tax assessor |
| Jinny Peterson | director, GoodJobs! employment service |
| Harland Peterson | president, the local Agway, and bank board member |
| Harvey Bozzel | president, Bozzel Advertising |
| Mark Anthony Jefferson | president, Hemlock Falls First National Bank |
| Charley Comstock | president, board of directors of the bank and insurance agent |
| Will Frazier | manager, Gorgeous Gorges trailer park |

And other members of the Hemlock Falls Chamber of Commerce

# PROLOGUE

*There had to be some way to kill him.*
*And it had to be soon.*

Everyone was gone. The meeting room still held a faintly congratulatory air, enhanced by the professionally decorated Christmas tree standing to the right of the wet bar. Two empty bottles of Moët et Chandon lay abandoned at the coffee station, jammed onto the plate of pâté, caviar, and the remains of soft French cheeses. The C-SPAN people had left an orange extension cord coiled under the windows overlooking Times Square.

*He'll be back in here in just a few minutes, full of himself. Crowing like a rooster. I could wind the cord around his neck from behind. Jerk it tight. Hold on for a sweet, sweet eternity until . . . no. That's stupid. You can't be anywhere near him when it happens.*

A brightly colored array of advertising brochures sprawled across the conference table, all that was left after the contracts had been signed, sealed, and notarized, the copies initialed, the files tucked away into the lawyers' briefcases.

# Claudia Bishop

The brochure read:

## PARADISE FOUND!
## THE INN AT HEMLOCK FALLS

The headline overprinted one of Sarah Quilliam's elegant paintings of the Inn in summer. The huge old mansion was centered in the middle of a velvet-green lawn, and surrounded by gardens blazing with roses. The grounds swept down to Hemlock Gorge, where the waterfall cascaded into the river. Quill's artistry was as vivid as ever. You could practically hear the rush of water. They needed a brochure for the winter months, too. Somebody would have to get on that.

*If the gorge is as steep as it looks—I could push him right over the top. He'd bounce all the way to the bottom.*

"What the hell are you grinning about?" Zeke Kingsfield blew into the conference room like the sickest of ill winds blowing absolutely nobody any good.

*Keep it mild. Keep it humble. Most of all, keep it sweet.* "Just happy with what's ahead. All of us at the magazine are." *A little smarm couldn't hurt.* "Another brilliant deal, Zeke. Really. Brilliant."

Kingsfield swelled like a pig bladder. "The crap with the Inn, you mean? Sure. Fine. Whatever. Just as long as that chef . . . what's her name?"

"Margaret Quilliam, Meg."

"Yeah. Her. Just as long as she keeps a lid on it." Zeke's eyes narrowed and his thin lips got even thinner. "If she doesn't?" Zeke shrugged. "She'll rue the day. I can tell you that. They don't call me the Hammer 'cause I play the drums. I'm in absolute control of the Inn deal. It's the trailer park deal that better work."

"If you don't mind my saying so, *that's* the deal that's going to catch the nation's eye."

Zeke smirked. Then he scowled and said, "And if I find

one word of *that* sucker's been leaked in Hemlock Falls, there'll be hell to pay. You can count on it."

"Everything's going to be fine, Zeke."

"It'd better be." He shot his cuffs and looked at his diamond-encrusted Rolex. "We've got the jet booked for tomorrow at noon. Add my skis to the list of stuff I'm taking with me. There is a ski run in this godforsaken village, isn't there?"

There was an insert in the most elaborate of the brochures. "They've just completed two new cross-country runs. According to this."

"'Kay. So get a move on. I'm taping that interview with Charley Rose in twenty minutes. And for God's sake, get this pit of a room cleaned up." He snapped the edge of the cheese tray with an irritable thumb and slammed out of the room. The tray teetered, then tipped and spilled its contents onto the monogrammed rug, obliterating a handful of Zeke's initials.

*There had to be a way to kill him.*

*And it had to be soon.*

# CHAPTER 1

"You're telling me if I don't sign this thing, we're going to lose the Inn?" Meg Quilliam sat directly opposite Mark Anthony Jefferson. Mark was president of the First National Bank of Hemlock Falls. The same bank that held a half-million-dollar past-due mortgage on the Inn at Hemlock Falls.

Not to mention an additional half-million-dollar line of credit. Also past due.

"Losing the Inn would be one outcome, yes," Mark Anthony Jefferson admitted.

Meg narrowed her eyes in a lethal squint, slammed both small fists onto the Mark's desk, and shouted, "And a *merry flippin' Christmas* to you, too!"

Sarah Quilliam ran one hand through her hair and wished, not for the first time during this meeting, that her little sister would just shut up. "Meg," she said as patiently as she could through gritted teeth. "Mark isn't saying anything of the kind." She added, under her breath, "I knew you wouldn't understand what's happening here. I just knew it."

Meg made a sound like a teakettle on the boil.

Quill bit her lip. If there was anything Meg hated more than a meeting about their mortgage, it was a condescending sister. "I didn't mean that the way it sounded," Quill amended hastily. "I'm sorry. I'm really, really sorry."

Meg folded her arms across her chest and asked coldly, "How *did* you mean it?"

Quill cleared her throat nervously, but she met her sister's eyes with her chin up. "Well, if you weren't such a drama queen, I could have prepared you for this."

"Me! Me the drama queen! As if this whole bankruptcy thing has just dropped on us out of the blue. You've known about this for months." Meg sank back into her chair and drummed her fingertips furiously on the chair arm. "And you waited until now to tell me. Right before Christmas, naturally. Perfect timing, sis."

"I wanted to be sure Kingsfield made us a real offer. An offer we can live with. An offer that will let us keep the baby *and* the bathwater." Quill made a face and added lamely, "So to speak."

Meg growled.

Mark Anthony Jefferson shifted uneasily in his large red leather chair. Someone—perhaps Clarice, Mark's chic and stylish wife—had piled a pyramid of blue and silver Christmas balls next to the inkstand. Quill thought about moving the ornaments out of Meg's reach. The eight-inch sauté pans in Meg's kitchen at the Inn were her sister's missiles of choice, but the ornaments would do in a pinch.

Mark looked at them both sympathetically. "It's been a rough year for a lot of small businesses, ladies."

"I don't get it," Meg said. "We've survived tough times before. Why is this different?"

Quill ran her hands through her hair, which was thick, red, and wildly springy. "I wish I knew. I'm the one that writes the checks. I'm the one that books the guests. If anyone knows anything about why we aren't getting more trade,

I should. But, Meg, as far as I can tell, there just isn't any business! There hasn't been for the last six months!"

"Come to think of it," Meg mused, "we did go under once before. We got fed up with trying to run the place a few years ago. We sold it to Marge Schmidt, remember? But then we bought it back again and things were just fine. So what makes this time different?"

"The new resort down the river has made a great deal of difference in the town's economy," Mark said.

"It's made a big difference to us, that's certain," Quill said gloomily. "They're very white linen"—she interrupted herself at Mark's questioning look—"their restaurant's very upscale, and that's direct competition for us. And they rotate their celebrity chefs. That's a huge draw. Plus, they have an indoor swimming pool."

"We had Mike the groundskeeper put in a cross-country ski trail around our property," Meg said. "That's helped."

"Except they use our ski trails and stay at the River Resort," Quill said wryly—"There *are* more people coming to visit Hemlock Falls. They just aren't coming to stay with us." She put her hand to her throat.

"You okay?" Meg asked.

"Just a little queasiness," Quill said. "On top of everything else, I'm probably coming down with the flu." She took a deep breath. It seemed to help. "Mark, I hope you don't think I've just been sitting around on my hands waiting for the bank to call the loan. I did a painting for our new brochure. Harvey's put ads in the *New York Times*. I've invited a billion travel agents to come and scope us out. And there certainly seems to be more people around than ever before. They just aren't staying with us."

"The town's growing," Mark said in satisfaction. "The past few years have been very good for the town. We're located in one of the most beautiful parts of the country. And people are discovering us." He beamed at them. "Harvey's making up new ads for the Chamber of Commerce. Did you hear about those? Hemlock Falls is becoming a vacation destination."

"Phooey," Meg said rudely. "I don't see what's good about more traffic and higher real estate prices. And you know what happens when you get tons of people moving in—more crime, that's what. It puts a huge burden on town services, too."

"Growth's not all beer and skittles," Mark admitted. "You two hear about the vandalism?"

"If you're talking about the punctured inflatable Santa Clauses on the courthouse lawn, I hardly think that rises to the description of vandalism," Quill said glumly. "And we're losing sight of why we're sitting here. We're sitting here so that Meg can sign Kingsfield's leasing agreement and I can stop having nightmares about losing everything we've worked for all these years."

"So, the economy's been good for everyone except us," Meg said bluntly. "Why?"

Quill shook her head. "I haven't the foggiest idea."

"You've talked to John Raintree?" Mark asked in a kindly way. John had been their business manager in palmier days.

"Of course I have. He says that boutique businesses like ours can be victims of faddism."

"Faddism," Meg repeated.

Quill threw her arms up in the air. "He meant that we're not the trendy thing to do anymore. He thinks we need to reinvent ourselves. And that's what this deal with Kingsfield is going to do. Help us reinvent ourselves."

"Oh, fine," Meg said sarcastically. "We're over the hill at what—you're thirty-six? And me at thirty-two?"

Quill sighed. It felt as if the sigh came from the soles of her feet. "I tried to tell you what was going on, Meg, but did you want to hear about it? No, you didn't."

"That's not fair," Meg said.

Quill bit her lip. "No," she said after a moment. "It isn't fair. And I didn't tell you as much as I should have about the financial problems because you get so upset." She blinked back a rush of tears. "Sorry. The stress is definitely getting to me. Weepiness isn't like me at all. Anyhow, you're the star attraction at the Inn, Meg. It's best that you're left alone to do what you do best. The money stuff is my job."

"That's fair," Meg admitted with what would have been sublime egotism if it hadn't been true. She *was* the best chef around for three hundred miles and one of the five best in the entire state of New York. She reached over and briefly clasped Quill's hand. "I'm sorry I yelled 'Merry flippin' Christmas' at Mark. It's not his fault. And I'm sorry I shouted at you, too. Well, pretty sorry."

Quill took a deep, affronted breath.

Mark rapped the surface of his desk with a gentle thump of his knuckles. "Ladies," he said. "May we get back to whether or not Meg is going to sign this contract?"

"No," Meg said promptly, "I'm not."

Mark was unperturbed with this obduracy. "You haven't looked at the considerable advantages of the Kingsfield offer. You're looking at a splendid opportunity."

"We are, huh?" Meg said sulkily.

Very few people other than Quill knew that this meant Meg was ready to be reasonable. But Mark was president of the largest bank in Hemlock Falls because he was a genius at picking up cues. He smiled at Meg and it was the smile of a man with the answers. A man with faith in the sisters' ability to pull the Inn out of its slump and keep the business out of foreclosure.

"A splendid opportunity," Quill repeated. "See, Meg?"

"That's because *he* doesn't have to put up with Lydia Kingsfield," Meg said flatly. "I can't believe you guys are asking me to do this."

Mark raised one eyebrow in Quill's direction.

"Lydia's editor of *L'Aperitif*," Quill explained. "Kingsfield Publishing's made the offer to lease the Inn to the magazine, but Lydia's the person that thinks the Inn offers the best background for the magazine's new TV show. She's the one that made the decision to offer this lease to us."

"And she's the one who's going to be up my nose," Meg interrupted. "Every flippin' second!"

"Of course I know who she is, now that you mention it," Mark said with an air of surprise. "Clarice has a subscription to *L'Aperitif*. I looked at the current issue before I met with you two today. She writes that 'From My Desk to Yours' feature, right? She seems a very pleasant person, in print."

Meg made a rude noise.

"We know her, actually," Quill said. "I mean, not because of the magazine. Kingsfield bought the whole thing a few months ago, and a lot of the editorial staff left to work other places. Before the buyout, all our contacts with *L'Aperitif* were with the old editor, Lally Preston. Lally's reviewers gave Meg her three-star rating a few years back. But Lally retired when the magazine was sold, or at least, that's what the news releases said. And Lydia took over as editor. She's made some interesting design changes in the magazine. Anyway, that's not why we know Lydia. We know Lydia from school."

Mark raised the other eyebrow.

"High school," Meg grumbled. "In Connecticut. She was a stuck-up pill back then and I'll bet she's a stuck-up pill now. You know how she made head cheerleader?"

"Meg!" Quill said.

"Bribed the head coach. It's true. Lydia's father made a ton of money as an arba-whatsis on Wall Street. Bought her everything she ever wanted, including being head cheerleader."

"Hm," Mark said.

"And do you know what Lydia got as a sixteenth birthday present? A brand-new BMW. I suppose that doesn't mean much to you guys now, but back then, that car was hot." Meg folded her arms. "Not to mention an unlimited charge card at Saks Fifth Avenue."

"Is that a fact," Mark said. Then, for good measure, "Mm-hm."

"Oh, for Pete's sake, Meg," Quill said in exasperation. "Lydia's changed a lot, since then. We've all changed a lot since then. We've had some terrific talks on the phone."

"Phooey," Meg exploded. "It's a question of character. She's married to Zeke Kingsfield, the biggest business shark in the United States of America. Did you see that *60 Minutes* piece of the two of them? They're joined at the hip. Devoted to each other and power mad, to boot. Like Anthony and Cleopatra before the Romans showed up to sink the ships at Actium. This is a woman who thinks people can be bought. And she's married to a man who's happy to write the checks. Up until now, there's been no stopping the two of them." She pursed her lips and gazed thoughtfully at Mark. "You know about Kingsfield, don't you, Mark? They call him the Hammer of Wall Street. Mean as a pit bull and just as likely to let me loose to do my own thing. Now, you just think about how happy *you'd* be if good ol' Zeke made an offer to buy your bank and you had *him* looking over your shoulder every five minutes."

Mark seemed somewhat discomposed at the thought.

"Now, Meg," Quill said.

"*And* nosing around your safe-deposit boxes, or whatever . . ."

"Meg!"

". . . and bossing your tellers!" Meg sat back with an air of satisfaction. "You think you'd like that, Mark? Huh?"

Mark coughed into his hand.

"All I can say is, you wouldn't like it any more than I'd like Zeke's evil twin buzzing around my kitchen. Lydia is a woman," Meg said darkly, "who ought to be purely ashamed of herself. And please don't laugh at me," she added crossly.

Mark folded his hands on his desk. "Laughing at you is the farthest thing from my mind. I want you to take a realistic look at the problem. What we have here is a default situation."

"You mean we haven't paid the mortgage for three months," Meg accused him. "Default situation, my foot. We're welshers. And you're going to call our loan and sell us out to the Demon Couple of Wall Street. *Just like Snidely Whiplash*."

Mark let this roll over him without a flinch. "Let me lay out a couple of options."

Meg brightened. "Options? You mean we don't have to sell the Inn to Loathsome Lydia?"

"Meg!" Quill'd had enough. "We are *not selling* the Inn to Loath . . . I mean Kingsfield Publishing. We are leasing certain rights to them. In return for a pile of money that will keep us"—despite her best efforts, Quill felt her voice rising to a shriek—"out of foreclosure!"

"I don't want that woman in my kitchen."

"Does she actually have to *be* in your kitchen?" Mark asked a little desperately. "Surely she's not moving in with you."

"Not year-round, no," Quill said. "As you can see from the contract"—she gestured at the two-inch-thick folder in front of the banker—"they are purchasing the right to use the Inn at Hemlock Falls name on a line of chutneys, jams, and jellies. Meg agrees to provide the original recipes, and this agreement stipulates that she comes up with at least two new products a year for the duration of the lease. Somebody from Kingsfield Publishing needs to be around when Meg is testing stuff in the kitchen, that's all. And it doesn't have to be Lydia. Necessarily.

"The other part of the lease is the right to use the Inn as the set of this new TV show *Good Taste* four times a year."

"I did mention that to Clarice," Mark said. "She was thrilled about the show being shot here."

"Four shows out of the season's twenty-seven," Quill said. "But Lydia's the host and at that point, yes, she *does* have to be in Meg's kitchen. For a week or so at a time."

"Hah," Meg said. "And what about the fact that the

11

Provençal Suite will be turned over to them for their permanent use?"

"They're paying for the room, all year, Meg, that's true, but this is a couple that has a town house in London, a huge apartment on Central Park West, and a whole darn island in Bermuda. They just want to keep their personal stuff here so they don't need to haul a huge amount of luggage around."

"They'll like it here better than all those places," Meg said tragically. "And we'll *never* be rid of them."

Quill got up and walked restlessly around the room. Mark's credenza held a stack of *Inc.* magazines, three golf trophies, and a ceramic Christmas tree that lit up from within. She picked up the Christmas tree and set it down again. "Meg, when I talked with you about the jams and jellies thing, you thought it was a great idea."

"True."

"And when I talked with you about *L'Aperitif* shooting the *Good Taste* show here, you thought that was a good idea, too."

"You didn't say we'd have to sign our life away to do it. You didn't tell me it was a ten-year lease!"

"No." Quill went back to her chair and sat. "No, I skipped over that part. But I'm telling you now. And I'm telling you why. And I *really* need you to make up your mind, Meg, because if you refuse to sign, I've got to call New York and cancel everything. Lydia and the crew are planning on getting in here tomorrow afternoon to set up for their Christmas show, so just *please* get a grip, Meg, and give me some help here. I mean, how bad can it be?"

Meg folded her lips together. She closed her eyes. She sat back in her chair and took several deep breaths. "Okay," she said to Mark. "What are the other options?"

Mark said with admirable calm, "They are less appealing, to my mind at least. You haven't been able to make a mortgage payment for three months. Technically, that allows us to begin foreclosure."

The word dropped into the room and sank like a stone in a pond.

"You padlock the door shut in a foreclosure," Meg said. "That's what happened to Peterson's Automotive and Water Softeners when George went bust. I remember. Padlocks."

"I hardly think padlocks will be necessary," Mark said in a kindly way. "No bank is ever anxious to foreclose. We'd have to run the Inn—and what do we know about running an inn? Ha ha ha."

Meg and Quill stared back at him.

"So. Foreclosure is a last-ditch option. A far better option would be to sell the Inn outright. Now, of course, that will take some time, to find a qualified buyer. Or even someone who is interested at all."

"There's a third option," Meg said. "You could lend us some more money."

Mark shook his head. "I really don't think so. There's the other matter of your line of credit. Between the money owed on the line of credit, the amount of your personal assets, and the mortgage arrears, you aren't a real good credit risk for us, frankly. If it'd been up to me—well, maybe I would have agreed to extend the credit line a little bit more. But I took this one to the board of directors. They said no."

"The board of directors doesn't want to lend us any more money?" Meg said indignantly. "Well, thank them very much for me, will you? When I think of the free food I've given those people, I could just spit." She slumped back in her chair. "I just don't get it. Harland Peterson's on the board. He's been a friend of ours for ages. Marge Schmidt is on the board and she's—" She interrupted herself. "Well, sometimes Marge is a friend, and sometimes she's more of a competitor, but she's always there to give us a hand if we need it. I can't believe they wouldn't extend the loan."

"I'm your friend, too, Meg," Mark said. "And I certainly can't recommend it, as much as I would like to. As a matter of fact, there's one more issue I'm going to have to bring up."

"Oh?" Quill said feebly. "Something else?"

"It's not the end of the world," Mark said reassuringly. "Let's get this contract out of the way, first. Now. Assuming that Meg agrees to license the Inn name and premises to Kingsfield Publishing?" He paused interrogatively.

"Ugh," Meg muttered. She drew a deep breath. "Sure. Fine. I'll do it. We don't have any choice. I see that. I see that quite clearly. I'm not even mad about it anymore."

"You aren't?" Quill said.

"No." She glanced at Quill, and then away again. "This has been hard on you, sis. I know that. It's just . . ."

Quill bit her lip and nodded. "Yes," she said. "It's not just ours anymore. We're going to have to share a lot of the decision making. But honestly, I've talked this over with John."

Mark nodded. "I was sorry to see him leave for larger pastures. But he's doing well in his business in New York, I hear."

"He's making billions," Meg said. "And he and Tricia are pregnant." She sat up, her face brightening. "Quill! What if we asked John for a loan? Did you try that?"

"No," Quill said. "I didn't ask. What's more important, Meg, is that he didn't offer. Anyhow, Mark, I've discussed this with Myles, of course, and Marge, as well as John. I think we've made the only possible decision here."

"And it's a wise move." Mark gave a small sigh of relief and rose from his chair. "If you'll just wait for a moment, I'll call our notary in, and we'll get the signatures witnessed." He smiled warmly. "You're in luck. Charley Comstock's in the bank, and he's a notary. If you'll excuse me?"

He went out the door, his step considerably lighter than when he had come in to meet them.

"Who's Charley Comstock when he's at home?" Meg asked.

"Our insurance broker. And president of the board of directors of the bank." Quill breathed a little easier. Her stomach was settling down. "You've met him before. Marge sold him part of her insurance agency last year."

"If I did meet him, I don't remember."

Meg shoved her chair away from the desk, put her elbows on her knees, and stared at her feet. Quill didn't know what she was thinking. The color of Meg's socks was a pretty good indicator of her mood but the weather was snowy outside and she was wearing boots. "Black," she said, following Quill's gaze. "In case you were wondering."

They both turned around as the door opened. Mark ushered Charley in. He was of medium height, compact, and at least ten years older than Quill, who at thirty-six was beginning to wonder about age-related things like hitting forty. Not to mention children, and the advisability of changing to a less stressful career. Like air traffic controller.

"Girls," Charley said genially, as he settled onto Mark's leather sofa. "It's good to see you. Especially under these circumstances. It's a red-letter day for the Inn!"

Meg stared up at him from lowered brows. "Girls?" she asked with lethal politeness. "I know haven't met this guy before, Quill. I would have remembered anyone who called us girls."

Quill kicked her ankle and mouthed, "Let it go."

"I think I've just about had it with letting stuff go."

"Pardon me?" Charley said amiably. "Did I miss something?"

Mark raised his voice a little, perhaps to forestall another explosion from Meg. "Things are going to get a lot better from here on in, you two." He pulled the stack of contracts into position and took out a pen. "Okay. Let's get this rolling."

Quill had to hand it to her sister. Meg didn't hold a grudge. She signed and initialed page after page with a composed air and didn't bite Charley Comstock's finger off when he pinched her cheek in farewell. "You girls are making the right decision, here," he said. "Big things are coming to Hemlock Falls. This is just the thin edge of the wedge."

Quill, who was staring with enormous relief at the substantial check Kingsfield Publishing had issued as a down payment on the lease, acknowledged this with an absentminded nod.

"And the expansion's not just due to business drawn in by the resort," Charley went on, perhaps to attract her attention. "Big things are about to happen in Hemlock Falls."

"Big things like what?" Meg demanded.

"I can't say too much about it, not that I want to keep you in the dark," Charley said. He laid a finger on the side of his nose and nodded wisely. "I can tell you this. We've had a very large depositor join our customer base recently."

Mark cleared his throat in warning. "Bank business should really remain confidential, Charley."

"Ah, don't be an old lady, Mark. It'll be out soon enough. Anyways, Quill, it's definitely a commercial operation. We just aren't sure what's going to happen with it. But it's bound to be big. Really big. So big that it's bound to give that failing business of yours a big kick in the pants." He chuckled. "A good kind of kick, of course."

Mark put his hand on Charley's shoulder. "You'll be wanting to get to your next appointment, Charles."

Charley wriggled. "Yeah. Well. Anyways. Mark? You'll talk to them about the other matter? The board's decision? And by the way, Quill, we need to sit down next week. I'm afraid we're looking at a bit of a premium hike next year. And we'll want to increase your fine arts policy. I saw in the *Wall Street Journal* that one of your acrylics went for twenty thousand dollars at auction."

This put a dent in Quill's good humor. She'd sold those paintings of hers that she'd wanted to sell and she was keeping the ones she wanted to keep. It was only when they belonged to someone else that they commanded amazing prices. Maybe she should retire from innkeeping and paint full-time again.

"I'll be in touch, girls! Don't do anything I wouldn't do."

Charley shut the door with a slam. Meg made a pistol out of her thumb and forefinger and cocked it. Then she aimed it at the closed door and said, "Pow."

"He means well," Mark said. "I think. Anyway—congratulations, ladies." He shook hands with each of them and handed Quill two copies of the contract.

Quill exhaled in relief. She hadn't realized she was so tense. She clasped Mark's hand warmly between her own. "You've been wonderful."

"All part of the job."

Quill moved to get up. Mark said, "There's just one other thing."

Quill sat back in her chair. "What other thing?"

Mark took a deep breath. "The money that you'll receive from Kingsfield is going to cover a good portion of your operating expenses from here on in. That's good."

"But?" Quill said.

"But we, that is, the bank and our board of directors, are concerned about your ability to pay back your line of credit, which is currently . . ." He leaned forward, shuffled though the pile of papers on his desk, and read aloud: "Five hundred four thousand twenty-two dollars and fifty-six cents."

There was a long, heavy silence.

"We've just been through our annual audit," Mark said. "The bank, that is, and the OCC is a little concerned about our loan-to-deposit ratio."

"Oh, dear," Quill said, in what she hoped was a sympathetic way. Then, "What's the OCC?"

"The Office of the Comptroller of the Currency."

Quill blinked in confusion.

"That's the feds," Mark explained. "It's that part of the government that makes sure banks are on the up-and-up. Part of Treasury."

"And a good thing, too," Quill said heartily. "But what does that have to do with us?"

"The OCC is a little concerned about the extent of our

liability." Mark sighed. "To make it short, the board wants a consultant on site."

"A consultant?" Quill said. "What kind of a consultant?"

"Think of it as an IRS audit," Mark said affably. "It's along those lines."

"An IRS audit?"

"It doesn't have a thing to do with taxes," Mark said in a reassuring way, "although, I must admit, tax issues arise with more frequency than one would like . . . never mind. I misspoke. Forget the IRS analogy. The consultant will be more like a business auditor."

"An auditor?" Quill frowned.

"Yes. He'll take a look at the way the Inn is run."

Quill felt herself flush. "You mean, at the way *I'm* handling things?"

"Well, yes," Mark admitted. "At the way you're handling things. The OCC comes in and takes a look at the bank every year in the same way." He scowled and said to himself, "And aren't they a bunch of troublemakers." He growled a little. "Never mind, forget I said that, too. He'll spend a few days at the Inn observing how you two are getting on. That's all." He sat back and beamed at them.

"You mean poking his nose into things?" Meg said. "Like Quill's office?"

"Like everywhere," Mark said ruefully. "The consultant basically has free rein. At any rate, the consultant will come up with a list of recommended actions. And we'd be grateful if you'd take his recommendations to heart."

"You mean you want some guy to poke around in my Inn and then tell me what to do?" Quill said indignantly.

"I'm afraid we're going to have to insist on it. Now, the fellow we've recruited has an excellent reputation, and his fees are pretty reasonable. Considering."

"Fees?" Quill said.

"Well, yes. I'm afraid he doesn't work for free. But you'll

more than make up his costs in the money he's going to save you."

"You mean *we* have to pay him? Now, look here, Mark . . . ow!" She glared at Meg. "What was that kick for?"

Meg gave Quill her sunniest smile. "What was that you said? How bad can it be having Loathsome Lydia tramping all over my kitchen? So how bad can it be having this nice old busybody tramping through your files?"

"Oh," Quill said.

Then, "Well, fine."

Then, "Whatever."

Then, because her queasiness was back, "Phooey."

# CHAPTER 2

"I still think you could have said something to me before all this blew up in our faces." Meg picked a bronze angel from its nest of tissue in the ornament box and held it up. One of the gauzy wings was crumpled. She straightened it out with a slight frown and cupped it in the palm of her hand. Quill was perched cheerfully on a ladder inside the windows. They were both finishing the holiday decorations begun the week before.

They were in the dining room of the Inn at Hemlock Falls. Outside the floor-to-ceiling windows, a long expanse of snow-laden lawn stretched to the gorge. The nine a.m. meeting with Mark Jefferson had only seemed to take hours; it was just after ten o'clock and the sun shone molten gold on the waterfall tumbling over the lip of the gorge.

"It didn't blow up in our faces, that's the point. Disaster has been averted. It's a terrific deal. The Inn's saved, Meg! What better Christmas present could we give each other than that? And you *did* know the bare bones of the deal. I told you I was going to call Lydia and talk to her. But you said, and I quote directly, 'If you don't leave me alone about this stuff, I'm going to go on strike.' You threatened that more than once."

Meg tugged absently at her hair. Like their Welsh father, she had gray eyes, pale, translucent skin, and hair as dark as a crow's wing. Quill's red hair and hazel eyes came from their mother. They didn't resemble one another at all, Quill thought, looking down affectionately at her. "What are you thinking?"

"That every time you did talk to me about this, it was in the kitchen. Usually in the middle of the dinner hour. You know how I get during dinner hour. You just didn't want the hassle."

Quill decided not to comment on that. She reached down for the angel and then tucked it among the pine boughs draped over the lintel. "There. How does it look?"

Below her, Meg peered up with a critical eye. "Move it to the left a bit. Now up about four inches. Good." She smiled. "Perfect."

"That's the last of it, then." Quill climbed down and together they gazed at the results.

Quill always greeted the approach of the holidays with a mixture of feelings compounded of hope, joy, and a glum anxiety. This year, anxiety had predominated, and she'd thrown herself into the task of decorating the Inn for the holidays wondering if it would be the last time. Every year was a challenge. This year seemed worse. The financial crisis only served to make the Christmas decorations an insurmountable hassle. And, although she tried to come up with new ways to decorate, there was only so much you could do with lights, tinsel, pine boughs, and ornaments.

Meg put her arm around her waist. "You've outdone yourself, Quillie."

"Not too bad, is it?" She'd taken eight-inch square blocks of rigid foam and turned them into red-and-gold houses, sleighs, churches, mosques, ships, camels, donkeys, sheep—anything she could think of with the remotest connection to the holidays. With the aid of a scalpel, a glue gun, and a ton of ribbon, glitter, fake jewels, and velvet, the figures stopped those who saw them for the first time in their tracks. "Our biggest problem is always the scale of things. We need big stuff. So I made big stuff."

The proportions of the Inn did require outsized decorations. The building had stood on the lip of Hemlock Gorge in one form or another for three hundred years and more. Originally a wayfaring stop for trappers headed north for furs, the original forty-by-forty-foot structure had grown to twenty-seven guest rooms occupying forty thousand square feet. The ceilings in the ground-floor rooms were over eighteen feet high. This grandeur swallowed up conventionally sized ornaments.

Every year, they put up the most luxuriant fifteen-foot pine trees they could find in the dining room, Tavern Lounge, and foyer. They hung wreaths in the mullioned windows, draped the stair rails and ceilings with pine boughs, and twined holly and mistletoe over the doorways. At night the Christmas lights cast rainbows of color into the shadowy corners of the elegant old building. The air was laden with forest scents. The effect was magical, a fantastically hued holiday universe that kept the world with its defaulting mortgages at bay.

"And a good thing, too," Quill murmured.

"What?"

"Christmas. Chanukah. Eid. All those middle-of-the-winter holidays that say there's hope ahead! Think how glum life would be if we didn't have the holidays to look forward to once a year."

"You sound like that repellently cheerful Tiny Tim," Meg said. Her mood, always volatile, had clearly taken a downward plunge. "Do you really think that Loathsome Lydia is going to bring us holiday cheer? Phooey. You'd better think again. I understand we didn't have any choice, Quill. But we're going to celebrate Christmas with a bunch of nosy, bossy, interfering strangers."

Quill, giddy with relief that the contract was signed and the substantial check deposited, didn't remind Meg that as innkeepers, their job was to host strangers. And she didn't ask her sister if she had nothing better to do than drive her crazy with mood swings, either. Which was, she reflected, quite noble of her. But she did give Meg the Look.

Meg made a face at her. Then, since she didn't wear a watch, she grabbed Quill's wrist and squinted at the time. "I've got a shipment of fruit due any minute now. It's okay if I go back to the kitchen?"

"What are you checking with me for?" Quill asked indignantly.

"Practicing. I'm practicing asking permission. How am I doing so far?"

"On the knuckle-sandwich scale? You're at about five hundred. Any higher and ka-pow." Quill made a fist.

Meg made a rude noise in return and marched through the swinging doors to the kitchen like a one-woman SWAT team.

"So she went ahead and signed it?"

Quill turned to see Dina crossing the dining room. Their receptionist carried a fistful of pink messages. "Hey, Dina. Yep. And the check is in the bank."

"That's terrific." Dina looked up at the garlands draped over the windows. "You finished them! Looks great. And you look a lot better, too. So was there a mighty battle?"

"There was a mighty resistance," Quill admitted, "but I wouldn't go so far as to call it a battle. For one thing, she didn't throw stuff."

"So we won't have to close, after all," Dina said. "It'd have been horrible if we'd been kicked out of the Inn just before Christmas. Like the Little Match Girl."

Dina was slight, with a fall of brown hair, a creamy complexion, and a pair of owlish spectacles with bright red rims. She was in the final year of her doctorate in limnology at nearby Cornell University, and unless it flourished in pond algae, she had a fuzzy grasp of realities. "We were in no

23

danger of being kicked out into the snow," Quill said sooth-
ingly. "But I was thinking seriously about cutting your pay."

"No kidding?" Dina nudged her glasses farther up her
nose with a forefinger. "You are kidding. Funny." She waved
the pink message slips. "There's a couple of messages you
might want to return right away. And somebody named
LaToya Franklin called to confirm that the Kingsfield group
is coming in tomorrow. I let Doreen know so housekeeping
could be sure and get the rooms ready. And I let Kathleen
know, so she can get some more of the waitstaff in here."

"Thank you, Dina. That's good work."

"And the Golden Pillar people called and made reservations for two people for the rest of the week. Two *separate*
people."

"Things are looking up," Quill said a little dryly. That
made two more reservations on top of the four rooms set
aside for the Kingsfield group. "Now if we just had twenty-
one more guest rooms rented, we'd be in terrific shape."

"Things are going to get a lot better now that the TV
show's coming here," Dina said confidently. "Now, you had
four phone calls while you were out." She thumbed through
the pink slips and began to hand them over one at a time.
"Sheriff McHale called. He's definitely maybe going to be
home for Christmas."

Quill sighed. She'd long ago given up reminding Hemlockians that her husband hadn't been sheriff for several
years now, but instead was an investigator for an interna-
tional security agency.

"And there's one from the mayor reminding you about the
Chamber meeting this morning."

Seeing that Dina was going to read every single one of
the messages before she handed them over, Quill turned and
headed through the dining room to her office beyond the
foyer, Dina at her side.

"John Raintree called." Dina gave her a meaningful glance.
"It's about how the meeting with Mark Anthony Jefferson

went, I expect. How did it go? About the line of credit, I mean? I know the mortgage is okay because of the Kingsfield check."

Quill looked at her blankly. For a brief period, she'd forgotten all about the consultant who was coming in to fix the incursions into their line of credit. "We aren't in default anymore with anything. But there is a sort of annoyance we're going to have to put up with for a while." She hesitated. She really needed John's take on the whole idea of the interfering consultant before she talked to any of the staff. But before she talked to John, she wanted to talk to Marge about why a member in good standing of the bank's board of directors hadn't given her notice of this particular cloud on the horizon. And the board had gone along and picked somebody without so much as a by-your-leave. "I'll get back to John later this afternoon. He'll want to go through the whole meeting. With the Chamber meeting coming up, I won't have enough time to go over things thoroughly." John had been the Inn's business manager for their first five years. Quill had wondered more than once if he could have kept them out of the current mess. He said not. Quill didn't believe him.

"And Mrs. Schmidt wants you to call her."

Quill stopped so abruptly Dina caromed into her. "Now Marge *is* somebody I want to talk to right this minute. I can't believe she didn't warn me about this person from the bank."

Dina blinked at her. "What person?"

"Mark says the bank wants some assurances that we're running things as well as possible. That I'm running things well, actually. And Marge knew Mark was going to spring that on me, and she didn't say a word. It would have been nice to know ahead of time."

"Know what ahead of time?"

Quill picked up her pace and crossed into the foyer, stopping briefly to replace a fallen angel in its assigned spot among the pine boughs in the oriental urns flanking the reception desk. She tucked the ornament in and went into her office, Dina at her heels. She sat down at her desk.

"The bank's sending in someone to take a look at the way we're running things. At the way I'm running things, to be specific."

Dina made a face. "So, like, who is it?"

"I don't know."

"And what kind of stuff is this person going to do?"

"I don't know, Dina."

"So what are *you* going to do about this examiner person?"

"Hit him with a stick," Quill said glumly. "Never mind." She held her hand out for the slips. "Nothing. I agreed to it. I didn't have a lot of choice. So I'm not doing a thing."

"Then why—"

"Dina! May I have the rest of the messages, please?"

"Whatever. Sure." She handed the slips over. "There's one from Jinny Peterson at GoodJobs! She's just checking on how Melissa Smith is working out in the kitchen. And then there's this last one."

Quill looked at the last one. "Hm. Who's this McWhirter? And you put a frowny face next to his name?" Dina had small, precise handwriting. This was due, she claimed, to having to keep lab notes in cramped and confined spaces. The frowny face was very neatly drawn, although quite small.

"He didn't say what he wanted. As a matter of fact, he *refused* to say what he wanted."

"That's why you drew a frowny face?"

"I drew a frowny face because he refused in a very rude way, and if you ask me, he's just some kind of very obnoxious sales guy selling cemetery plots or whatever and I would have thrown the message in the trash can if you hadn't yelled at me about taking each and every message no matter what. He was," Dina repeated with some heat, *"rude!"*

Quill obligingly threw the note from the cemetery salesman McWhirter into the wastebasket.

The phone rang. Dina said, "I'll get it!" reached across Quill's desk, and chirped, "Inn at Hemlock Falls and the good news is we've been saved by the bell and we're not going broke! May I help you?" And then, "We were just talking about you, Mr. McWhirter." Suddenly she turned bright pink. "You still don't want to tell me why you're harassing Ms. Quilliam? No?"

Too late, Quill jumped up and reached for the phone. Dina blew a raspberry into the receiver and hung up.

Quill sat down again and sighed. "Dina."

"That," Dina said, her voice trembling, "was *very* satisfying."

"Just how exactly was he rude?"

"Mean," Dina said. "Just out of nowhere. For no reason." She blinked away tears, and then sat down on the couch. Quill loved the fabric—large bronze chrysanthemums on a background of cream and red. Dina's bright purple sweater clashed horribly with the flowers. "Sorry. I must be PMS-y or something. But you know how stuff just hits you all of a sudden? When you aren't, like, really prepared for it?"

"What did he say?" Quill persisted.

"Well, after I said that we were just talking about him, he said that he knew what to do about snippy little pieces like me."

"Oh, dear." Quill tugged at the curl over her left ear and regarded her receptionist. "Maybe it's better not to . . . chirp when you answer the phone . . ."

"Chirp?"

"Chirp," Quill said firmly. "As in giddy. It doesn't excuse this person, of course, and if he calls back one more time, you can be sure I'll give him a piece of my mind, but really, Dina, no chirping."

Dina thought about this, sighed, and then said, "I was just expressing my personality."

Quill maintained a prudent silence.

"You want coffee or anything?"

"Coffee'd be fantastic. Thanks." She addressed Dina's back as she went out the door. "And if you must know why I'm calling Marge back first, it's because I want to find out how come my practically best friend in Hemlock Falls failed to warn me there was a bomb in my bus. To wit, this consultant."

Dina turned around. "Mrs. Schmidt is practically your best friend?"

"After you and Meg, of course," Quill said generously as she dialed Marge's cell phone number. "Coffee. Please. That's what best friends do—offer up coffee when the times get tough."

"Schmidt, here," a voice said in her ear.

"Marge, Quill here. How are you?"

". . . I can't come to the phone right now. Leave a message."

Marge was not only the richest but the thriftiest person in Hemlock Falls. Once answering machines had come on the market, she'd fired her own receptionist and relied on them exclusively. Quill left a message to please call back, then called John Raintree's office to see if she could drive to Syracuse and meet him for dinner, but discovered he was out. She knew there was no way to reach Myles. She didn't really need to call the mayor because it was the second Tuesday of the month and the Chamber of Commerce meeting was always held in the Inn's Tavern Lounge and she never forgot that, although occasionally she skipped meetings. Elmer had a talent for reminding people of the obvious.

She felt, suddenly, useless. And terrible about crushing Dina's personality. All those management courses she'd taken at nearby Cornell University hadn't done a thing for her management skills. She bit her thumbnail and brooded until she remembered that Jinny Peterson was expecting a phone call and Jinny always cheered her up.

She keyed in the GoodJobs! phone number and was delighted to finally hear a human voice.

"Thank you for returning my call, Quill."

"I'm always glad to talk to you, Jinny. The agency's helped us through some tight times. Dina said you were checking on Melissa Smith."

"Is she doing well?" Jinny, one of the younger members of the prolific Peterson clan, was related by blood or marriage to half the indigenous population of Hemlock Falls. She'd gotten a master's in social work from Ithaca College and was the logical choice to take over the directorship of GoodJobs!, the new Tompkins County service to help the unemployed.

The program had been a godsend; the county picked up half the wages for those employers who agreed to take what the *Hemlock Falls Gazette* rudely referred to as the "hard-core unemployed." Doreen had taken on two maids for the housekeeping staff, and Meg had agreed to take Melissa on as a dishwasher, a position normally reserved for recent graduates of the Cornell School of Hotel Administration who wanted to work their way up to a responsible position in the kitchen.

"I think Melissa's working out very well. But to tell you the truth, I've been so occupied with other things, I haven't really had a chance to sit down and talk with her."

"You *have* been through the mill," Jinny said. "But everyone's been rooting for you. How did the meeting with the bank go this morning?"

Quill was too used to the speed and efficiency of village gossip to take offense at this intrusiveness. "Quite well. Lydia Kingsfield's coming in with her camera crew tomorrow. She plans to get some preliminary background for the Christmas show."

"It'll be such fun to see it!"

"It won't air until next year at this time," Quill warned her. "But we're looking forward to it, too. From what I gather, there's going to be a feature on the Inn in that month's issue of *L'Aperitif*."

"Exciting times," Jinny said. "And it sounds as if you can take on a couple more of my clients."

"I'll do my best. But I haven't kept up with the ones we've taken on. Let me go talk to Melissa and see how she's doing. I'll call you back."

"I'll see you at the Chamber meeting, won't I? It can wait

until then." Jinny rang off with renewed good wishes for the Kingsfield project.

Quill sank back with a sigh of contentment and looked at her desk. It was free of the stacks of invoices, overdue notices, reminders, red slips, and overdraft notices that had haunted her for months. She'd dropped the backed-up bills in the mail as soon as she'd deposited the Kingsfields' check.

She'd go to the kitchen and talk to Melissa. And then it would be time to celebrate the Inn's salvation with a good lunch, a glass of the best red their sommelier, Peter Hairston, could recommend, and a large dish of Meg's Christmas mousse.

Meg looked up from her clipboard as Quill came through the swinging doors into the kitchen and said, "Hey."

"Hey," Quill responded. "Anything for lunch? And after lunch, is there any of your mousse? I'm in the mood to celebrate."

"Give me a second. I'm taking tomorrow's lamb off the menu."

"Why?"

"Because Loathsome Lydia loves it."

Quill sighed.

There were two places in Meg's kitchen where Quill liked to sit. The first was a stool at the birch-topped prep table, where Meg stood now with her clipboard. The second was the rocking chair by the cobblestone fireplace, where Quill's dog Max lay curled blissfully asleep. She settled into the chair by the fireplace, reflecting that there were *only* two places to sit. Not for the first time, Quill thought that the kitchen could do with a bit of reorganization. The one time she'd mentioned it to Meg, she'd bounced two eight-inch sauté pans off the cobblestone fireplace mantel.

The room was large enough, with a bank of windows overlooking the herb and vegetable gardens in the back, a line of Sub-Zero refrigerators on the east wall, and sinks and dishwashers on the west wall. Meg's ten-burner Aga stove was to the left of the doors to the dining room. The huge oak beams crossing the ceiling had been exposed, and bunches of dried herbs, sauté pans, fry pans, and pot lids hug from them all year round. Salamis, cheeses, sausage, and an occasional ham swung from them in fall and winter. Large rubber mats covered most of the flagstone floor. At this hour—about forty-five minutes away from lunch—there was a crowd of people in the kitchen, from Meg herself, and Elizabeth Chou and Mikhail Sulaiman, the two sous-chefs, on down through the dishwasher.

"I see Melissa isn't in yet?"

Meg didn't look up from her clipboard. From the speed of the pen, it was clear she was planning the week's menus, a task that took all of her attention.

"Meg?"

"She comes in at noon on Mondays."

Quill looked at the clock. Quarter to. She set the rocker going with a shove of her foot. Meg glanced at her. "How do squash soup, Parma ham with caramelized onions, and my spinach sound?"

"For lunch?" Quill said hopefully.

"For tomorrow's lunch special."

"It sounds terrific."

"Good."

"Does Lydia Kingsfield like squash soup?"

"Hates it," Meg said cheerfully. "Especially with heavy cream. Have you noticed that *L'Aperitif* has been featuring a lot of low-cholesterol recipes lately?"

Quill got up and stepped around Max, who acknowledged her existence with a lazy thump of his tail. She pulled a stool a little way from the prep table and sat on it.

"So why the change in attitude? You weren't exactly over the moon about the deal when we were in Mark's office, but you didn't declare war on it, either."

Meg put her hands over her eyes and held them there for a brief moment. "Sorry. Sorry. I'm doing the best I can."

"You know why you hate this deal?"

"Because I'm giving up all rights to a free, independent existence?"

"Because we didn't have a choice."

Meg nodded her head in slow, grim agreement. "Oh, are you right about that."

"If we'd had a choice," Quill continued stubbornly, "we would have jumped at it. Think about this, Meg. The largest and most successful gourmet magazine in the United States is going to market the Inn at Hemlock Falls' jams and jellies and pickles. Just for a start. And we get some money every time a customer buys one of those jars. And not only will the line use some of your own recipes, Meg, but you get to approve each product that goes out under the label."

"There's a bunch of other people that approve it, too," Meg said sourly. "I have a vote, sure. But that's it."

"And four months out of the year—in the off-season, yet—*L'Aperitif* is going to tape the new cooking show right here in the kitchen! We'll have swarms of people booking huge amounts of time. We'll be so busy we'll have to add more rooms! Expand the kitchen! I mean, let's face it, Meg. The kitchen could do with some major remodeling."

"But I don't want expansion to happen," Meg said quietly. "Do you? You remember that trip to Italy we took a few years ago to visit Corisande?"

"Of course I remember it. It was a terrific trip." Both of them had enjoyed the time with their niece.

"And you remember that little bistro we found just outside Pompeii?"

"In the distance you could see the sea," Quill said. "Oh, yes. I remember."

"And just around the corner . . ."

"McDonald's."

"McDonald's." Quill sank her chin onto her hands. Those golden arches had been quite a shock. The restaurant had also been enormously busy.

"We wanted a unique, boutique-style restaurant when we started this place, and that's what we have. I don't want to screw it up with expansion. As a matter of fact, neither do you."

"True."

Meg reached up, sliced an end off the Parma ham, and dropped it onto the chopping board. She went to the dairy Sub-Zero and brought back a selection of sweet cheeses. "We've got Irish soda bread today. It works with the ham, weirdly enough. So"—she kept her head down as she prepared the lunch plates—"here we are. Snatched from the precipice by a conglomerate. How long do you suppose we're going to be able to keep things the way they are?"

"I don't know," Quill said soberly. "Maybe never. Marge says it's the Wal-Mart effect."

"The what?"

"We can't compete with big luxury chains in terms of services. And we can't get into a price war. We can't afford to operate on the prices we're charging now."

"So you're saying we were doomed anyway?"

"Yes," Quill said cheerfully. "We were. So isn't it better to end up with this little compromise?"

"And you're cheerful about this because . . ."

"Because, Meg, I'm starting to believe what Marge and John and Myles, too, have all been telling me. Not being able to pay the mortgage—it's not totally my fault. I've been feeling just awful about all this. Marge said from the beginning she doubted there's a thing I could have done differently. As a matter of fact, she says that calling up *L'Aperitif* with this idea was the smartest thing I've ever done. In business, that is. Of course, to Marge, business is what makes the world go round."

"The smartest thing you've ever done, huh?" Meg laid her chef's knife deliberately across the wooden board and rolled her eyes.

"Yeah." Quill pushed her chin out in a mildly defiant gesture. "Which brings me to the point. This isn't Loath . . . I

33

mean Lydia Kingsfield's fault. She didn't come roaring in with her lawyers to take over our business. She responded very nicely to an idea I suggested. So please, please, *please* don't serve her food she hates or that's going to send her cholesterol sky-high, and don't encourage the housekeeping staff to put awful stuff in her bath salts."

"Okay," Meg said.

"Okay? You mean . . . you aren't going to start a campaign of terror against Lydia?"

"Not," Meg said, "unless she starts one first."

Quill thought this over. "Look, even if she does come across in a kind of obnoxious way, it'd be a good thing to remember the Innkeeper's Oath."

"Quill, I never had a thing to do with that Innkeeper's Oath. That was all your idea. Rule One: Don't Belt the Guests. Rule Two: If You Have to Throw the Guest Out, Make Sure There's Someplace for the Bozo to Go. Etcetera, etcetera. Besides"—Meg waved a pan of caramelized onions in the air—"there's not one rule that applies to . . . whatever the Kingsfield people are. Intruders, that's what they are." Meg scooped a bit of the caramelized onion onto the ham, shaved some Parmesan over it, and cut a neat slice of Irish soda bread. She handed the lot to her sister. "Here."

"Thank you." Quill eyed the plate carefully.

"What are you looking for?"

"Not poison exactly. Maybe a bit of ipecac?"

Meg smiled. "I'm over it."

"Are you sure?"

"I'm sure."

Quill eyed her sister narrowly. "You're lying to me, aren't you?"

"Like a rug."

The back door to the kitchen opened. A small woman came in, bundled in a cheap, bright red parka and frayed rubber boots. She hung her parka on a coat hook, removed her snow boots, and neatly lined them up beneath her parka.

"There's Melissa now," Meg said. She raised her voice. "Hey! Mel! Come and have a slice of ham."

Quill had conducted the initial interview, and she'd been struck at the time by both Melissa's shyness and her intelligence. She was pale and walked with her shoulders hunched, as if expecting a sudden blow. Jinny Peterson hadn't known where Melissa had lived before she'd arrived in Hemlock Falls; she'd no friends that Quill knew of. But she did have an adorable six-month-old baby named Caleb, and Quill asked after him now.

"Oh, he's great," Melissa said with a soft smile. "And you know we've moved, Caleb and I."

"To a larger apartment, I hope." Melissa had been living over Marge's latest business acquisition, the Croh Bar. The late-night noise and the glare of the neon sign hadn't been the ideal environment for the baby, and Quill was glad to hear they'd found a different place.

"Oh, even better than that, Ms. Peterson arranged for me to get a mortgage on a single-wide out at Gorgeous Gorges."

"That's terrific." The trailer park was neat and orderly; its chief asset was its location on the banks of the Gorge River. It was a beautiful spot.

"Two hundred dollars a month," Melissa said with a determined jut of her chin. "With this job, and the one I just found on the night shift at the grocery, I can afford the payments, if I'm careful."

"And you've found a good place for Caleb?"

"There's the nicest old lady that lives one trailer over from mine. Mrs. Huston. She's a widow. She has eighteen grandchildren and not one of them comes to visit. She's always talking about them and how badly she feels that they're so . . . neglectful." Melissa paused and twisted a strand of lank brown hair around her forefinger. "I think they're ashamed she lives in a trailer park. But I'll tell you something, after the life on the streets in Syracuse, it seems like paradise to me. Anyhow, I've been leaving Caleb with her, and it's worked out just fine, although," she added wistfully, "it's hard, not seeing him all day."

"And this job seems to be working out for you?"

Melissa directed an inquiring look at Meg. Meg grinned at her. "The only thing Kathleen tells me is that you're a little shy with the rest of the guys. The work you're doing here is just fine."

Melissa shrugged. "Well, washing dishes. You don't exactly have to be a rocket scientist, do you?"

"If anything else comes up here, we'll let you know," Quill promised. Melissa nodded, in a nicely judged combination of friendliness and aloofness. She wrapped her apron more firmly around her slim middle and went to her post by the dishwashers.

"Life on the streets in Syracuse," Meg said softly. "That's the first time I've ever heard her say a thing about where she's from."

"She's going to make it, though, don't you think?"

Meg nodded. "Oh, yeah. I think it's the baby, myself. There's got to be something very focusing about a baby. I wish we could make things a little easier for her, though."

"I wish we could let her bring Caleb to work, instead of just for little visits. Her whole life's a struggle, Meg." Quill shook her head. "And here we are complaining that we have to cede a little space to a perfectly pleasant and probably very interesting person."

"Yeah." Meg rubbed her nose. "Makes you think. And I'm glad you said what you did about keeping an eye out for something a little more challenging. In the meantime, I've got work to do." She ducked out of Quill's sight and clanked around the pots and pans stored under the prep table. "Sheesh! It's a mess in here."

Max, attracted by the metallic rattle—undoubtedly, Quill was sure, because it was a pleasant reminder of his forays into village Dumpsters—joined Meg under the prep table. Max had wandered into their lives several years ago. He was a stray, with courage and a loyal heart. He'd been an abused and neglected mess when Quill had taken him to the vet. Not the best dog food available or the most dedicated grooming could make Max other than a sorry example of the canine gene pool. His coat was a mixture of muddy browns, dismal gray, and streaks of black. It looked as if someone had thrown a can of motor oil over him. Quill scratched what she could see of his haunches. He wagged his tail furiously and wriggled further under the prep table.

Meg shrieked in protest. "Quill, this dog is not only the homeliest dog in Hemlock Falls, he's the pushiest. Max, get *off* of me."

Quill slipped off the stool and crouched down. "Come on, Max. Do you want to go for a walk? Walk, Max?"

"Um, Quill?" said a familiar voice from behind her.

Quill, having gotten on all fours in order to pull Max out from the pans, swiveled around to see two pairs of feet.

The first, size-seven clogs with a pair of knee socks embroidered with frogs, she recognized as Dina's.

The second, highly polished wingtips and topped by dark blue wool trousers, she didn't recognize at all. Nobody in Hemlock Falls wore wingtips. Not even Elmer Henry, who took his position as mayor seriously enough so that he never was without a tie, or Howie Murchison, the town's most trusted lawyer and justice of the peace.

Quill backed away from the prep table and straightened to her full height. A tall, thin gentleman in a dark blue suit, striped tie, crisp white shirt, and the sourest expression Quill had seen looked her directly in the eye. He held Dina firmly by the shoulder. Dina looked nervous. The suited gentleman looked stern. Quill frowned at him and said, "I'd appreciate it if you'd take your hands off our receptionist."

He gave a supercilious sniff.

Meg gave Max a final shove and emerged from beneath the prep table, her dark hair ruffled around her pink face. She smiled politely at Dina's escort. "Nobody's allowed back here but staff, sir. I don't mean to be rude but we really need to get you back into the dining room. And while you're at it, perhaps you could unhand our receptionist? If you wouldn't mind."

"Sorry, Meg," Dina said. "But I couldn't really help it. Mr. McWhirter wouldn't let me come and bring you out to him."

"McWhirter?" Quill said.

"Albert McWhirter," he said. His voice was as acidulous as his expression.

"Mr. McWhirter," Dina continued, "says he's been sent here from the Office of the Comptroller of the Currency. And he says he's not leaving until he sees every book in the place."

# CHAPTER 3

There was a prolonged and uncomfortable silence. Dina took the opportunity to sidle next to Max.

"Yikes," Quill said. "Well. Um. How do you do?"

"Not at all well, at the moment," McWhirter said sourly. He directed a fulminating glace at Dina. "This young lady appears to be laboring under a misapprehension about my credentials."

"He's not a cemetery salesman," Dina said meekly.

"No," Quill said. "I can see that."

"Miss Quilliam? We need to talk."

"It's Mrs. McHale, actually," Quill said a little frostily. "And I think it would be a good idea to have our discussion in my office," she added firmly.

"This is the guy Mark sent?" Meg said. "Yikes, indeed. Tell you what, Quill. You go right ahead and take Mr. McWhirter back to your office. I'll send Melissa in with some coffee."

"I'd prefer tea," McWhirter said.

"Tea it is." Meg grinned at her sister and waved. "Ta-ta."

McWhirter was dourly silent as he followed Quill back to

her office. It was a nervous-making silence, and despite an heroic attempt to shut herself up, Quill began to prattle.

"This," she said as they passed through the dining room, "is our dining room."

McWhirter looked at the tables, seating from four to six people, most of them filled with guests reading the menu of the special of the day. "It seems an appropriate use of the space."

"We can seat one hundred and forty-six people at a time. We aim for two turns in an evening if we can. But we usually just have one. A turn is one sitting."

"I know what a turn is." He gave her a thin smile. "I specialize in restaurant turnarounds."

"Yes, well. And we go through the archway here to our reception area." She stopped short and gestured toward the east wall. "And there's the wine racks, of course. And here, as I say, is our reception area. We have a very good receptionist. Well, of course, you met her. Dina. Dina Muir. A very smart, very polite, very valuable employee."

McWhirter raised one eyebrow in a saturnine way.

She patted the waist-high sign-in desk. "This nice old piece dates from the late-nineteenth century." She edged her way past the desk to her office door and flung it open with a flourish. "And this is my office." She craned her neck and stared straight up. "The ceiling's made of tin. I fell in love with those wonderful decorated squares. Well . . ." At last, thankfully, she faltered to a stop.

He stopped in the doorway and looked around. There was a faint expression of distaste on his face. With his thin legs, beaky nose, and wattled chin, he reminded Quill of a turkey buzzard. She gestured grandly toward her little Queen Anne conference table. "Please sit down, and let me know how I can help you."

"Do I know him, Quill? Sure. They call him Scrooge McWhirter," Marge Schmidt had a gleam of humor in her basilisk eye. She hefted a large slice of icing-topped cinnamon bread from the napkin-covered basket between them and slathered butter over the whole.

"Scrooge, huh?" Quill swallowed and looked past the bread to a poster of the Grecian Isles on the diner wall. She was overdue for a vacation. "Any particular reason? For calling him Scrooge, I mean."

Marge laughed unfeelingly. "Well, it ain't because he's filled with the old Christmas spirit, that's for sure." Quill's stomach lurched. She wasn't getting the flu. She was getting an ulcer.

"Scrooge McWhirter," Quill said, as if this third repetition would invoke a kindly Christmas spirit.

He'd requested all her accounts and her appointment diary. He intended to interview each one of the staff in the coming week. And he had been quite nosy about training programs for staff—particularly staff that answered the phone.

Nonetheless—with a feeling that it was all in the lap of the gods, and they'd been treating her pretty well, lately, considering everything—she'd gone about her business the rest of the day in a mostly optimistic frame of mind. Until her breakfast date with Marge Schmidt the following morning.

"Tough, is he?" she asked Marge.

"Tough enough."

She'd wakened that morning determined to get a grip on anything that needed gripping. And the day was shaping up to be a pleasant one. The Kingsfield contingent was due to arrive. They wanted to start shooting background for *Good Taste* right away. She talked to Meg, and they decided to offer a reduced menu in the dining room until after Christmas, since the guests were few and the walk-ins even fewer. She called the bank to make sure that the very large check, which sealed the contract to lease the name and premises of the Inn, was still residing in the company bank account. Everybody would get a Christmas bonus. The mortgage was paid up.

New York State Electric and Gas would put the Inn back on its Christmas card list. The terrible anxiety—the sense of failure—that had dogged her for the past few months was gone. She was in charge, and things were going well. And then Marge had called and asked her to come to breakfast.

"Well, he's certainly living up to his name," she said.

All but one of the twenty-seven guest rooms at the Inn could compete with luxury hotels anywhere in the world. There was one cramped single, in the northwest corner of the Inn with a view of the now-defunct paint factory on the outskirts of the village. Quill put McWhirter in it because he'd asked for it.

Quill nibbled at a bit of cinnamon roll. "He ordered consommé and toast for dinner, and oatmeal with skim milk for breakfast. He knows he has the pick of the menu, too. Can you imagine anyone passing up Meg's food? Especially when he doesn't have to pay for it? And he asked for the cheapest room we had, which I almost never use for guests, unless it's an emergency, and he seemed perfectly happy with it."

"He's not real big on the comforts of life," Marge said briefly, "or so I hear. Did he have any first impressions? I'll say this for him: he doesn't waste any time."

Quill unfolded the napkin covering the bread basket. "Well, it was a bit like going to the dentist, to tell you the truth. More wincing than actual pain, at least on my part." There was freshly baked cranberry-orange bread, right next to the cinnamon bread. It looked terrific. Quill didn't think her ulcer would object to Betty Hall's cranberry-orange bread. It had a statewide reputation.

They were sitting in Marge's diner—the Hemlock Falls All-American Diner! Fine Food! And Fast!—that the businesswoman owned with Betty. Quill put a piece of cranberry-orange bread on her plate. Then she added a slice of the cinnamon bread. She was sure she'd read somewhere that cinnamon was an aid to digestion.

"He didn't seem too impressed by the Kingsfield deal,

though. I thought that was a little odd." Quill pulled a frowning face in imitation of McWhirter. "Anyhow, after he got settled in his room, he spent the entire afternoon and half the night prowling around my inn."

"Prowling, huh?" Marge burped discreetly and took a long drink out of her coffee cup. People meeting Marge for the first time refused to believe she was the richest person in Tompkins County. She was dressed, as usual, in chinos, a bowling jacket, and a checked shirt. As a concession to the weather, she'd added a bright red sweater with black reindeer galloping across the front. She had short, ginger-colored hair and the expression of a tank commander. Quill was extremely fond of her. "He's pretty thorough. We put the word out that we were looking for someone to come in and take a look at your operation a few weeks ago. He jumped at the chance."

"Which reminds me." Quill put the cinnamon bread down. "Why didn't you tell me the board voted to do this to me?"

"For one thing," Marge said tartly, "bank business is confidential, or darn well ought to be. For another, I thought your day-to-day operations might benefit from an objective eye and I didn't think you'd agree to the expense unless I put a little pressure on. And McWhirter knows what he's doing. That chain of steak houses—Muriel's, you know it? He practically turned that chain around single-handed."

"I know *of* it," Quill said scrupulously. "I've never actually eaten there. But that's not much of a recommendation as far as I'm concerned. There's no way that a chain pulls in the same kind of customers that we do, Marge. I mean, two-pound steaks? Whole fried onions? And all of it frozen and trucked in once a week, if I'm to believe the trade magazines. That isn't us at all."

"Has he said anything about the operation yet?"

"Nope. He's just been stalking around. And making notes in a little handheld tape recorder." Quill put her thumb in the middle of the cinnamon bread and squashed it flat. "In this horrible droning cackle," she added crossly. "Like a raven of doom."

"Raven of doom, huh?" Marge reached across the salt and pepper shakers and moved Quill's bread plate out of reach. "You gonna eat that or play with it?"

Quill made an apologetic face. "Sorry." She dabbed butter on the bread and ate it. "We got off to a bad start. I apologized and I made him as welcome as I could. But he's so cranky, Marge. And sour as a Key lime."

"You'd be smart to make the best impression on him you can. Show him you got a real grip on the business."

"Well. Of course." Quill had never been sure she had a real grip on the business. If she'd had a real grip on the business, crabby old McWhirter would be driving some other poor innkeeper crazy. "And I told everyone not to worry, that he'd be gone in a few days, and to treat him like a guest instead of a food inspector. Poor Melissa runs off every time she even thinks she hears him coming. I just hope he doesn't put everybody's back up. This is Tuesday, which is the day we do the linen count, and you can just bet he's going to be driving Doreen absolutely crazy."

"You'd better keep her away from the mops," Marge advised unsympathetically. Doreen, the Inn's head housekeeper, had a notoriously short fuse.

"Well, what can he do to us, after all?" Quill said with a renewed surge of optimism. "Mark Jefferson said he'll give the bank a list of recommendations, and how bad can that be?"

"Is that a question?" Marge demanded.

"I guess so."

Marge raised one chubby finger after the other as she counted off: "First, let's say he thinks you're overstaffed. He'll want you to fire a bunch of people. Second, let's say he finds that the kitchen budget is too high. He'll want Meg to make less expensive food. You want me to go on?"

"Nope," Quill said decisively.

"This guy will look at where you're spending money, and how you're spending money, and make a big fat list of what needs to be done to cut your costs. Worst case, he can tell us the business isn't viable and that we should call your loan."

"We?" Quill said.

"The board of the bank," Marge said impatiently. "Jeez, Quill. D'ya think we sent this guy on over to you because there's nothing to watch on cable TV? You want to keep on doing business in Hemlock Falls, this is the guy you got to listen to."

"You're kidding me."

"I never kid about business."

Quill ate her piece of cranberry bread and said philosophically, "Marge, I've been getting your advice about running the Inn, and John's, too, ever since I realized the Inn was in trouble. I don't know anyone as smart as you about business, except John, of course, and to think that some crabby coot recommended by the . . . what is it?"

"Office of the Comptroller of the Currency."

"Right. Anyway, do you really think that he's going to find any major problems? I don't believe it for a minute. The way Mark presented this, it's a necessary step to getting the mortgage continued. Like getting an engineering inspection when you sell your house."

"You think so, huh?" Marge might have been Hector skeptical about the contents of the wooden horse outside his city's gates. "Well, what's gonna come will come. You planning on finishing that cinnamon bread? We've got that Chamber of Commerce meeting and for once, it'd be nice if you were on time."

Quill swallowed the rest of the bread and edged out of the booth.

"Tell you what," Marge continued, "you drive. I want to walk back downtown after." She patted her substantial stomach. "Doc Bishop thinks I need to get a little more exercise."

Quill followed Marge out of the diner. She'd parked the

Honda close by—it was rare to have a parking problem in the village—and they drove the short distance back to the Inn in silence. Marge was lost in thought. Quill herself—her optimistic mood temporarily dashed by Marge's grim reading of the McWhirter powers—grew progressively more cheerful as they proceeded down Main Street and past the Christmas decorations.

The residents of Hemlock Falls loved the holiday season. They decorated with the enthusiasm of little kids. Each year, the explosion of holiday decorations gave the whole village the look of a print by Currier and Ives. Most of the buildings in the village were of cobblestone. And while the founding of Hemlock Falls itself dated back to the late seventeenth century, most of the town's expansion had occurred just after the Civil War, at a time when Carpenter Gothic was the favored architectural style in upstate New York. So icicles dropped dramatically from the elaborately carved eaves. Snow topped the slate roofs like frosting on particularly elegant gingerbread houses. The December sunlight bounced dazzling prisms of light from the ice-wrapped trees.

Pine garlands twisted down the lengths of the lampposts lining Main Street. An illuminated plastic Santa, sleigh, and reindeer marched across the top of Nickerson's Hardware store. Large wreaths decorated with colorful ornaments and red velvet bows hung over the doors to the shops. Two-foot-high Christmas trees sat in the middle of the black-iron planters. At the end of Main Street, a life-sized crèche complete with bejeweled Magi sat in front of the Hemlock Falls Church of the Word of God, next to a ten-foot-high menorah that lighted up at night and a twelve-foot minaret. All of this goodwill, Quill thought, puts Scrooge McWhirter in his proper perspective. "And besides," she said aloud as she parked the Honda in her regular spot near the Inn's front door, "it wouldn't hurt to sit down and give him a little bit of advice about how the business is really run. Maybe I'll take him to lunch."

"It's you he's going to have for lunch," Marge said bluntly, "and I'm not talking about his picking up the tab. Best to leave him alone. Come on. Let's get the lead out."

The Hemlock Falls Chamber of Commerce meeting was held in the conference room at the Inn. Marge and Quill arrived at quarter to ten, which, Quill reminded Marge, was earlier than necessary and they could have had a second slice of Betty's cinnamon bread. Quill looked into the room. "And the only person in there is Harvey. So I've got time to go check on things."

Marge grasped her firmly by the elbow and hauled her into the room. "You leave McWhirter alone. We're not early. We're right on time. Harvey wants to talk to you."

"Harvey?" Quill stopped dead. "You set up a meeting with Harvey?" Harvey Bozzel was president of Hemlock Falls' best (and only) advertising agency. He was responsible for several notorious campaigns in his career: the Little Miss Hemlock Falls Beauty Contest (which ended in a fistfight among the six-year-old contestants), the Civil War Days reenactment (the gallant Hemlockians in the Fourteenth Division had lost), and the Fry-a-Way Chicken contest (a corpse ended up in the deep fryer). Quill was extremely dubious about the results of meetings with Harvey.

A wide grin split his face as Marge hauled Quill to the conference table, and he hurried up to meet them. "Merry Christmas, Quill." He took Quill's hand in both of his own and shook it heartily. "And a Merry Christmas to you too, Marge. Well! Let's sit down and have at it."

"Have at what?" Quill asked warily.

Harvey patted his sculpted blond hair, cleared his throat, and took a deep, dramatic breath. "The First Annual Hemlock Falls Christmas Chorale!"

"Oh," Quill said in mild surprise. "That doesn't sound too bad."

"Doesn't sound too bad? Quill! Marge! It's fantastic!"

"Are you planning a concert, then?" Quill asked.

"We've got that special meeting of the Chamber coming up day after tomorrow, and I thought we could have the chorale debut at it."

"Oh," Quill said. She'd forgotten about that. Zeke Kingsfield was famous for his real estate seminars. To the delight of the mayor—and most of the businessmen in the village—he had agreed to present a shortened version of it at a special Chamber meeting.

"And then the Reverend Shuttleworth wants us to sing at the midnight carol service, of course. And I thought maybe we could get up a caroling group to go around the village. Adela's got the Ladies Auxiliary knitting hats."

"Hats?" Quill said. "We're going to be wearing special hats?"

"Oh there's big stuff coming down in Hemlock Falls," Harvey said importantly. "And we have to be prepared for any and all contingencies."

"What does that have to do with hats?" Marge demanded. "And what are you talking about, 'big stuff coming down in Hemlock Falls'?"

"Just a few of us are in the know, if you get my drift. The mayor made a couple of calls yesterday. Just to the movers and shakers, if you get my drift."

"You're drifting all right, Harvey." When Marge's temper was roused, as it appeared to be now, she had the belligerence of a tank. "Nothing big goes down in Hemlock Falls without me hearing about it."

This, Quill knew, was not a boast, but a fact.

Harvey smiled and put his fingers to his lips. "It's big. Very big. I can tell you that. It's going to put Hemlock Falls on the map. That's what Elmer said."

"All that means is you don't know a thing about it, either," Marge said.

Quill looked at her. "Charley Comstock did say something yesterday morning about some new business at the bank meeting, come to think of it. But he was very vague.

You haven't heard anything, Marge?" If anyone was a mover and shaker in Hemlock Falls, it was Marge.

"Charley?" Marge looked thoughtful, but she let it drop. The members were filing in to the meeting. She marched forward to take her usual spot next to Harland Peterson at the head of the table. Quill herself retreated to the corner farthest from the mayor's podium. The room was long and narrow, and the rear was ideal for those Chamber members (like Quill herself) who preferred to sit in meetings unnoticed. Back in the mid-1900s, the conference room had been a keeping room for food storage. Such a space offered few usable options. Quill had installed a beige Berber carpet, painted the walls a soft cream, put up some whiteboards at the far end, and added a credenza with a sink to accommodate coffee service.

Chamber meetings were the only time that she was thankful for the proportions of the room. The space really wasn't usable for anything other than meetings.

But it was a good place for that. She'd scrounged a rectangular table long enough to seat all twenty-four members of the Chamber of Commerce from an auction of old public library furniture. The chief advantage of the table as far as Quill was concerned was that the farthest corner hid her from the active, highly vocal members clustered at the front, like Harvey.

Harvey followed Quill back to the end of the table, an A-frame tucked under his arm. "I've made some preliminary sketches of the program, here."

"Oh," Quill said again. "I see. You'd like me to design the cover?"

"We sure would!" Harvey placed the A-frame on the table with a flourish. "The cover cries out for the Quilliam touch!"

"For God's sake, Harvey. Are you trying to cadge off Quill again? Tell him you won't do it, Quill." Miriam Doncaster swept into the room. She dropped into the chair next to Quill's and shook her head in some disgust. Miriam had moved to Hemlock Falls more than twenty years before, with a husband in tow. The husband had picked up and moved on, leaving Miriam with a ten-year-old to support and a large mortgage to pay off. She'd taken a job as town librarian and paid off the bank. The ten-year-old was grown up and practicing as a lawyer in Cleveland. And Miriam had settled into the village with the ease of a Hemlockian born and bred. "You realize what he did with your sketches for the Texas Longhorn Cattlemen's thingie, don't you? Sold them. Sold them on eBay as original Quilliams. He got a pretty price for them, too."

"I personally donated the money to the high school," Harvey said frostily.

"That you did," Miriam agreed. "For the Harvey Bozzel Career in the Arts Scholarship."

"It doesn't matter," Quill said hastily. "I'd be glad to do it. What with all the money hassles, I haven't been working at all lately. This will be a good project to limber up, so to speak."

"And if we do decide to put the sketches on eBay, the money will be put to a good cause," Harvey said.

"The library, perhaps?" Quill turned to Miriam with a twinkle. "I know the state's been hacking away at your budget, Miriam."

"Bless you, my child," Miriam said. "You heard that, Harvey. The money's mine."

"So," Quill said, "let's see what you're proposing here, Harvey." She turned back to discover that Harvey had charged to the head of the table, where Mayor Henry stood rapping his gavel on the tabletop with an air of having to practice.

"You've lost him, momentarily, at least." Miriam put her hand on Quill's arm and said with unaccustomed warmth, "By the way, I was so glad to hear that you and Meg are out of the woods. And with the Kingsfield Publishing consortium, no less. Quite a coup."

"Yes," she admitted. "I don't have to tell you how worried I was. The light at the end of the tunnel is *not* an oncoming train, thank goodness. I'm very grateful to them."

"And Meg?" Miriam asked with a shrewd glance. "How's she going to feel about the temporary invasion of her kitchen?"

"It'll be fine," Quill said with more confidence than she felt. "I hope. Lydia Kingsfield is checking in this afternoon, with, I think, some of the crew for the cable show. So I'll know soon enough."

"And her infamous other half, Zeke, 'the Hammer'?"

Before Quill could answer, Elmer Henry rapped his gavel and called the meeting to order. Quill scanned the table and saw that most of the Chamber members had turned out for the meeting: Harland Peterson, the big, weather-beaten president of the local Agway, sat next to Marge. Howie Murchison, the town's attorney (and Miriam's occasional date), was present, as well as Dookie Shuttleworth, minister of the Hemlock Falls Church of the Word of God, Esther West (West's Best Dress Shoppe), and Charley Comstock. Charley sat next to Carol Ann Spinoza, the village tax assessor and Quill's least favorite person in the entire world.

There were some new faces, too: Jinny Peterson from the recently formed GoodJobs! agency and Tom McHugh, who'd taken over Peterson's Auto after poor George's bankruptcy sale. Quill looked at them all with varying degrees of affection. "I feel quite sentimental about everybody today," she said to Miriam. "It'd have been horrible to leave all this and have to move back to New York." She looked around the table once more. "Oh, phooey," she said under her breath.

Miriam craned her neck in the direction of Quill's gaze. "What? What's wrong?"

Albert McWhirter, immaculate in a gray pin-striped suit and crisp white shirt, had been hidden behind Harland Peterson's broad back. He'd taken a chair from around the table and set it against the wall. He sat with his feet together, his back straight, and a supercilious look on his face.

"Who *is* that?" Miriam asked.

"The bank thinks we need someone to take a fresh look at

the way we're running the Inn," Quill said warily. "That's the someone."

"Quill!" said Mayor Henry with all the decisiveness his portly five feet five inches could muster. "Didn't you hear me call the meeting to order?"

"I did. I did. Sorry, Elmer."

"No offense taken, Quill," Adela Henry said graciously. The mayor's wife—who dominated her husband both physically and politically—nodded in an amiable fashion. Adela, fond of bright colors, had added an orange chiffon blouse to her favorite purple pantsuit this morning.

Elmer nodded agreement and tapped the gavel again. "Before we start, I'd like to introduce a guest to these proceedings. This here is Albert McWhirter, from Syracuse. He's here for a few days on bid-ness, and as a member in good standing of the Syracuse Chamber of Commerce, we welcome him as a brother member." Elmer clapped his hands to start the applause, which was polite and perfunctory. "Now, Quill. Perhaps you could have the minutes ready to read, after the reverend leads us in prayer."

Obediently, Quill fumbled in the pocket of her long wool skirt for her sketchpad. Dookie Shuttleworth thanked the Lord for the many blessings given to Hemlock Falls. Elmer rapped the gavel and asked for a motion to read the minutes. Esther West somewhat testily pointed out that they always opened the Chamber meeting by reading the minutes and why did they have to take a vote? The several minutes it took to settle this point of order gave Quill the chance to flip through her sketchbook to the November meeting. The relevant page was embellished with a sketch of Elmer dressed as a Pilgrim, a sketch of Adela Henry in the guise of a ferocious Apache wielding a tomahawk in Elmer's direction, and an attractive series of swooping lines that looked like a Dada-esque version of a lemon pie with the figure $233.43 written underneath.

"Minutes of the last meeting," Elmer said, with a thwack of the gavel.

Quill looked at the otherwise blank page and said in an authoritative voice: "The November eighth meeting of the Hemlock Falls Chamber of Commerce was called to order by Mayor Elmer Henry at ten o'clock."

"No, it wasn't," Esther said fussily. "We started an hour late, Mayor, because you and Adela had that huge argument over the Thanksgiving Day Parade."

That accounted for Adela's ax and the panicked expression on the Pilgrim mayor's face. Quill made a little note next to Apache Adela.

"Did you make that correction, Quill?" Esther asked.

"I did. Thank you, Esther." Quill cleared her throat. "Old business centered around a discussion of the Thanksgiving Day Parade and the success of the Veteran's Day bake sale, which yielded a profit of two hundred and thirty-three dollars and forty-three cents."

"Actually, the bake sale profit was a hundred and ninety-eight dollars and sixty-six cents," Esther said. "I paid myself back for the coffee cups and napkins I had to buy because we ran out right in the middle of the sale. And the reason we ran out is because nobody listened to a word I said about how many coffee cups and napkins we were going to need."

"You spent thirty-five dollars and change on coffee cups?" Carol Ann Spinoza demanded. "That is a total abuse of public funds." Carol Ann had the blond, athletic good looks of a high school cheerleader. Her hair was drawn up in a neat ponytail. She always smelled of shampoo and soap. She was the cleanest person Quill had ever met in this life. She was also the scariest. As town tax assessor, Carol Ann gave new meaning to the term "abuse of power."

The meeting descended into familiar squabbles, with Carol Ann's high, sticky-sweet voice dominating the uproar.

Quill drew her charcoal pencil from her other pocket and

---

## Claudia Bishop

turned to a clean page in her sketchbook. She drew a tropic island, a peaceful beach, and a little swimsuited Meg and Quill lying under a palm tree. By the time she'd sketched in a muscular beach boy carrying a pitcher with paper umbrellas sticking out of the top, the acrimony over the bake sale expenditures had died away.

"And what about new business, Quill?" Elmer said.

Quill paged back to her November notes. "Golly, Elmer. We didn't have any new business."

"We didn't?"

"Nonsense," Carol Ann said. "I have some new business."

Since Carol Ann's interruption violated Robert's Rules of Order, everyone felt safe ignoring her.

"Nothing," Quill said cheerfully. "And a good thing, too. It's a perfect time to take a vacation. You've worked hard all year, Elmer. We all have. I think we should just kick back and maybe have a party. We have the one hundred and ninety-eight dollars from the bake sale, after all. That'll buy a few rum toddies down at the Croh Bar."

"I find that a very frivolous suggestion," Adela said reprovingly. "And you've been quite remiss in your taking of the minutes, Quill." The words "as usual" hung in the air. "Harvey here brought up the formation of the Hemlock Falls Choir at the end of last month's meeting."

Quill bit her lip guiltily. "Oh, dear. You're quite right, Adela. I do apologize. Again."

"Well, you had quite a lot on your mind, what with running the Inn into bankruptcy and all," Elmer said kindly. "We all know about that. Anyhow, as your mayor, we've got some great—"

"I didn't run the Inn into bankruptcy," Quill interrupted. She darted a glance at McWhirter, who stared impassively back. "And," she added in what she hoped was an impressive way, "I had quite a lot on my mind. Some of you may know I was in negotiations with the Kingsfield Publishing Group."

Elmer gave a knowing chuckle. "Otherwise known as

54

Zeke 'the Hammer' Kingsfield. Now, about Zeke," he added with confidant familiarity.

"I've seen him on that show, *The Assistant*," Esther broke in. "You know, the one where he makes big business executives out of taxi drivers and that. It's sort of a talent show. We all have an inner executive, Zeke says."

Elmer gave Esther a skeptical glance.

"Yes. Well," Quill said. "Lydia Kingsfield, editor of *L'Aperitif* and her husband, um . . . Zeke, have made my sister, Meg, and me a simply terrific offer. They're going to lease the Inn four times a year as a set for the new *L'Aperitif* TV show, *Good Taste*. Not to mention the line of special foods that will have the Inn at Hemlock Falls label. We are going to have tons of money around. We'll be rolling in it." She stuck her chin out at a defiant angle.

There was an impressed silence. Swept up in the drama of the moment Quill realized she had risen to her feet. She sat down again. She met Miriam's amazed glance with an apologetic air.

"Always glad to welcome new millionaires to Hemlock Falls," Elmer said. "As a matter of fact . . ."

Quill felt her cheeks turn hot. "Well, we aren't going to be millionaires, precisely."

"Everybody who works for Zeke Kingsfield is a millionaire," Esther said in a hushed voice. "My glory, Quill. And to think it happened to you."

"We aren't working for him," Quill said hastily. She got up again and faced them. "And I didn't mean to imply that we're rolling in more than a . . . a sufficiency. I just meant . . ."

Miriam gave Quill's sleeve a sharp tug. She sat down again with a thud. Miriam winked one big blue eye at Quill and said loudly, "I make a motion that we get on with the choral society, Elmer."

"I make a motion that we pay attention to my new business issue," Carol Ann said furiously. "I hope you realize that some vandal is going around assassinating Christmas lawn décor with a paintball gun and I move to start a volunteer police force to track these vandals down."

"No," Howie Murchison said. "No vigilantes, Carol Ann. You've tried this on us before. I second the motion to discuss the choral group."

"Carried," Elmer said with considerable relief. "Harvey, you want to show us your plans? And then I've got an announcement about a special Chamber meeting day after tomorrow." He beamed at them. "Always save the best for last, I say."

"I suppose I got a little carried away," Quill said to Miriam in an undertone.

"You certainly did."

"It's because Mr. McWhirter is sitting there. I didn't want to look like an idiot."

"The examiner that came recommended by the OCC?" Miriam said with interest. "Is that him? Hmph. Looks like he ate lemons for breakfast."

Quill tugged at her hair miserably. "Do you suppose everyone in Hemlock Falls is going to think we're millionaires?"

"You'd better hope Carol Ann doesn't." Miriam smiled. With her short, sun-streaked hair and large blue eyes, she was attractively middle-aged. The softening of her jawline and the wrinkles around her eyes made her appealingly warm. "Well, let's say you're probably going to be getting a lot of offers you wouldn't have gotten before."

"Time-shares," Quill agreed glumly. "Hot tips on surefire stocks. Yuck."

"Quill?" Elmer's tone was unusually polite. "We were wondering what your thoughts were on the matter."

"I'm sorry." Quill stopped herself and made a fierce internal vow to never say she was sorry again. At least not in the next twenty minutes. "What . . . ?"

"My choral group," Harvey said proudly. He set the A-frame upright. "I have to say, with all due modesty, that bringing a fresh approach to this product would be a challenge to Saatchi himself."

"You mean a fresh approach to Christmas?" Quill said.

"Christmas," Harvey agreed. "But I don't think there's anywhere in these great United States of ours that you'll find an idea like this!" He flipped the A-frame open with a flourish.

" 'The Big Guy and the Angel-ettes,' " Elmer read out slowly.

"You got it," Harvey said. "The classic Christmas choir, with a modern twist! We take your basic chorus, sopranos, altos, tenors, what have you. And we take your basic Christmas carols, like, say, the 'Hallelujah Chorus . . . ' "

"Actually," Miriam said, "the 'Hallelujah Chorus' is more of an Easter piece. And I wouldn't call it a carol, Harvey. It's a choral piece from one of the greatest oratorios ever written."

"You bet," Harvey said. "But has anyone brought Handel into the twentieth century? I think not!"

"What do you mean, bring Handel into the twentieth century!" Miriam exploded. "Handel's perfectly fine in the eighteenth!"

Harvey snapped his fingers in a one-and-ah-two-ah kind of way. "Rhythm, guys, rhythm. You want to *syncopate* that old warhorse. Jazz it up. Get the Angel-ettes moving!"

"And who," Dookie asked in a bewildered way, "is this Big Guy?"

Harvey beamed. "That's the hook! You don't get a product without a hook! We never actually see the Big Guy. A big bass voice offstage would give just the effect I'm looking for."

"You mean, God?" Nadine asked with a confused air.

Several of the members of the Chamber of Commerce looked skyward.

Miriam grabbed her hair with both hands and put her forehead on the table. Quill bit her lip, but it didn't help. She pinched her knee hard, but that didn't help, either. She kept her head down, waved in an abstracted way to the assembled group, and escaped to the corridor, closing the door behind her.

"And what's so funny, missy?" Doreen Muxworthy-Stoker stumped down the hall toward her, pushing a utility cart stacked with brooms, buckets, and bottles of cleaner.

"Harvey's taken on Christmas." Quill groped in her skirt pocket for a tissue and blew her nose. "It's the most supremely awful idea he's ever had."

"Christmas's survived worse, I bet." Doreen scowled. With her aureole of frizzy gray hair and beaky nose, she looked like an angry chicken. "I'm not so sure we will. You got to get yourself down to reception." She pushed the cart forward with a rattle, and Quill fell in step beside her. "Is Mr. McWhirter making himself a nuisance?"

"It was not my intention," said a dry voice behind her.

Quill bit back a shriek. "Mr. McWhirter. My goodness. I hadn't noticed that you left the meeting. Surely it's not over?"

"From the sound of it, the meeting will go on for some considerable time."

"It usually does when an idea of Harvey's is involved," Quill admitted. "Is there something I can do for you? Are you getting all the information you need?"

"Rome," he said testily, "was not built in a day. Which is to say I have made a fairly productive start. There are a few situations that require immediate redress, however. We need to discuss them."

"Of course," Quill said anxiously. "We could talk about them now. If it's about Dina, for example, I know she may not be quite the ideal receptionist at first glance, but when you get to really know . . ."

"I have taken care of Miss Muir."

Quill had a sudden, unwelcome vision of Dina slumped over her desk, dead as a doornail.

"And I'm not ready to run down my preliminary list just yet. So perhaps we could arrange to meet later in the day."

"Plus," Doreen said. "You got to get yourself down to reception."

"Fine," Quill said irritably, "I know, I know. If you could just give me a hint, Mr. McWhirter, I could maybe be thinking about things."

"That's a good first step, Miss Quilliam."

"What's that?"

"Thinking. I'm glad you're open to the idea. Shall we say one o'clock? Your office?"

He didn't wait for a reply, but stalked off down the corridor like the buzzard he resembled. Quill bit her lip and suppressed a word that would have dismayed the Reverend Mr. Shuttleworth. "The old goat must be driving you bananas, Doreen. I'm really sorry."

"Him? Not so's you notice. Now, he's not the most cheerful cuss I've ever seen, I'll give you that. But he appreciates a good cleaning job."

"That's because you've trained the best maid staff in upstate New York," Quill said loyally. "Nobody could find fault with the way you run the housekeeping staff. So, if it isn't Mr. McThing that's bothering you, what is it?"

"If I was you," Doreen said mysteriously, "I'd head on out to reception and take a look for myself."

# CHAPTER 4

"This *all* has to come down," Lydia Kingsfield said. "Every last pine bough, every last colored light, and for God's sake, get rid of those tacky foam things."

The words weren't addressed to her, but they brought Quill to a halt in the archway that led from the conference room to reception. A tall woman with hair like a raven's wing and a Barbie-doll figure had the Inn's groundskeeper backed against the wall. Mike Santelli was quiet, short, and muscular. He got along much better with mulch and fertilizer than human beings and the look on his face was that of a hounded stag. Lydia shook one long, crimson-nailed forefinger in his face and he stared at it cross-eyed until Quill tapped Lydia on the shoulder. He slid sideways against the wall, ducked under Lydia's arm, and headed for the oak front door at speed.

Quill said, "Lydia?"

Lydia Kingsfield turned with a shriek of delight. "Sarah Quilliam! My God! If it isn't herself!" She rushed forward, grabbed Quill by both shoulders, and sent a kiss past her left cheek. She pushed Quill back, looked her up and down, and added, "If I hadn't seen your picture in *Art Today* a few months ago, I wouldn't have recognized you. But then people with fair skin tend to age if you don't keep at it. And it's only been . . . what? Eighteen years since high school?"

"And you," Quill said, "haven't changed much at all."

"Aren't you sweet!"

Lydia hadn't gained an ounce since she was eighteen and the head cheerleader for the Waterford Wanderers high school football had team. Quill hadn't gained an ounce, either. But Lydia's figure had all stayed in the same place. Quill had an unusually good eye for the spatial, and nothing in Lydia's face or figure seemed to have been affected by the pull of gravity at all. She must, Quill thought, have a ferocious exercise routine. Not to mention annual visits to surgeons specializing in discreet nips and tucks and hefts, if plastic surgeons engaged in hefts.

Her chocolate hair glowed with health. Her skin was dewier—and, thought Quill unkindly, a lot smoother—than it had been at eighteen. Her teeth were the bright, unnatural white that came from continuous visit to dentists with whitening machines.

She made Quill feel like a forty-watt bulb in a hundred-watt chandelier.

"And aren't I just tickled purple to be here!" Lydia gave her a big, bright, insincere smile.

Quill caught herself smiling back in exactly the same way and bit her lip in annoyance. "We're glad to have you, of course. Has Dina gotten you checked in?"

Lydia looked around and said in a vague way, "Dina? That little person with the owlish spectacles? Yes. She has. At least, she sent that other person, with the muscles, to get my bags, and of course as soon as I saw him I knew he could give me a hand getting this taken care of right away." She craned her neck and peered into the dining room. "Where'd he go?"

"Get what taken care of?"

"This!" Lydia waved her hand at the foyer.

Quill had a number of favorite places in her building, and the foyer was one of them. The huge oak door at the entrance dated from the early nineteenth century. The oak flooring was just as old; the planks were a foot wide and polished to a warm, caramel sheen. The oriental rug that lay in front of the fireplace was a mixture of Quill's favorite colors: peach, celadon, cream, and robin's egg blue. The four-foot oriental vases that flanked the mahogany reception desk were excellent reproductions of the imperial T'ang dynasty.

And the cobblestone fireplace behind the two leather couches was just plain beautiful.

"This? You mean the foyer?"

"I mean the country look, sweetie, is so over I can't begin to tell you."

Quill sorted these locutions out with some difficulty. She looked at her watch. Lunchtime. It felt more like four o'clock in the afternoon.

"Not to mention this holiday stuff." Lydia waved her arm at the pine garlands with their load of carefully designed ornaments. "Ugh. It's practically Victorian." The amount of venom she injected into that innocent adjective would have killed a pig. "There is *no way*, Quill, that I can use this crap as a set for my new show. None," she added flatly.

Quill had learned a lot in her ten years as an innkeeper. The first rule of innkeeping was don't belt the guests. The second rule of innkeeping was if you do belt the guests, make sure that you don't really need the income before you do it. "Why don't we talk about this later? Let's get you settled, first."

"No, we need to get this settled first," Lydia said decisively.

"Okay, then." Quill took a deep breath. "Forget it. There's nothing in our leasing agreement about changing the premises in any way."

"There most certainly is. And I quote directly because I wrote the clause myself. *L'Aperitif* has the right to 'make those changes necessary for the quality of the show.'"

"Those changes don't include changing the look of the Inn beyond recognition," Quill said with some heat. "The Victorian look is part of what attracts the guests."

"Oh. The guests. You're turning them away at the front door, aren't you? I forgot about that."

Quill counted backward from fifty. She'd reached thirty-two when the oak door banged open and Zeke "the Hammer" Kingsfield marched in. Quill knew it was Zeke "the Hammer" Kingsfield because his face was all over the Internet when she logged on to retrieve her e-mail in the morning, and all over the *New York Times* whenever she had time to read it, and even on infomercials selling his real estate seminar on TV.

"Darling!" Lydia said with pleasure.

Zeke stopped short inside the door, put one hand on his hip, and surveyed the foyer with a sly, expectant expression that reminded Quill of Rupie Farnsworth, the terror of her sixth-grade homeroom. Lydia hadn't known Rupie Farnsworth as well as Quill and Meg had, but she knew him nonetheless. She wondered at a woman who could marry somebody that resembled that little sixth-grade bully.

On the other hand, Zeke "the Hammer" Kingsfield was worth half a billion dollars, so perhaps that explained it. Lydia had always been somewhat mercenary.

Zeke's shock of bright blond hair, the pugnacious jaw, the small but intensely alive brown eyes were the stuff of caricaturists the world over. He was also, Quill discovered, very tall.

"There you *are*," Lydia said.

"Here I am," he said, with a wink. He posed for a few moments longer, then ranged across the floor and stopped in front of Quill, hand extended. "Zeke Kingsfield," he said modestly. "And you are?"

"This is little Sarah Quilliam, Zeke. My best friend from high school. And the owner of this place."

Quill's best friend in high school had been Caro Gilliam. And Meg. But she said merely, "Hello," and shook Zeke's hand.

Zeke held onto Quill's hand much longer than necessary. Not, Quill thought, in a flirtatious way, but so she couldn't escape. "Not little Sarah Quilliam, Lydia. But Quilliam, the artist. Part and parcel of the reason why we've made this deal, isn't she? Brilliant debut, short but brilliant career, then—retired to the country to take care of her abruptly widowed little sister. And we've got her on ice!" He shook Quill's hand back and forth. "Am I right? Am I right?"

Quill counted backward from twenty and stopped at ten. She said, "Welcome to the Inn at Hemlock Falls, Mr. Kingsfield."

"And a fine welcome it is." He threw his head back, scanned the ceiling, and raked the rest of the room with his penetrating gaze. "Love this old-timey look. Just love it."

Quill bit her lip and darted a glance at Lydia. She stood with one hand on her hip, a rueful expression on her face. But she said merely, "It's so you, darling," and gave Quill a catlike smile.

Kingsfield exhaled in noisy satisfaction. Then his chin went up. He stared past Quill's shoulder. For a brief moment, he looked furious. Puzzled, Quill turned around. Albert McWhirter touched his forefinger to his temple and gave Kingsfield an ironic salute. Then he disappeared into Quill's office.

"What's he doing here?" Kingsfield demanded.

"The bank asked him to come in and take a look at the way the Inn was running day to day," Quill said. Then, for no reason she could figure out she said, "He's been quite helpful, so far."

Kingsfield grinned without amusement. At that moment,

Charley Comstock and the mayor came down the hall, on their way to the parking lot. Kingsfield darted a brief glance their way, turned his head to his wife, and ignored them.

"Say!" Elmer said in awed excitement. "Aren't you . . . I mean to say . . ."

Kingsfield turned to them with an expression of artificial surprise. "Yes?"

"Mr. Kingsfield," Charley Comstock said with solemn gravity. "It's good to see you again. Welcome to Hemlock Falls, sir."

Elmer nudged Charley sharply with his elbow. "Introduce us, Charley."

"Mr. Kingsfield? The mayor of Hemlock Falls." Charley elbowed Elmer aside. "I was hoping that we could spend a little time together before the larger meeting? The one where you're delivering your real estate seminar?"

"Talk to my people about that," Kingsfield said abruptly. "Set it up with LaToya. Lydia," he said with irritation. "Just where is LaToya?"

"With the crew for the show. Give her a call on your cell phone."

But Kingsfield's attention had skipped on. "I just got here, for God's sake. Give me a day or two. Good to meet you, Mayor. See you again." He waved dismissively at them, and then walked toward the arch into the dining room.

"Jeez," Elmer said in an impressed undertone. He followed Charley to the front door, stopped, and looked back wistfully. "He's a big guy, isn't he?"

"He is," Quill said with some surprise. "Well over six feet."

"Six-four," Lydia said.

Kingsfield ignored them with a lordly air, and sauntered through the archway to the dining room. It was twelve thirty and the weekday lunch service was in full swing. He stopped a few paces into the dining room, put one hand on his hip, and surveyed the area with that same sly, expectant look. The room rustled with the sound of geese on a pond. "Zeke! It's him! The Hammer himself."

He took several strides forward and disappeared from Quill's view. Fascinated despite herself, Quill walked to the archway. The Hammer was working the room. He bent over the tables, shaking hands, slapping men on the back, putting a familiar (and, Quill recalled, sweaty) hand on women's shoulders.

"Quite a performance," Lydia said in her ear. She smiled proudly.

Quill jumped. "Yes. Well. Um. Lydia. Let's get you settled." She led the way back through the foyer to the staircase that swept up to the second and third floors and began the walk up to the second floor. "We've put you in the Provençal Suite, as you requested."

"It looked the best of the lot in *Architectural Digest*," Lydia said in a discontented way. "But, Quill, that spread was almost ten years ago. Design's moved on since then."

"Oh, I don't know. I've always believed in the Platonic ideal, myself. There are some shapes, some combinations of color and line that are eternal, don't you think?"

Lydia didn't answer. They walked the rest of the way to the room in silence. Quill used her master key and opened the door to the Provençal Suite, then stepped aside to let Lydia enter. "This room has always seemed exceptionally restful to me. I hope you find it so."

Quill had used the blues and yellows of classic French country design in the bedspread, the drapes, and the several area rugs that lay on the floor. This room—like five others in the Inn—had its own fireplace, and a view of the falls through the French doors that led to the outside balcony.

Lydia walked restlessly around the living area. "It's very nice, Quill. But it's so nineties! I suppose that's what comes of holing yourself up in a backwater for the past ten years."

"Hemlock Falls isn't a backwater." Quill bit her lip. This,

she reminded herself, was the woman whose checkbook had saved the Inn. She made an effort to sound reasonable. "The Inn's on the New York State historic buildings register, you know. It'd violate the spirit of the architecture to . . . just what do you think it should look like, anyway?"

"Simplicity," Lydia said. "My design team for the show is going to puke. They're devoted to me. We think alike. I can't imagine what's going to happen when they see your kitchens. But I can tell you right now what they would like to see here. What I would like to see here. Bare wood floors, polished to perfection. A platform bed instead of this four-poster monstrosity. Built-in cabinets, hidden in the walls. And all those grotesque lights and ornaments and pine-tree crap downstairs? A single strand of white lights would be far, far better." Lydia waved her hand in the air. "Keep the damn firs in the forest."

"It seems awfully cold," Quill ventured. "And joyless."

Lydia stared sharply at her, poked her head into the bathroom, kicked at the pile of suitcases on the floor, then flung herself onto the four-poster bed and closed her eyes. "I'm exhausted. We had to fly up on a commercial jet, you know. Ours developed some kind of engine problem. And the plane was jammed with fat people and screaming kids."

"How difficult for you," Quill said politely.

"You have no idea."

Quill let the silence drag on. Then she said, "We keep birch logs in the baskets by the fireplaces. If you'd like to get a fire going, I'll send someone up to get it started."

Lydia covered her eyes with one hand and sighed deeply.

"I'll let you freshen up a bit, shall I? And ring downstairs if you'd like anything." Quill straightened the vase of fresh roses Doreen had placed on the coffee table and looked around the room once more to make sure that everything was in place.

"Quill?" Lydia said.

"Yes?"

"I'm sorry." Her voice was dry. "I used to be nice. It's just . . . you don't know what it's like."

Quill couldn't find anything to say to this. She headed out the door.

Dina sat in her accustomed place behind the waist-high reception desk, absorbed in a textbook. She looked up as Quill came down the stairs. "There you are."

"Here I am," Quill agreed. "Here are the two of us, as a matter of fact. Where is everybody else?"

Dina marked her place in the text with a yellow sticky note and closed it. "Mr. Fred Sims checked in just before Mr. and Mrs. Kingsfield got here and just after the *Good Taste* crew checked in. Quill?"

"I'm right here."

"The director is the single most handsome guy I have ever seen in this life. He is hot."

"Okay," Quill said agreeably. "Has he ousted Davy Kiddermeister in your affections?"

"I am not kidding. And no one ever said Davy was hot. I mean, he's hot, but not in a good-looking way."

"Dina!"

"Anyway, this Fred Sims is *not* hot. Not by a long shot. So, where was I?"

"Planet Dina?" Quill suggested.

"Mr. Kingsfield bombed on out of here to check out the cross-country skiing. The production crew checked in before them because the Kingsfields sent them on by train. This was because of all the equipment. They hauled all this stuff in just after you went into the Chamber meeting."

"I suppose I should go and welcome them." Quill sat down on the leather couch. Mike kept the fireplaces in the public rooms alight in the wintertime, and she frowned into the flames.

"You could, I suppose," Dina said cautiously, "but they

were fussing about getting the shoot ready so they might be pretty busy. On the other hand, you have to see this guy Ajit to believe it."

"The shoot," Quill said. "I'd forgotten about the shoot."

"You know, the *Good Taste* cable show. When you had the staff meeting about all the changes that were going to happen, you said we were leasing out the Inn as a set for *L'Aperitif*'s new TV series. Well, you said it *might* happen if you and Meg and Kingsfield Enterprises came to an agreement. And the crew's fussing around trying to find a place to set up."

"Right." Quill sighed. "I guess I shoved all that to the back of my mind. I suppose that's why Lydia thought she could complain about . . . Dina? Do *you* think our Christmas decorations are hokey?"

"Hokey?"

"Outdated, passé, and corny? You don't think, for example, that we should throw out all the pine trees and my little decorated houses and animals and put up single strands of pure white light?"

"There's single strands of pure white light all around Peterson's used car lot," Dina said. "So you can see all the used cars if you decide to buy one at night, I guess. And in operating rooms, so you can see the guts of people that are getting operated on. But if you ask me, and," she said, pushing her glasses up her nose, "you just did, I think our Christmas decorations are fabulous."

"So do I." Quill jumped to her feet. "So I'll go find the crew and tell them how *glad* I am that Loathsome Lydia has decided to lease the Inn for her show. And that if they touch one of my handmade ornaments, they'll die! Where are they, by the way?" She froze, as a sudden, horrible thought stuck her. "Not in Meg's kitchen?"

"*Good Taste is* a cooking show. So yeah, they're in the kitchen."

"Yikes." Quill grabbed her hair and tugged at it. "Why

didn't you say something? How long have they been in there? Has Meg thrown anyone out?"

"I haven't heard any explosions," Dina said. "Yet. Don't look so worried."

"I'm not worried." Quill wondered why it was so annoying to have someone tell you that you looked worried, especially when you were.

She forced herself to walk calmly through the dining room and not run madly off in all directions. Maybe Meg wasn't smacking innocent heads with her eight-inch sauté pan. Maybe pigs could fly.

She even paused and smiled at the few remaining diners. Four of the thirty tables were filled with late lunchers lingering over coffee, and in the case of one elderly couple, a couple of brandies. She checked, as a good, responsible innkeeper should, the readiness of the dining room to receive more guests, just in case business picked up. The unoccupied tables had been cleared, then reset with clean cutlery, glasses, and linens. And with the last of the Christmas decorations up the day before, she had to admit the room looked wonderful. She rotated the color of the tablecloths according to the time of year—and, she admitted to herself, her own particular mood. This Christmas, she'd decided on a heavy cream, with an underskirt of taffeta striped in green. Each centerpiece featured sprays of holly in a low crystal lotus bowl. Three slender green tapers were nestled in the middle. The tree in the corner adjacent to the wine cabinet filled the room with the welcome scent of pine. Outside the long windows facing the gorge, a feathery snow was falling. Quill looked at the room with an objective eye and thought: *Lydia Kingsfield is nuts. The room is warm and happy. She's an idiot. And I didn't even* like *her in high school.*

A crash and a shriek from beyond the double doors to the kitchen jerked her attention to the present. The *Good Taste* crew had found Meg. Or perhaps it was the other way round. Quill stiffened her spine, walked into the kitchen, and found

Meg collapsed in the arms of the most gorgeous male Quill had even seen, both of them bent over with laughter.

"Hey, Meg."

"Hey to you, too." Meg straightened up, gave the gorgeous male a kiss on the cheek, and bushed herself off. "Have you met Ajit? Ajit, this is my sister, Quill."

Quill extended her hand. "Welcome to the Inn at Hemlock Falls."

"I'm Ajit Hadad." He was tall and superbly conditioned, and he moved like a dancer. He wore his black hair a little long, and it sprang back from his classic features like birds' wings. Dina was right. He was gorgeous. Too gorgeous to paint, as a matter of fact. Quill preferred more irony in her work. "I'm Lydia's director. And it's an honor to meet you, Ms. Quilliam. I'm a devoted admirer of your work, especially your acrylics. As for what you've done with this wonderful old place." He gestured widely. "It's magnificent!"

Quill blushed and lapsed into confusion.

"She doesn't know what to say when people talk about her painting," Meg said kindly. "Or when she gets compliments about the Inn. But she's glad you like it. Bernie and Benny like it, too, Quill. It was the first thing they asked about when they came into my kitchen."

A short man in his midthirties—who reminded Quill of the '60s movie star Albert Finney—a very tired Albert Finney—gave Quill a beaming smile. "I'm Benny Pitt. Set design. And I have to tell you I just love what you've done with the place, too. It's classic Victoriana. Never goes out of style. And this is my partner in life, Bernie Armisted."

"Fabulous," the man next to Benny agreed. "I'm Bernie Armisted who would be Bernie Pitt, if there were any justice in the state of New York, which there is not. Costumes. We're the two Bs. You can tell us apart because I'm the better-looking one." He was slim, rangy, with tousled dark hair and day-old stubble on his chin.

"Actually," Quill said, "You're both . . . um . . ."

"Gorgeous," Meg said cheerfully. "Loathsome Lydia hasn't changed a bit. She still doesn't like keeping company with plain old ordinary human beings. Everything around her has to be beautiful. The diva with the cheekbones and the cornrow braids over there is LaToya Franklin."

"She looks like Naomi Campbell, doesn't she?" Benny said. "Only much better-natured, thank God."

"Just call me the Assistant," LaToya said with a soft smile. She wasn't as tall as the supermodel, but she had the same kind of slim, imperial elegance. "I'm Ajit's assistant. And Lydia's assistant. Not to mention the Bs and Zeke, too. The assistant qua assistant, that's me."

"Oh!" Quill said, remembering. "You were on Zeke's television show last year."

"That's right. I won the big corporate job over all those fierce competitors."

"This job?" Quill asked, then immediately regretted the surprised emphasis on the adjective. Assistant on a cable TV show didn't seem like a big corporate job. Perhaps things had changed since she'd moved away from New York. To this backwater, as Lydia called it. "Backwater my foot!" Quill said aloud, to general bewilderment.

"Of course not this job," Bernie said, as though explaining things to a small child. "You notice Zeke never announces for how long the winners keep that big, fat paycheck and the corner office? You worked there for how long, sweetie? A month? Longer than any one of the others. She had to leave to make room for the next one. Zeke doesn't talk about that on TV."

LaToya spread her hands in a "that's life" gesture. "And she was good at what she did there," Benny went on with wry indignation. "She's good at everything she does. We're lucky to have her here."

LaToya rolled her eyes. "And to think how my mamma sacrificed to get me that Harvard MBA. But I love you both, darlings. I'd love you, too, Ajit, if you weren't better looking than I am. And the job's not so bad, Quill. At least I'm in television. I've got to start somewhere."

Meg clapped her hands together, "And these, as I started to tell you guys before my sister waltzed in and interrupted me, are the members of *my* crew."

Quill sat in her accustomed chair by the fireplace, and, with some bemusement at the dramatic change in her sister's attitude, watched Meg introduce the kitchen staff. The reason for her sister's good humor became clearer after the introductions were over, and everyone had found a place to lean, stand, or sit.

"Ajit," Meg announced, "is going to remodel my kitchen. For free!"

Quill opened her mouth and closed it again. Then she bent over and looked at the color of her sister's socks, that excellent barometer of her sister's moods. The socks were sort of a blushy pink. Like a newborn. A color receptive to new experiences. Then she said, "You don't mind changing the kitchen?"

"Mind? You've got to be kidding me. This kitchen's driving me crazy."

"But, Meg, you did the layout yourself when we bought the Inn. I thought you loved the kitchen!"

"So I did. More than ten years ago. Up until then, I'd cooked in other people's kitchens. It's different when you're in charge. For example, the stove"—she pointed at the ten-burner Aga by the kitchen doors—"should be right where the prep table is."

"We've got a dual-fuel Garland on a truck headed this way even as we speak," Benny said. "And we're going to surround it with two prep sinks and acres of countertop. Then we'll be able to rip out the wall ovens between those windows and put in a bread hearth."

"A bread hearth!" Meg said. She ran her hands through her short dark hair, making it stand up like a porcupine's quills. "I always wanted a bread hearth."

"This is the first I've heard of it," Quill said.

"I didn't want to upset you when I knew we couldn't afford it," Meg said with a noble air. "Do you have any idea how that's going to affect the baking? There'll be a line down Route 15, begging for the peasant breads."

"And with the stove in the middle of the kitchen, we'll have room for the elves," Benny said. "The bread hearth's going to give us a perfect backdrop."

Quill closed her eyes and opened them again. "The elves?"

"Just for the holiday show, sweetie," Bernie said. "We don't like to encourage Herself to take things too seriously."

"Herself?"

"Pssht!" Benny poked Bernie in the ribs. "They were best friends in high school," he hissed.

"No, we weren't," Meg said. "Lydia was a cheerleader. Lydia was cool. We hated Lydia's guts."

"Meg!" Quill, exasperated, began to rock furiously back and forth.

"Okay. We didn't hate her guts," Meg said. "We didn't even know her all that well. It's now that I hate her guts."

"She's rich, she's gorgeous, she's the editor of one of the most successful magazines in America, and she's in love with her successful husband," LaToya murmured. "What's not to hate?"

"It's not that," Meg said sunnily. "If somebody's going to be rich, gorgeous, and successful and it's not you, why not somebody you know and like? Nope. I hate Lydia's guts because she's a snob. She's got lousy taste. And she's a bully. Other than that I can't think of a thing wrong with her."

"She's been in your kitchen recently." Quill guessed.

"She was in this very kitchen before she even got checked in," Meg said in an agreeable tone. "And I escorted her right out of this kitchen this morning." She gave her eight-inch sauté pan an affectionate pat.

"Let me guess. She said the kitchen design was so over, she couldn't believe it."

"She did," Meg agreed cordially.

"But you're totally fine with Benny and Bernie remodeling it?"

"They love it the way it is right now," Meg said earnestly. "But they did think it'd be more efficient if we moved things around. And once we got talking about how much ground I cover during the day, I told them we needed a change."

Benny gave Quill a tremendous wink. Quill decided the two of them needed to sit down for a nice long talk. Anyone that could handle her volatile sister in the course of a single morning had a magic Quill wanted to borrow.

"So Meggie ran into the Wicked Witch of the gourmet trade a little sooner than expected," Benny said. "Which makes it easier on us, because Meg knows what she's dealing with right off the bat and we don't have to make like little hypocrites and pretend we like the . . . witch."

Quill found herself feeling sorry for Lydia. "And the elves?" she said, hoping the change in topic would give Lydia's reputation a rest.

"The elves," Ajit said. "Yes. We were hoping that you could give us a hand with that, Quill."

"You were?"

"Lydia is going to have help in the kitchen when she cooks, of course. This is a professional cooking show, and we'll have a complement of sous-chefs and dishwashers on the show on a regular basis. Bernie's going to see to it that the actors are well choreographed. But we haven't had time to cast it, you see. And we want to get as much background work done here as possible. So we're short one elf."

"One elf," Quill said. "But he or she won't be the same person in subsequent shows."

"Not to worry." Benny swept to the prep table. With one hand, he held aloft a red jerkin with a green pointed collar and a black belt. With the other, he held up an elaborate belled hat with a point that came low over the nose. "Ta-dah! And the makeup's not to be believed, clown white with rouged cheeks and cute little Rudolph noses."

Quill decided, suddenly, that she needed a nap. Things were very confusing. "I suppose," she said after a moment, "I could call the high school and see if the cheerleading squad is available."

"Phuut!" Meg said. "We've got real kitchen assistants right here. Let's make one of them the elf."

Quill looked at the five members of the kitchen staff that had been on the lunch rota when Ajit and company had descended on the kitchen. She raised her eyebrows interrogatively. "What do you all think about that?"

"It'd be a hoot," Elizabeth Chou said. "I'm a sous-chef, by the way, Ajit. So if Lydia needs anything sautéed, I'm your woman."

"And I can cut up a chicken in ten seconds flat," Mikhail Sulaiman said eagerly. "But only if the elf's nonsectarian."

Peter Hairston, their sommelier, pulled a face, rolled his eyes, and responded reluctantly. "Sure. Fine. I'm in, if you can't find anyone else."

"I'd be privileged," Kathleen Kiddermeister said. Her face glowed. Her job as head of the waitstaff didn't offer many opportunities like this one. "Wait till my kids hear about this!"

"And how about our pot girl?" Bernie said brightly.

"What about you, Melissa?" Quill said kindly. "You haven't been with us very long, but I think you'd enjoy it."

"I don't know," Melissa said. "I don't think I should."

"It'll be fun," Elizabeth said, "and goodness knows we can all use a little of that."

"It isn't a job requirement, Melissa," Quill said, "So please don't feel you have to."

"We'd be all made-up?" Melissa said. "And dressed in those cute costumes?" Timidly, she reached forward and gave the belled hat a little shake. The chimes rang cheerfully through the kitchen.

Ajit clapped his hands. "Good. I choose Melissa. And that has to be a record time for recruiting an elf. Okay, everyone, we've got a ton of work to get through in the next four days. I want to begin to lay tape tomorrow, so let's not waste any time."

"An excellent policy," Albert McWhirter said as he came through the doors from the dining room. "Miss Quilliam? It's past one o'clock. You are late for our meeting."

Quill leaped to her feet. "Mr. McWhirter, so it is. I'm so sorry."

"Now, elves," Quill heard Benny say as she followed McWhirter back into the dining room, "I want everyone to line up to get measured tout de suite. Elizabeth? Peter? And Melissa. Now, where did Melissa get to?"

# CHAPTER 5

Albert McWhirter pointed a bony finger at one of the two chairs at the small conference table in Quill's office. She sat down in one; he sat down in the other.

"I do not appreciate the misuse of my time, Miss Quilliam."

Actually, he didn't sit, so much as perch on the chair opposite hers. His beaky nose and wattled neck increased his resemblance to a buzzard.

"I'm afraid staff concerns are of more immediate concern to me than you realize," Quill said loftily. "Although I regret the inconvenience to you. Of course." She glanced at the clock on her desk. "It *is* a whole ten minutes after one. Golly. What an inconvenience."

McWhirter seemed unperturbed by the sarcasm. He lifted his briefcase to his knees, opened it with precise swipes of his thumbs *(Click. Click.)*, and removed a small, elegant laptop.

"That computer," Quill said with enthusiasm. "is perfectly adorable."

"It's an adequate machine," he acknowledged. He tapped the keypad with his forefinger. "This is a preliminary to the in-depth report that I shall forward to the bank just after the Christmas holidays," he said. "First, *(tap)* efficient deployment of your workforce. Second, *(tap)* appropriate use of available cash. Third, *(tap)* management's grasp of key issues." He leaned back in his chair and regarded her with icy gray eyes. "Shall we begin?"

"I wanted to tap his little pea brain right out of existence," Quill said with warmth of passion she didn't know she had. "I wanted to wring his scrawny little buzzard's *neck*!"

"Whoo-ee." Meg shook her head and took a swig of the red zinfandel Quill had brought up to her room after a late dinner. "Have another glass of this stuff. It's terrific."

"I'd better not." Quill glanced at the clock over the mantel in Meg's rooms. "Myles usually tries to call about eleven. I don't want to be three sheets to the wind."

Meg reached forward and filled Quill's glass. "You're perfectly coherent when you're two and a half sheets to the wind. And listen to me, it's either that or large doses of Prozac."

Meg occupied a third floor suite of rooms overlooking the falls. There was no kitchen. She'd told Quill the last thing she wanted to do at night was look at any kind of appliance. There was a bright rug on the living room floor, piles of pillows in red, yellow, and green on the black chenille couch, and at least 300 cookbooks piled in precarious stacks all over the floor. Quill settled her heels on the stone slab Meg used as a coffee table and continued her rant.

"He wants me to lay off half the staff."

"Impossible," Meg said shortly. "I'm stretched to the limit in the kitchen as it is. If I worked those guys any harder, they'd fall over dead from stress."

"Not the kitchen staff. He says that's the one place where 'labor appears to approach maximum efficiency.'"

"Appears to approach?" Meg shrieked. "We damn well *are* efficient."

"He says that it's due in part to one of the owner-operators contributing directly to the success of the operation."

"He means me?"

"Yep."

" 'Owner-operator'? Did he talk like that the whole two hours?" Meg demanded.

"Yes. He did."

"And wait a second. What was that stuff about my contributing directly to the blah blah blah?"

"It's because you cook. As opposed to us hiring a chef. As opposed to me, who doesn't do anything. He thinks I waste too much time in frivol."

"Frivol?"

"He doesn't call it frivol. He calls it being an indirect. Indirects are bad. Very bad."

" 'Indirect' isn't a noun," Meg said.

Quill heaved a sigh. "Apparently a business like ours doesn't have enough money to support indirects."

"What part of speech *is* 'indirect,' anyhow?" Meg gazed in a puzzled way into the depths of her glass of wine.

"An adjective," Quill said. "I've been reduced to an adjective. And apparently it's an adjective the Inn can do without."

Meg gasped, inhaled her wine, coughed, and shouted, "He wants you to fire yourself?"

Max, who had been curled asleep by the small fire in the grate, awoke with a start and began to bark.

"Is he *crazy*?" Then, in a calmer tone, "Hush up, Max. There's a good boy. Now let's get serious about this, Quill."

"I am serious," Quill said testily. "He's not crazy. He's probably right. He said I'm spending far too much time in 'activities ancillary to profitability.' "

"Such as?" Meg said in a dangerous way. Then, to the ceiling, "The *nerve* of this guy."

"Oh, being secretary of the Chamber of Commerce. He doesn't see that as a useful civic contribution. As a matter of fact," she added, in a burst of honesty, "the Chamber probably doesn't find it very useful, either. I've never taken very good minutes."

Meg patted her on the shoulder. "I am going to put something very nasty in his oatmeal tomorrow morning."

"And the breakfasts and lunches with people like Marge. He says those don't contribute a thing. And he asked to see my appointment books for the past few years, and, of course, I handed them right over. And he took exception to the time I've spent investigating cases."

"You keep our murder cases in your daybook?" Meg said in an awed sort of way. "Like, 'break into Ro-Cor construction, eleven p.m.'?"

"Of course not. But there's a lot of unaccounted-for time, naturally, and I explained that our murder cases took up a certain amount of it. Then there was the week I spent in jail, and the time I was buried in the basement for two days, and the couple of trips I took to Syracuse and wherever to look for clues."

"So, once you explained it, what did he do?"

"He turned pale. And then he looked aghast. And then he asked if we did all this for free, which, of course, we do. We can't charge anything for our detective work. We don't have a license."

"Hm."

"And I must admit we're usually detecting by default, as it were."

"Hm."

"Of course, there are those who think we're just plain nosy, but I told him we had a sincere dedication to justice."

"True. What did he say to that?"

"He said that I should get a real job."

"Wow." Meg thought about this for a minute. "You mean, like take over the bookkeeping, instead of farming it out to Blue Man Computing in the villages? And maybe answering the phones and booking guests, instead of having Dina do it? And doing our own business plans, instead of getting advice from Marge and John? That kind of job? Not a real job like at, say, Kmart."

Meg appeared to be asking this in all sincerity. Quill looked at her for a long moment, then swung her feet to the carpet and grabbed the wine bottle. "How much of this stuff have you had, anyway?"

"I did have a drink with Ajit in the Tavern Lounge," Meg said with dignity. "Vodka. Neat. You know how I like vodka. Neat."

"You haven't had more than three ounces of vodka at one time in your life," Quill said. "I've never seen you drink much more than a half bottle of red wine at a time, either. You are remarkably abstemious for a chef. You know what? You're blotto!"

Meg waved her hand airily over her head. "I feel great."

"I'll bet you do."

"So," Meg said, her hand still suspended in the air over her head, "what else did McWhirly have on his little pea brain?"

Quill gently guided Meg's hand to a more comfortable position and debated her answer. In her current condition, if Meg did throw anything, she was liable to miss what she was aiming at. She decided to go for it. Just in case, she moved the wine bottle well out of her sister's ambit.

"His next suggestion was that we buy in bulk."

"Bulk? We already buy in bulk. Toilet paper, tissue paper, dishwashing powder. We buy all that in bulk."

"We don't buy food in bulk."

Meg shook her head and laughed. "No, no, no, no, no."

"He thinks we should . . ."

". . . Sure, I get it. Buy sides of beef and freeze them. Whole hogs. Those liquid eggs. I know what you're talking about." Meg took another sip of wine and winked. "He's an idiot. He's a dope. He just doesn't get it. No, no. No. No. No."

"Meg, you don't understand the power this guy seems to have. If we don't take at least some of these recommendations to heart, he'll tell the bank to call the loan. And then we'll be in the soup. I suppose we can borrow against the lease that we have with the Kingsfields, but the interest rates would be ruinous."

"No, no, no, no, no." Meg patted Quill on the knee, and kept on patting. "The Inn at Hemlock Falls is famous for the quality of its food. The fineness of its linens . . ."

". . . And that's another thing," Quill said. "No more six-hundred-count sheets."

". . . the excellence of its chef. Nope. This guy doesn't get it. It's not possible. No, no, no, no, no."

"I had hoped," Quill snapped, "that you'd have more constructive comments than 'no, no, no, no, no.' And *stop* patting my knee!"

"I *do* have a constructive comment. It's more than a constructive comment. It's a solution! Wait here." Meg heaved herself up from the couch with an "oof" and disappeared into her bedroom. She reappeared moments later with a pistol.

Quill felt all the air rush out of her lungs. When she did speak, it was in a whisper. "Where did you get that thing?"

"It's a paintball pistol!" Meg said gleefully. "A little teeny derringer that shoots little balls of paint! Jerry Grimsby gave it to me as a Columbus Day present."

"A Colum . . . a what . . . a . . . Meg!" Quill clapped her hand over her mouth. Then she said, very quietly, "You're the Christmas vandal! You've been shooting inflatable Christmas ornaments all over Hemlock Falls!"

"I hate those inflatable thingies. But who says I'm the Christmas vandal? It could be one of *hundreds* of right-thinking people." She waved the gun, steadied, and pointed at the wall.

Quill yelled, "Don't shoot!"

A large splotch of orange paint knocked the clock off the mantel, and then dribbled down the brick.

"Pow!" Meg said. She swiveled the gun around.

Before she could change her drapes from cream to orange,

Quill wrestled the little pistol away from her. "Jerry Grimsby has a lot to answer for."

"Jerry Grimsby," Meg said dreamily, "is my sweet patootie." She opened her eyes and said, "So that's what we'll do to McWhirter. We'll turn the bugger orange. Or purple."

"What a good idea," Quill said cordially. Meg reached for the gun and Quill, who was at least four inches taller than her sister, kept it out of reach. "Oh, no, you don't. I think I'll keep this with me."

"I think you won't. Give it back."

"You promise not to shoot Mr. McWhirter?"

"No."

"You promise not to shoot Mr. McWhirter tonight?"

"Yes."

Quill gave her the pistol. "Good night, Meg."

"G'night, Quill."

"Good grief, Myles," she said into the phone some half hour later. "What am I going to do?"

"Is anybody dead?"

"Nope. Nobody's dead."

"Then it'll wait until I get home."

"You are coming home for Christmas?"

"I'll do my best, my love. You know that."

"I do know that. I love you, Myles."

"I love you, Quill." He paused. Quill was sure she could hear the sounds of gunfire in the distance. She bit her lip to keep from asking him where he was. She knew he couldn't tell her until he did return to Hemlock Falls, and then it would be information for her ears alone. "Quill. You will keep that paintball gun out of your sister's clutches?"

"I will."

"And get that ulcer looked at." There was a world of amusement in his voice. "If it is an ulcer. You could always try Maalox."

"I put a call in to Andy Bishop. He says it sounds like the start of an ulcer. Maybe." Actually, Andy, too, had advised Maalox, which made Quill feel quite old and subsequently, quite cross. She patted her stomach. "Myles? If you're on your way home, I'm feeling better already."

# CHAPTER 6

Zeke Kingsfield slapped his hand on the table and said loudly, "There's nothing like an early morning cross-country run to set up the appetite."

"You enjoyed the skiing, then?" Quill moved the small tray containing the raw sugar and the brandied raisins closer to his bowl of oatmeal.

"It's quite beautiful out there over the gorge," Lydia said. "The view from the crest is fabulous. Just fabulous. I don't know how you stay in business with that beautiful hotel perched right on the river. I hear it's doing quite well?"

"Very well," Quill said. "There were some problems at first, but I understand they're running close to full capacity now."

"Shame about that little trailer park downriver, though," Lydia said. "Quite spoils that wonderful view. Don't you think?"

"It's affordable housing," Quill said, trying hard not to sound defensive. "And the residents keep the grounds up. Several of our housekeeping staff live there."

Lydia looked at her husband and smiled in a secretive way. "Do they? Now, Quill, do tell me why it took you so long to decide to fix up that cross-country trail."

Quill shrugged. "No real reason, I guess. Although we did think that it might attract guests in the winter. We put the run in last year. The property extends for some way down the gorge, and it's really lovely out there any time of year. But especially in the winter, I think."

"It's supposed to snow later this afternoon and tonight," Lydia said. "If the forecast's reliable, that is. The trail could use another couple of inches." She frowned at the raw sugar and dumped several spoonfuls of wild blueberries into her yogurt. "How many miles did you lay out?"

"You saw how twisty it is," Quill said. "Our land runs to about half a mile, but Mike was very clever about the design. There are two trails. One goes by the gorge. That's a mile round-trip. The course you took this morning is three miles one way." She looked at Lydia with unfeigned admiration. "And a lot of it's uphill. If you both got around that at six o'clock in the morning, I'm truly impressed."

Zeke leaned over and smiled into her eyes. "You want to be truly impressed, you should take a little trip with *me* this morning."

Quill drew back a little. Zeke smelled of soap, toothpaste, and a men's scent so expensive she had no idea what it was called, although it'd been in the air at the men's counter at Bergdorf's the last time she was in New York City. "Thank you, Zeke. But I have a pretty full schedule this morning."

"Cancel whatever it is," Lydia advised. "You have people, don't you?"

"People?"

"People to take care of whatever."

Not if Mr. McWhirter has his way. Aloud, Quill said, "Maybe another time."

Zeke scowled and hunched a little closer. If she backed up any further, she'd be in the lap of the couple at the adjacent table. "My guess is there's been a few rumors about the old Zekester floating around town."

"A few," Quill admitted.

"Then you'll be one of the first to know." His eyes narrowed in an assessing way. After a long moment, he leaned back and said casually, "It's big, Quill. What I'm planning is big. And it's going to affect every single person in the town of Hemlock Falls."

"I see," Quill said coolly. "And this—big—plan is to be announced at the special meeting of the Chamber tomorrow afternoon, I take it."

He struck the table with the flat of his hand and shouted, "Yes! So, you ready to rock and roll?"

"Let me take care of a few things first. I'll meet you at the front door in twenty minutes?"

"Make it ten. I'll have the car brought up."

Quill turned to Lydia. "And you'll be coming with us?"

"Not a chance. They're bringing in your new kitchen this morning. I want to be ready to start this shoot this afternoon."

"This afternoon?" Quill said, astonished.

Lydia folded her napkin and rose. "It's all in the organization, dear. See you at lunch? There are a few things about the Christmas decorations we need to discuss."

"Certainly." Quill's spirits, which hadn't been all that high to begin with, sank a little lower. "About one o'clock?"

"See you then!"

Quill excused herself, promising to be at the Inn's front door in ten minutes' time, and escaped to her office. She left a note for Dina and a message on Meg's cell phone, and rescheduled a meeting with Jinny Peterson, who had another job candidate to interview. An impatient horn sounded outside her office window. She went to the window and drew the drape aside. A large limo idled in the circular driveway. Zeke must have rented one from Ithaca. Quill sighed, pulled on her wool coat, wrapped her muffler around her neck, and promised herself no matter what, she wouldn't give in to the temptation to smack the Hammer right over the ear.

"Sorry about the fact it's a Cadillac," Zeke said as the chauffeur settled her into the passenger seat opposite him. "We're too far upstate to have easy access to a Bentley."

He was perfectly serious. Quill looked at the rosewood bar, the Bose sound system, and the calfskin seats. She wished she'd worn her knitted hat. She could have pulled it over her face as they drove—slowly—down Main Street. Kingsfield waved out the window with the genial affability of Idi Amin in a hometown parade as they rolled past Nickerson's Hardware, Blue Man Computing, and Harvey's advertising agency. People swarmed out on the sidewalks to watch the limo passing by.

"Will this take very long?" Quill asked politely. "And where are we headed?"

"It takes as long as it takes. As for where we're going, I'll leave that as a surprise. Now. I bet you didn't know my people have been scouting upstate New York for quite a while."

As they left Main Street and turned onto Route 15, Zeke slumped back in his seat and stretched his legs next to hers. Quill edged a little further down the leather and said, "Not exactly."

"Not exactly?" His eyes sharpened. "What does that mean?"

"Your name wasn't mentioned. And certainly nothing specific's been said. But both my banker and our mayor have been dropping hints about some . . ." Quill paused and picked her words carefully. ". . . benefit to the village in the near future."

"Benefit." Zeke seemed to savor the word. He smirked in pleasure. "I guess you could call it that. And I'll tell you something, girlie, I guess you could call it the biggest thing to hit your little village since . . . well . . . ever in its history, I guess."

Reminding herself that Hemlock Falls had survived worse things than the Hammer—the Spanish flu in 1918, two Civil War battles, and the Depression—Quill said, "Oh?"

Zeke drew his legs under him, put his arms on his knees, and hunched over, an expression of deep sincerity on his face. "People tend to overlook upstate New York."

"They do?"

"State's got a bad rep. High taxes. Big-city crime. Declining population. Thing is—all those problems are going to be hitting your other big states quicker than you want to think. Florida. South Carolina. California. And look what you've got here." He swept his arm in a wide arc. Quill looked out the window. "Snow?" she ventured.

"Psh. Your weather's nothing like the northern half of the U.S. of A. Look at North Dakota. Minnesota. Hell, even Michigan. Now that's bad winter weather. Nope, what you've got here is ninety-two percent of the fresh water in the whole damn globe, some of the richest farmland, low population density . . ."

Quill watched the woods and the fields roll by. They were making an arc around the village. They had passed the newly minted grandeur of the Resort and had turned on the road that ran along Hemlock Gorge. "And some of the most beautiful country in the world," she said.

"Real estate," the Hammer said with a fat chuckle. "And it's goddam cheap." He leaned forward and pressed the intercom button next to the rosewood bar. "Turn here, Frank. I want her to see the site."

The big car lumbered left and bumped down a dirt-covered road. Suddenly, Quill knew where they were headed. "Are you going to buy the Gorgeous Gorges trailer park?"

"Who told you that?" he asked sharply. "Nobody knows that but me and my private banker."

Quill raised her eyebrows at his unpleasant tone. "It's not hard to guess, is it? The trailer park sits on the lip of the gorge. It overlooks that wonderful lichen-covered shale and the river that winds through it. The trailer park is on one of the loveliest sites in this part of the state."

The limo came to a stop in front of a single-wide trailer with a hand-lettered sign to the left of the front door that read OFFICE. Zeke eased himself out of the limo with a grin, and stood, bareheaded, with his chamois wool coat flung carelessly around his shoulders.

The park was laid out on a grid, like a giant tic-tac-toe board. Each of the nine squares held five trailers. The dirt paths that separated the squares were mounded with dirty snow. Green street signs with white lettering stood at each intersection: Waterfall Drive, Stone Steps Lane, Granite Street. The house numbers began at 35, for some reason.

Most of the trailers in the grids were double-wides, and most of those had small front yards, each with a mailbox on a white post, a row of empty window boxes under the living room windows, and a Christmas lawn ornament. Inflatable Santas bobbed gently in the light breeze. Six-foot-high inflatable Christmas trees glowed brightly even in the sunlight. One giant bubble had snow—or something very like it—falling inside the sphere, around the shoulders of kid-sized inflatable skaters.

"What time is it?" Zeke demanded.

Quill looked at her watch. "A few minutes before ten."

"You better get out of the car. You aren't going to want to miss this."

The sound of wheels on gravel drew Quill's attention to Gorges Lane. A media truck from the NBC feeder station in Syracuse parked in the middle of the drive. Local anchor Sandra Hotchner got out, along with her cameraman. A second van pulled up behind the first. Quill recognized the reporter from the news on CNN. He wrote for the *Wall Street Journal*. Behind that van, a tow truck made a distant third.

Zeke walked up and down the short path to the office, hand on hip, head up, sharp brown eyes scanning the trailers. After a long moment, the door to the office opened, and a guy in a John Deere cap, a bright orange hunter's vest, and laced-top boots emerged. He stood on the small square that was his front porch and stared at the limo. Then he stared at the reporters. Zeke waved cheerfully at him, and continued his march up and down.

The door to number 43 opened, and a short, broad woman with long, heavily bleached blond hair stood there, arms akimbo, a cigarette dangling from her lower lip. She wore pink bunny slippers. Then an elderly lady with a cane and a down coat came out from 63. A spry old man bent almost double scooted out of 46. Two Mexican men, a Haitian, a young Spanish mother with two toddlers hiding behind her snowsuit—the park was filled with people.

And a tired-looking young girl with a baby on her hip emerged from number 37. Melissa Smith and her little boy.

Quill opened the door to the limo and got out. She wasn't sure what was going to happen. Whatever it was would probably be too noisy for a six-month-old baby.

Zeke stopped, put his hand on his hip, and looked at the assembly. "It's good to see you all here today," he said in a loud, genial voice. "You must have gotten the letters I sent out that said I'd be dropping by for a visit. That if you were home at the time and wanted to talk, you'd hear something to your advantage."

The man in the John Deere hat came closer. Quill recognized him. It was Will Frazier, from Peterson's gas station. He nodded at Quill. Then he turned to Zeke. "Yeah," he said nervously. He dug into the pocket of his hunting vest. "We all got this."

"Could I see that, Will?" Quill asked. She took it. It was a standard 8½-by-11 sheet. Goldenrod, Quill thought. That was the standard name for the color. The sheet had been run off a cheap printer.

**WANT MONEY?**
**IF YOU OWN A TRAILER AT GORGEOUS GORGES**
**YOU'LL GET SOME**
**10:00 AM DECEMBER 12**

Zeke grinned at her. "Short and sweet. Pulls 'em in every time."

Will frowned at him. "So what's this all about, mister? I'm thinking maybe I should have called the cops to be in on this? I mean, if they ain't headed here already." His uneasy glance raked the reporters, who had begun to crowd around Zeke, microphones at the ready.

Zeke shook his head and delivered his sly, sideways grin. "It's Will Frazier, isn't it? You sure you haven't seen me before?" He raised his hand, turned his thumb and forefinger into a pistol and delivered the signature line from *The Assistant*, "Get a grip!"

There was a shocked silence.

"You the Hammer?" Will said incredulously. He looked at Quill, who nodded matter-of-factly. "You're kidding me. You're kidding me! Hey, folks! It's Zeke Kingsfield! This is . . . this is pretty amazing, Mr. Kingsfield. This is amazing."

"But not as amazing as what I am about to tell you." He raised his voice. It was a big voice and when he shouted, it was impossible to ignore. "I am here," he said, "to make a millionaire out of each and every one of you!"

For the first time in her life, Marge Schmidt was astounded into speechlessness.

"I was there," Quill said flatly. "It's a fact." She, Marge, and Doreen were seated in the dining room at the Inn. It was late afternoon.

"A million bucks," Doreen said, awed. "Holy cripes." She picked up her teacup, looked at the contents as if she'd never seen them before, and set it back down again.

Quill had spent most of the morning watching Zeke Kingsfield write out ten-thousand-dollar checks as a deposit to those residents of Gorgeous Gorges who agreed to sell their trailers—and their shares in Gorgeous Gorges, Ltd.—to Kingsfield Enterprises. By the time the last check had been written, and the last contract signed, Route 15 was choked with media vans, reporters, cameramen, and satellite feeds. A WYKY news helicopter circled endlessly overhead. Quill hid in the limo and drank club soda. The whole show concluded with the tow truck dragging one of the single-wides off to the dump. Zeke had given the residents a week to move out, but the large woman with the bunny slippers and the cigarette had been so excited that she'd volunteered her trailer for destruction right away.

When Marge did manage to speak, it was in a husky whisper. "He offered the forty-five people in Gorgeous Gorges a million dollars *each* for their trailers?"

"Forty-four," Quill said. "Old Mrs. Sanderson died two months ago and she had no heirs." She clasped Marge's hand briefly. "He didn't tell anyone what he was actually going to do, you know. Just dropped heavy hints at the bank. Charley knew something was up because the checks Zeke signed this afternoon were all drawn on an account at the First National here in town. CNN did a direct feed, and it was on the news live. Everyone from the village was down there in about five seconds, after that."

Marge shook her head in disgust. "And this was the day I picked to go to Syracuse. But why a million bucks each? I mean, I can see why he'd make an offer for that property. It's prime."

"It's larger than I thought," Quill said. "There's almost five hundred acres deeded to the trailer park, Marge, and it's all riverfront."

"Five hundred and two point six," Marge said. "If you want to be exact about it. Don't look so surprised, Quill. There isn't a developer this side of Syracuse who hasn't looked at the piece. Like I said, it's prime. But it's also a limited partnership with forty-five . . ."

"Forty-four."

". . . owners. It's a legal nightmare trying to get everyone to agree to a buyout. You'd be dead and in your grave before the first contract was signed." She shook her head. "But who's going to turn down a million smackeroos? How in Hades does he think he's going to recover the cost of that sucker?"

"I can think of a couple of ways," Quill said dryly. "You remember Briny Breezes?"

"Every real estate pro in the universe remembers Briny Breezes," Marge said. "Two hundred and thirty-three owners selling a whole dam' town for a million dollars each. And I see where you're headed." She rubbed her chin thoughtfully. "If I wasn't so gob-smacked over this thing, I would have figured it out for myself. Look at the publicity Briny Breezes got. It made the world news, for Pete's sake. Look at the publicity the Hammer's gotten already. By the time he decides to parcel out those five hundred acres into town houses, condos, whatever, there will be a line of dam' fools down Route 15 just begging him to get in on the deal."

"A million bucks," Doreen said. "Each. Dang. Stoke and I talked about buying one of them double-wides as kind of a summer place. They got a little beach right on the river, you know. Dang." She took a large gulp of tea.

"Yeah, well, I wouldn't be too sure of that million myself," Marge said cynically. "There's all kinds of ways to wiggle out of forking over that amount of cash, and you can bet Mr. Big Britches Kingsfield knows each and every one of 'em." She pushed herself away from the table with a grunt. "I'll tell you what fries my behind, though. How did a deal this big go down without me hearing about it? I'm telling you, Quill, I must be losing my touch."

"He dropped heavy hints to Charley at the bank, and to Elmer, but they had no idea this was going to happen. If it helps at all, of all the people in Hemlock Falls Zeke was worried about, it was you, Marge."

"Me?"

"He said it was important to keep the whole thing under wraps in case speculators, like, started buying up the trailers before he made the announcement. But that's a lie. You wouldn't cheat those people out of their money. I think he knows you would have raised a lot of sensible questions right up front. The first one, of course, you've already asked. Are all these people actually going to see their million dollars? But it's too late now. The chauffeur driving that limo was a notary, if you can believe it, and each one of those contracts was signed, witnessed, and notarized. There's no drawing back at this point."

"That's going to be some Chamber meeting tomorrow," Marge said glumly. "I guess he's going to give us the benefit of his inside take on the real estate business. What a load of hooey. And I'll be darned if I'm going to sit there with that fathead crowing like a rooster on a pile of chicken manure."

"Speakin' of which, you comin' to practice tonight, Quill?" Doreen asked.

"Practice?"

"It's the first rehearsal of the Angel-ettes," Doreen said. "And seeing as how our debut performance is tomorrow afternoon at the Chamber meeting, you'd better not miss it."

Quill thought of a hip-hop version of the "Hallelujah Chorus." "Gosh, guys. I'd love to. But I've got a whole list of things I have to talk to Mr. McWhirter about."

"Well, you can talk to him when we get an intermission," Doreen said. "So that's no excuse."

"What?"

"We signed him up. As a matter of fact, Dookie signed everybody in the Chamber up to sing. You know how hard it is to say no to that Dookie."

This was true. Their gentle, otherworldly pastor had hair

like a blown dandelion and a will of iron when it came to churchly matters.

"Besides," Doreen said, "he talked Harvey out of calling us the Angel-ettes, on account of the men in the chorus."

"Thank goodness."

"But he was kind of taken with the idea of the Big Guy," Doreen added.

"Oh, dear."

"Besides," Marge said, "you need to be there. Practically everybody in town's going to be there, including me." She smiled grimly. "That is, after I do a little poking around about this Gorgeous Gorges business."

"I don't have to come," Quill said a little crossly. "I've just had the weirdest week of my life, practically, and what I have to have is a nap."

"If you don't come," Doreen said with inexorable logic, "people will think you're stuck up on account of you got a million dollars from Zeke Kingsfield, too."

"I didn't get anywhere near a million dollars," Quill said even more crossly. "What money we did get goes straight to New York State Electric and Gas. And the bank."

"If you can convince the town gossips of that, good luck to you," Doreen said. "Anyways, see you at seven at the church, then."

"I'll see you there, too. Right, now, I got a couple of calls to make and maybe a big ego to puncture." Marge stood up with a glimmer of her old self-esteem.

"I don't know what to do next," Quill confessed. "This has been a totally confusing day. I've got to talk to Melissa Smith about where she's going to take the baby. The TV people loved the shot of the tow truck dragging away that trailer. Zeke told them he's going to have the whole park cleared in a week. Of course, with a million dollars, she's probably going to quit her job and it won't be my problem anymore." She rubbed her face with both hands. "But she's young enough to think that a million dollars is enough to last her a lifetime."

Marge tapped her on the shoulder. "Melissa and your financial advice can wait. Right now, judging from the sounds coming from Meg's kitchen, you'd better get in there and see what's what."

A hideous clamor was, in fact, coming from the kitchen.

"Ugh," Quill said.

"I'm off," Doreen said briskly. "I got to make sure Stoke's got everything he needs for the story on the new millionaires."

Doreen's third husband—perhaps it was her fourth, Quill wasn't sure—was the publisher of the weekly paper, the *Hemlock Falls Gazette.*

"It's been a heck of a news week," Doreen said with satisfaction. "What with Mr. Kingsfield bringing all this excitement to town."

"I'm off, too." Marge stumped out of the dining room, leaving Quill to face whatever awaited her in the kitchen. She dawdled at the table for a bit, finishing up the raspberry scones and drinking the rest of the tea.

The thumps and shouts continued.

She wasn't sure she wanted to intervene; she was even less sure when Max butted his way out of the swinging doors, gave her a guilty look, and trotted determinedly off to the reception desk, where Dina would undoubtedly give him the remains of her lunch.

"And where have *you* been all day!" Meg demanded as soon as she entered. The kitchen was empty of people other than her sister. It was also transformed.

Quill saw at a glance that Meg was hot, cross, and seriously annoyed with her universe. She stood in the middle of a pile of pots and pans, her face red and her hair a mess. Quill also spied the remains of a loin of lamb on the floor near the back door. "This," she said, "is obviously Max's work." She picked the meat up, looked around for the meat recycling can, and discovered that a dishwasher had taken its place. She gestured around the room with the lamb. "And this is obviously the work of Lydia's elves. Where *is* everybody, by the way?"

Meg held her weapon of choice, an eight-inch sauté pan. She reached up to hang it in its accustomed place on the beam and encountered a clump of mistletoe. She tossed it to the floor, where it landed with a very unsatisfying bump on a soft rubber mat. "They were helping me put the rest of this stuff away. I don't need any help. I suggested that they all take a nice long hike while I got reacquainted with my kitchen. So they did."

A brand-new twelve-burner Garland occupied the center of the kitchen. The stove formed the middle of a U; on either side, black granite counter tops stretched nine feet toward the back wall. A prep sink sat in the middle of both of the ells. Behind the stove, a brick bread oven took the space between the mullioned windows that had formerly been occupied by the stainless-steel sinks. The pot sinks and the refrigeration units—unlovely appliances at the best of times—had been moved to the east wall. On either side of the cobblestone fireplace, piles of pans, racks, pots, oven mitts, and kitchen towels lay jumbled against the cupboards that held provisions. What was most remarkable was the stripped-down-for-action, elegant utility of the space. What had been a warm, sloppy, excitable country kitchen was now a high-tech performance vehicle.

"Good grief," Quill said. She moved a rack of spices off her rocking chair and sat down. "Wow. How in the world did they accomplish this in eight hours?"

"They didn't," Meg said briefly. "The electrician and the plumber were here all last night. Ajit and the Bs promised me that the equipment would be down only for breakfast and lunch, and they were right. We're ready for dinner as soon as I get the pots and pans put away. Everything's operational. Although I've still got to store that junk"—she pointed at the jumble of towels, spatulas, ladles, and egg whisks on either side of the fireplace—"but Elizabeth, Peter, and Mikhail could clear it up in twenty minutes if I asked them to. If I wanted to, we could start on dinner."

"Do you want to start on dinner?" Quill asked after a moment.

Meg rubbed her nose. "There won't be much of anyone in the dining room, that's for sure."

"Do you like it? Not the lack of guests—the new kitchen."

Meg looked around uncertainly. "I don't know. Do you like it?"

"I love it," Quill said. "I think it's terrific. I can see that the traffic pattern's going to allow you maximum access to every part of the kitchen from the central point of the stove. It was brilliant of—who designed this?"

"Benny."

"It was *so* smart of him to put the prep sinks on either side of the stove. You're going to save yourself a ton of walking, Meg. And the sous-chefs can stand on the other side of the sink and work from that end. Yes. I like it." She bit her lip. "What about you?"

Meg walked inside the U from one end to the other. She turned the water in the sinks on. She bent down, grabbed two saucepans that were stored under the counters, and put them on the burners. She turned around and looked at the bread oven. Then she burst into tears.

"Meg!" Quill said, stricken. She sprang from the rocking chair and rushed to her sister. "Oh, Lord. I should have had all my teeth pulled before I called Lydia Kingsfield. I'll regret it to my dying day!"

"It's terrific!" Meg sobbed.

"What?!"

"It's terrific! I love it!" Meg was still in her toque. She rubbed her nose with her sleeve. "Jerry is going to turn pea green when he sees this!" She stood with her head down for a moment, heaved a deep sigh, and said in a tear-free voice: "Would you like a cup of cappuccino from my brand-new totally awesome espresso machine?"

"Sure."

"Decaf?"

"Sure."

Meg bent over and pushed a few buttons to the side of the sink on her left. A faint whirring struck Quill's ear.

"And maybe some berries and cream?"

"I missed lunch," Quill admitted. "And there weren't enough scones at tea. Sure."

Meg turned to the right-hand sink and pulled out a drawer. "Look," she said. "A refrigerator drawer." She took a few steps down the aisle. "And look here. A microwave drawer."

"Holy crow."

A buzzer chirped. Meg put a large white cup of cappuccino in front of Quill. "The stools aren't here yet, but you'll be able to sit on the opposite side of the counter from me, if you want."

Quill sipped the cappuccino, which was excellent. There was a confusion of noise at the back door: the clatter of boots on the floor, excited voices, a stamping of feet.

"The guys are back," Meg said. "Ajit and the Bs got Mike to help them bring the equipment in. They want to do a run-through of the elves dancing."

Quill looked around for the elves.

"Oh, LaToya's got all of them in the Tavern Lounge. They have this cute little number. You'll never believe who wrote it for them."

"Harvey?" Quill said.

"Me!" Meg beamed with modest pride.

"You?"

"I was inspired by the kitchen. And to think of all those years you've made fun of my singing."

"I've never made fun of your singing."

"You most certainly have." Some distant memory made Meg's cheeks flush with indignation. "Anyhow, I wrote a little verse and hummed the tune for Bernie, and once he figured out the tune, he said he's going to record it using his keyboard thingies and he thinks that Lydia's going to use it on the show as a theme song."

Quill found herself unable to say anything at all.

"And," Meg added, "I get paid for it. Anyhow, everyone's in the Tavern Lounge tapping their little hearts out. Go see how they're doing."

Quill took the long way around to the Tavern Lounge to give herself time to calm down. An innkeeper's days could be stress-filled and busy. She should be used to it, by now. She'd survived the visit of the Church of the Rolling Moses and the mighty Moses himself, a giant wrestler turned evangelical preacher. She'd coped with the Civil War reenactors' mistaken charge of the Inn, rather than the hill north of the vegetable garden. And she'd handled the brawls between those two irascible chicken kings, Colonel Kluck and his nemesis, not to mention the invasion of Leo "Boom-Boom" Maltby and the Boom-Boom girls.

So she was ready for dancing elves. She just wasn't sure she was ready for dancing elves on top of the sudden addition of forty-four millionaires to the village of Hemlock Falls all in the same day.

# CHAPTER 7

"And step and kick and step and kick. Terrific. Great. La-Toya, get those legs up higher." Bernie walked up and down in front of the laboring dancers, waving a broomstick in lieu of a conductor's wand. "Good Taste," he hummed in a surprisingly tuneful voice. "It's just Good Taste / a-a-and quite a place / to be h-a-a-a-ppy."

Quill moved quietly into the Tavern Lounge, to avoid breaking the performers' concentration. Nate the bartender was behind the long mahogany bar cleaning wineglasses with a soft cloth and grinning at the sight of Bernie, LaToya, and Melissa giving the Rockettes a run for their money. At least Quill thought he was smiling. With his full brown beard, stocky build, and shock of bushy hair, it was hard to tell. Quill walked up to the bar and settled in front of him.

"Hey, boss."

"Hey, yourself."

"The usual? Or something a little stronger?"

"Vodka, please. It's been a day."

Nate poured a jigger of Grey Goose into a tumbler filled

with ice, added a slice of lemon peel, and place it in front of her. Quill took a grateful sip.

"Is it true? What they're saying about that trailer park? They say you were there."

"It is true," she said, "and frankly, I have no idea why Zeke Kingsfield wanted me there, but I was."

"That part's easy." Nate resumed glass polishing with an angry vigor. "The Hammer wanted you there to make it legit."

"Make it legit?"

"Everybody knows you can't be bought. Or they're pretty sure, at least. So yeah, he wanted a reliable, hometown witness and he got one."

"My goodness," Quill said. "You really think so?"

Nate set the glass down and leaned forward. "But all I want to say is that there's no justice. No, sir. Why those forty-four people instead of me? And a bunch of trailer trash to boot."

Quill took a larger sip of vodka. She'd never seen Nate act this way before. Resentment. Name-calling. A dangerous hostility. There'd be a lot of that in the coming weeks. Money was the snake in Eden. Zeke Kingsfield had a lot to answer for.

Nate scowled in the direction of the kitchen elves. "You know that welfare dishwasher you and Meg took on?"

Quill turned on the barstool. Melissa stood between Elizabeth and Mikhail, their arms linked, all three giggling their heads off. Her hair had fallen free of its ponytail and she looked young, and happy, and for the first time since Quill had hired her, carefree.

"I heard that she's one of them that got the money. I'm a taxpayer, right? The government takes its slice out of what you pay me every week. And the government *gave* her that trailer. With *my* tax dollars."

"GoodJobs! gave her the opportunity to buy the trailer because she has a job with them," Quill said. "Marge Schmidt made her the loan."

Nate wasn't listening. "Since when are government agencies buying people houses?"

"Well," Quill said vaguely, "Katrina, you know."

"And the last hurricane in Hemlock Falls was when?"

"Please pay attention to me, Nate. She has part of her mortgage deducted from her paycheck every week. She's a single mother, Nate, and she works hard, and she's doing her best for her little boy." She smiled at him. "And you know what? When I came back into town with Kingsfield, there were a couple of people from the trailer park outside the Croh Bar, already, drunker than skunks. One of them was Dooley Norton, who works at the paint factory, and I know for a fact his shift started at one o'clock. But Melissa showed up for the lunch shift. This million dollars hasn't made a difference to her work ethic."

"That's only because she's going to be on TV."

"I didn't get the impression that was a real motivating factor for her," Quill said wryly. "But maybe you're right."

Nate sighed, put the polished wineglass in the rack, and started on another. "Well, maybe she does deserve a break, the poor kid. As for Dooley Norton." Nate chuckled. "That fathead don't know his ass from a hole in the ground, excuse my language, Quill. And he's pretty damn dumb about poker. I just might go down to the Croh Bar after I finish up here and relieve him of some of the money that's burning a hole in his pocket."

"Take five, elves," Benny caroled. "And then into the costumes! We want lay some tape this evening. That was wonderful, LaToya darling. Kiss-kiss."

"Oh, kiss my butt, Benny," LaToya said good-naturedly. "Oh, the depths to which I have descended."

"They look pretty hot and sweaty," Nate said to Quill.

"You're right." Quill raised her voice a little. "Benny? Would everyone like something cold to drink at the bar?"

"You are a lifesaver, Quill darling!" Benny clapped his hands sharply together. "No alcohol, loves. Not until we've shot a few scenes in the kitchen. Then you can get soused to the gills, for all I care." He settled on the barstool next to Quill and announced, "I, on the other hand, not having to keep time other than with my watch, am going to have a glass of your finest red."

After a moment's hesitation, Melissa joined them.

"You've had quite a day," Quill said. "It's good to see you here, Melissa."

"I couldn't let Meg down," she said in her soft voice. "Quill? Is it true? Do you think we're going to get our million dollars?"

"It would seem so," Quill said carefully. "Do you have plans for it?"

She grinned. "Now there's a silly question. Of course I do! I took that ten-thousand-dollar check right down to the bank and you know what, Quill? I bought a car! I took Caleb right down to that used car place."

"Peterson's," Quill said.

"And I found the cutest little Ford Escort. Used, of course, but it's guaranteed for a year. And as soon as I get a chance, I'm going to check out Ithaca College and go back to school." She sighed. "It's like a dream come true."

"Just don't let the dream turn into a nightmare, honey." LaToya leaned affectionately against Benny's side and asked for a Diet Coke. "With a lot of ice, Nate, if you don't mind." She turned to Quill. "That little song Meg made up is just great. If Benny here can approximate the tune on his keyboard, we're thinking of passing it by Lydia and using it as the show's theme song."

"Meg," Quill said with heartfelt sincerity, "never ceases to amaze me."

"How's the weather?" LaToya asked abruptly.

"It's supposed to snow. As a matter of fact, it's started already." Quill gestured toward the French doors that led to the flagstone patio outside. The floodlights illuminated one of those snowfalls consisting of big, fat, feathery flakes.

"Now that ought to please His Lordship," Benny said. "The man's a fool for skiing. Uh-oh, attention, troops." He raised his wineglass in the direction of the archway to the main part of the Inn, where Lydia was walking rapidly toward them. She looked surprisingly young and vulnerable. "Oh, hell, Benny," she said. "I'm sorry. I put my head on the pillow for twenty seconds around three and look at me. Out like a light for hours. If housekeeping hadn't tapped on my door, I'd be asleep yet." She yawned and blinked at Quill. "Well. You're back, I see. I hope you don't mind, but I sent that Mike of yours out to do some work on the ski trail. And I talked to that dreadful chicken-looking person, Doreen? About the linens. Mine are to be changed every day." She held an admonitory hand up. "I know a lot of the luxury hotels have started the practice of using the same sheets two days in a row, but I don't put up with it at home, I'm certainly not putting up with it here. And oh, since La-Toya's tied up with this dancing-elf crap, I gave your little Dina a few things to do for me. I'll need her again tomorrow, too."

Quill realized she was gritting her teeth. She wiggled her jaw to relax it and said mildly, "She's not 'my' little Dina, Lydia. Slavery became illegal in 1862."

"Tell that to that arsehole Zeke," someone whispered.

Lydia whirled. "Who said that?" She was greeted by a profound, uneasy silence. Her gaze raked Ajit, Benny, and the others. "All of you," she said, her voice heavy with threat, "need to remember which side of the bread has the butter."

Quill raised her voice a little. "So perhaps you could let me know when you need something, rather than go to my staff directly?"

"Fine. Sure. Whatever." Then Lydia smiled, catlike. "And how did *your* morning go?"

"Full of surprises," Quill said.

"I'll bet. I caught a little of it on TV. Do you know where Zeke got to, after all the shouting died down?"

"He said he was going to take the car into Syracuse." Quill looked at her watch. "That was about five, or so."

"But the chauffeur's off duty. He's planning on driving himself?"

"CNN has set up a live feed at one of their satellite stations there."

"That explains it, then. He'd go to the ass end of Death Valley for an interview." She shook her head. "I swear to God that the man would shrivel up and die without attention. I'd better go with him. He hates to drive. So, Benny. The kitchen's ready? Are you planning on laying tape this evening?" She snapped her fingers. "C'mon, folks. Time's money. I'll go catch Zeke."

Nate and Quill watched as Lydia swept out of the Lounge like a particularly ill-tempered sheepdog. She narrowly avoided Mr. McWhirter, who was headed into the Lounge, with a seedy-looking man at his heels.

"Who's that?" Quill asked.

"Name's Fred Sims. Checked in yesterday."

Sims was a short, stout man with a sullen lower lip and narrow little eyes. He sat down with McWhirter. The two of them engaged in desultory conversation. Quill tugged at her lower lip. She felt like Dorothy Parker: What fresh hell was this? "He looks kind of . . . sneaky?"

"Yeah?" Nate said indifferently. "We get all types in here."

"True," Quill said. "And just because McWhirter's out to totally dismantle my inn doesn't mean that he's bringing in sneaky-looking guys to help him do it, does it?"

"I don't see how," Nate said sensibly. "Now, about this Lydia. You guys were best friends in high school?" Nate said. "Was she like that, then?"

Quill, realizing that denying she had been Lydia's best friend in high school was as futile as reminding people Myles was no longer sheriff, addressed the second question. "She wasn't arrogant. And she wasn't bossy. But she did focus on things neither Meg nor I had time for, like cheerleading and the prom queen competition. But she was smart, Nate. Not that cheerleaders aren't smart, but she was a terrific student, and I remember that she aced her SATs."

Nate grinned at her. "And you ended up cheerleading anyways, didn't you?"

"You mean here?" Quill laughed. "Yikes. I suppose you're right. Anyhow, what I remember most about Lydia is that she was absolutely bound and determined to marry a rich man."

"Huh," Nate said. "She accomplished that, I guess." He looked at his watch. "Shift's over in five minutes."

"Are you leaving, Nate?" Benny said from the other end of the bar. "Then I suppose we ought to go back work. Come on, ducks. And Melissa. Where's our Melissa? Let's go, people!"

Quill watched them file out of the Lounge with a smile.

Nate nudged her. "You going to go sing at the church? Or are you going to go watch them dancing in the kitchen?"

"I suppose the church." Quill sighed. "Are you?"

"'Course," Nate said.

"I thought you were planning on going down to the Croh Bar and taking Dooley Norton for every penny he's got."

"Nah. It's Christmas. I'll catch him later. I'll just let Kathleen know I'm outta here early, and I'll drive the both of us to church."

"When Meg and I were little," Quill said as they drove through the Christmas-lit dazzle of Main Street some five minutes later, "our family did the same thing every Christmas Eve. After dinner, and before the midnight carol service, Dad would drive us through the neighborhoods to look at all the Christmas lights. I've loved driving at night during the holidays ever since."

"We opened our presents on Christmas Eve," Nate said.

"You didn't!" Quill paused, not sure how to pose her

question without sounding like an idiot, then she decided she didn't care. The strings of lights under the eaves of the cobblestone storefronts made her feel positively swampy with holiday good sprits. "You guys didn't believe in Santa Claus?"

"We're Swedes. We don't have Santa Claus. The next day," Nate went on with satisfaction, "we visited all the aunts and uncles, one by one. That was the chance for all the aunts to bring out the *lefse*, the lutefisk, the smorgasbord, the works." He sighed happily. "On Christmas Day, we made our way up one side of Lake Minnetonka and down the other. We didn't have time to miss Santa Claus."

"Meg believed in Santa Claus until she was eight."

"What happened when she was eight?"

"Rupie Farnsworth," Quill said. "He ratted Santa Claus out. He was in my class in sixth grade. A born bully, Rupie was."

"With us Swedes, the oldest girl in the family puts a lot of candles on her head and we all sing and maybe say a prayer."

"Santa Lucia," Quill said. "Sure. It must be a beautiful ceremony."

"Not very," Nate said dispassionately. "The candle wax got in my sisters' hair all the time. And one year the head-dress set my sister Ingrid's hair on fire."

They pulled into the Hemlock Falls Church of the Word of God parking lot. The life-sized carved wooden figures of Mother and Child were illuminated by the soft amber glow of lights from a tall menorah. The saddles of the three camels accompanying the Three Kings glowed with glass rubies, diamonds, and emeralds. The kings had been placed in a procession toward the crèche. The display glowed in the light of a seven-foot-high minaret with a miniature prayer platform at the top.

"Looks pretty good," Nate said.

Quill, who thought that the unorthodox display of the three great religions displayed a true holiday spirit, said, "It looks wonderful," and she and Nate walked up the stone sidewalk and onto the church steps in perfect accord.

Like most of the cobblestone buildings in the village, the church had been built more than 175 years ago. The pews were made of polished mahogany. The scuffed oak aisles were partly covered by a long, worn runner of that indeterminate red carpeting characteristic of old churches everywhere. The walls were wainscoted, surmounted by moldings carved with fruits and vines. And like all old churches, the scent was faintly musty, a combination of worn leather hymnals, furniture polish, and the passage of time itself. The aisle ended at a shallow step that led up to the nave. To the right of this step was a spinet piano. Esther West sat at a bench in front of it, studying sheet music.

At the far end of the church, a fair-sized pipe organ occupied the left side of the nave; to the right was the entrance to the robing rooms and the sacristy. The altar cloth was gold and white, and urns of white Christmas roses had been placed just beneath the marble altar itself.

Three steps down from the altar were the pews for the choir, two rows on either side. Harvey was busily directing basses and altos to the right, sopranos and tenors to the left. Nate took his seat with the basses with a cheerful wave. Quill stopped in the middle of the aisle, not sure where she should turn. Except for an occasional outburst in the shower, she hadn't sung a note since high school.

Harvey, dressed in a red vest, tartan-patterned trousers, and a white button-down shirt, was in the middle of a heated discussion with Harland Peterson and Marge. He caught her eye and waved her closer. "There you are, Quill, at last. Would you *please* remind both these people that the choirmaster's decisions are final? Final. You, Harland, are a tenor. You, Marge, are a contralto. Contraltos to the right. Tenors to the left."

"I told you this was a bad idea," Harland said to Marge. He took off his John Deere hat, wiped his forehead with his sleeve, took a glance at the altar, and tucked his hat in his back pocket. "What d'ya mean, tenor? I'm the same as Johnny Cash."

Marge jerked her thumb in Harland's direction. "He thinks Harvey thinks he sounds like a girl. And he thinks if he doesn't sit next to me, he'll lose the tune. I sing loud enough so he won't go off the key."

"Mario Lanza," said Quill firmly, "was not a girl. Mario Lanza wasn't even remotely girly, Harland. And Mario Lanza was a tenor." Then, in a moment of inspiration, she added, "So was Dean Martin."

Harland remained dubious.

"I'll tell you something that's not generally known," she added. "John Wayne was a tenor."

"That ain't right," Harland said skeptically,

"Sure it is," Marge said, with a large wink in Quill's direction.

"Can't be. The Duke?" Harland shook his head, and muttered, "What the hey, it's Christmas," He took his place next to Dookie Shuttleworth and the high school principal, Norm Pasquale, with a resigned air.

Harvey heaved a huge, beleaguered sigh. "Okay. Now, Quill. I'd say you were a soprano?"

"I have no idea," she said humbly.

Harvey hollered, "Esther?! Give us a note!"

Esther played a cadenza on the piano. Harvey motioned at Quill. Quill opened her mouth and closed it. Esther played the cadenza again. Then a third time. Quill took a breath and sang: "Ah-ah-ah-ah."

Harvey frowned. "Are you doing that on purpose?"

"No, Harvey. I am *not* doing that on purpose."

"Well." He scratched his head. "Sit next to Marge, okay? Harland's right. She sings loudly enough so that if you sing along with her, you won't lose the note."

Quill sat next to Marge in a state of mild dudgeon. "I *told* Harvey I didn't want to do this."

"You need to warm up," Marge said. "That's all. You warm up, you'll be surprised at what you sound like."

"I just hope no one else is surprised."

"You want surprise, I got a surprise. You see Will Frazier anywhere?"

Quill scanned the ranks of would-be choristers. Will caught her eye and nodded. He sat between Frank Harley and Ossie Newcome; Quill recognized both men from her occasional appearances at church. She nudged Marge. "He's over there." She watched the three men for a moment. "You see that?"

Marge craned her neck around. "I see Will and I want to talk to him. What else am I supposed to see?"

"Well, Frank's manager of the QuickStop. And Ossie's a teacher at the high school. I'm pretty sure both of them know Will. But see how they're sitting, Marge. Both of them are shoved over. It's as if they don't want to touch him. And they're talking across him, as if he isn't there. And Will looks just furious about it. It's that money. People resent it."

Marge gave her a cynical look. "You can think about it this way. At least they're not trying to *borrow* money from him."

Quill bit her lip. Marge marked a page in the hymnal with a piece of tissue and settled back in the pew with an air of having something to say. She looked at the three men and raised her voice. "Ossie, you switch places with Will. I think he might want to hear what I have to say." She waited until Will had resettled himself behind them. "Listen up, the both of you. I put in a few calls this afternoon. To a couple of friends of mine in Chicago."

Marge's friends tended to be people in rarified financial circles.

"You two ever hear anything about the Kingsfield corporation that issued those checks?"

"Me? Of course not," Quill said.

Will shook his head.

"It's called Bigger Fields Direct, Inc. And I've got a five-dollar bet with a friend of mine in the SEC the thing's owned by a series of other companies. I think the corporate veil's so thick around that company you couldn't pierce it in a hundred years."

Quill grasped about one word in three in this conversation. "You think there's something dicey about it?"

"He's trying to cheat us out of our million bucks?" Will said. His eyes were wide with dismay.

Marge snorted. "I sure do. But it's a legal cheat. I think BFD's a shell corporation and I think Kingsfield's up to his usual tricks. He's after the publicity. He's made a huge splash with this thing. *WSJ*'s giving him a story above the fold tomorrow—and this, mind you, in the middle of a pile of articles claiming that he's not as rich as he claims to be—so all of a sudden he's looking pretty good to investors."

*WSJ*, Quill knew, was the *Wall Street Journal*. "I'm not sure I'm getting the whole picture here."

Marge gave Quill's arm an impatient thump. "If this project of Kingsfield's falls on its keister—which I'm betting it's going to do—the Gorgeous Gorges trailer park people are going to be left with a ten-thousand-dollar check and a nice warm doorway to sleep in. That's what I'm sayin'."

"He's getting all those folks out of there so he can trash their trailers?" Will said. "He can't do that."

"You just took his ten thousand bucks, didn't you? Sure, he can do that."

"But they signed a contract to get a million dollars each from Zeke Kingsfield!" Quill said. "And he may not be a multibillionaire for real, Marge, but there's no denying he's worth a lot of money."

"Haven't you been listening to me? Will Frazier, here, and his friends didn't sign a contract for a million dollars' worth each of Zeke Kingsfield's money. They signed a contract with BFD. And from what my friends in Chicago tell me, BFD has a net worth of four hundred forty-six thousand dollars."

Will looked stunned. Then he looked mad.

Marge turned to him. "So what you want to do, Will, is get yourself on back to that trailer park right now and tell Kingsfield he's gotta wait thirty days before he starts haulin' those trailers out. You got that? Then if things go bust, at least you all will have a roof over your heads through the winter."

Before Marge had concluded this speech, Will had struggled out of the pew and was on his way out. "Looks madder than a warthog with a thistle up his butt," Marge said in satisfaction.

Quill watched Will bang out the church door. A few moments later, she heard the roar of his pickup truck. "Good grief, Marge," she said soberly. "Do you think you should have dropped it on him just like that?"

"It was the fastest way I could think of to keep those poor suckers from running bills up all over town. Will's the manager of the trailer park and the president of their board. Not, of course, that the board exists anymore. Kingsfield got more than two-thirds of the partnership signed over to him today. But he'll put the brakes on the spending, as far as anyone can. And he'll keep those trailers in the park for a spell."

"Do you really think Kingsfield's that cruel?" Quill said indignantly.

Marge shrugged. "You don't make those kind of bucks by playing Mr. Nice Guy. It's a fact. I'll tell you what burns my behind. If I'm right about this, and it's a scam, he's got that five hundred acres on the river for less than half a million bucks."

"But if the residents aren't paid the full amount, how can he?"

Marge patted her arm. "Slides the land into another company before he goes belly-up, that's how. Now, just relax, Quill. There's nothing more to do right now."

"You saved those people, Marge," Quill said. "That was a terrific thing to do."

"Maybe." She smiled. "But I sure put a spoke in the Kingster's wheel, didn't I?"

"I think, folks," Harvey shouted, "that we're finally ready to start. People? People? May I have your attention, please? Let's not waste valuable rehearsal time here! We're scheduled to give our first performance tomorrow. And I think," he added with a twinkle, "that in view of the terrific news some of our friends at the Gorgeous Gorges trailer park received today, and in view of who will be the guest of honor at our debut tomorrow, we want to begin with 'Good King Wenceslas.' "

A ripple of appreciative laughter swept the choir.

"Now, Marge? I want you to take the part of the Page. Elmer? You take the part of the King." Adela, decked out in a red velvet pantsuit with a bunny fur collar, nodded approval. "Ready? And a one and a two and ah . . ."

Quill stood up. Melissa was at the Inn with Meg. She would have to know what Marge had just told her. She really ought to get back. And it wasn't, she told herself, that she was afraid she would croak like a frog in front of everybody. "Harvey? I'm sorry. I just remembered that . . . I told Meg I'd give her a hand with the elf costumes."

"The elf costumes?" Harvey looked both puzzled and curious.

"The bells, you know," Quill said vaguely. "I'm sorry. I'll be back as soon as I can. You guys go on without me."

Quill was halfway down the aisle before she remembered that she hadn't brought her car. She stood on the steps of the church and debated; she could call Meg, or she could walk all the way back to the Inn. The snow was still falling in lazy, halfhearted swirls. The heavy sky was breaking up and a handful of stars shone through the thinning clouds. It was just cold enough for the snow to pile up without melting, but not so cold that she was in danger of freezing to death. Not if she kept moving. The twinkling Christmas lights, the fresh stillness of the air, and the occasional glimpse of the moon decided her. She'd walk. The past week had been filled with too many people and too many events for her peace of mind.

She had a penlight attached to the car keys in her purse in case the moon disappeared altogether. And she would be blissfully, totally alone for the twenty minutes or so it would take to walk home.

There was a shortcut to the Inn through Peterson Park. In the summer, when she had errands in the village, she almost always walked the half mile, and the terrain was totally familiar. She entered the park gates and crunched past the statue of General C. C. Hemlock on his horse, making up a mental list of things to do right now and things to do in the morning.

The very first thing was to sit down with Melissa Smith and talk to her about the supposed windfall from Zeke "the Hammer" Kingsfield. Marge had seemed pretty certain cash backed the ten-thousand-dollar checks he'd handed out like so much Halloween candy. If Melissa hadn't deposited it in the bank, she needed to do it right now. And if Kingsfield continued the dramatic removal of the house trailers, the residents of Gorgeous Gorges could end up homeless. On the other hand, if he was the owner of the property, Marge seemed to think he could kick them out anyway. So the second thing she needed to do was talk to Howie Murchison to see if there was any way an injunction could stall things.

She reached the perimeter of the little park and the narrow trail that led up the side of the hill to the Inn. It was slippery here, and she paid attention to where she put her feet. Her boots slipped on the icy patches so she stopped and directed her penlight to the brush. It'd help if she could find a branch to use as a walking stick.

Something large moved in the brush beyond her.

Quill swept the light breast-high and shone it into the thickets. There were deer in Peterson Park—too many of them, as a matter of fact. She made a soft, chirruping sound.

The rustling movement stopped.

Quill shone the light into the depths of the trees. Nothing. And paradoxically, the light made it harder to see in the dark. She switched it off entirely and waited for her eyes to adjust to the dim moonlight. A twig snapped. Uneasy now, she abandoned the search for the walking stick and began to hurry up the incline. She slipped and fell forward into complete and painful blackness.

# CHAPTER 8

Quill dreamed it was summer. She was washing her face in a warm pool of water in a forest glade. The washcloth kept moving out of her hands. It was rubbery and a little rough. She made a grab for it.

She woke up.

She was flat on her back and Max was licking her face. And her bedroom was dark. Max's breath smelled like Alpo. And there was something wrong with the furnace because her feet were so cold they hurt. Her head hurt, too.

She put her hands up and pushed at the furry chest. "Stop," she said.

Max whimpered and settled himself flat on her chest.

"Max, darn it. Get off. I can't breathe!"

Quill struggled upright. Max weighed close to eighty pounds. And he was stubborn. She rolled the dog over and pushed him off into the snow.

And she realized, with a jolt of absolute panic, that she was lying in the middle of a woods in the dark and it was snowing hard.

Max jumped to his feet, shook his coat free of snow, and shoved his solid body against her shoulder. Quill steadied herself with one hand on his back and pulled herself to her feet. "Aren't you a good boy," she said breathlessly.

Her memory crept back to her in fits and starts, like floats bumping into her in a river. She'd left the church to walk home. She'd slipped on the ice on the path up the hill. She'd knocked the brains out of her skull when she'd fallen.

Except that she'd fallen forward; she was certain of it. And she'd wakened on her back.

She felt her forehead gingerly with one gloved hand. There was a terrific lump. And it was scraped raw. It stung in the frigid air. She must have hit a rock or a tree trunk the size of Alaska when she'd tripped. She was still clutching her key chain. She switched the flashlight on, and the beam pointed straight down. Shakily, she directed the beam to the ground in front of her.

The path was free of debris, except for a thin carpet of snow and a swirl of paw prints, footprints, and boot prints. The prints were filling up rapidly as the snow came down. But there was no boulder, no tree trunk the size of Alaska or otherwise.

She crouched down and nearly fell over from dizziness. She steadied herself with one hand and ran the flashlight over the roiled-up snow with the other. The paw prints were Max's. The boot prints were hers. The footprints belonged to somebody with a pair of smooth-bottomed shoes.

"Somebody's been here," Quill said aloud.

Max pushed himself against her knees and she nearly fell over again.

"Max, who the heck would be out in the snow in shoes? Their feet would freeze off." A sudden stab of pain in her skull made her gasp. She hadn't fallen. She'd been hit over the head. "Which I hope they did, by God. Froze off, I mean."

She took a deep breath. Her purse must be lying somewhere around here. There, at the side of the path, half its contents lying soggy in the snow. She picked her purse up and retrieved her cell phone, wallet, and sketchpad. The sketchpad was a total loss. All her money and credit cards were still in her wallet. And her cell phone was deader than a doornail, either because she'd forgotten to charge it or because its complicated little innards didn't take to storage in snowbanks.

The ache in her head ebbed. The snow slowed and stopped. The clouds drifted on and the moon shone down, illuminating the path up the side of the hill to home. It was either back through the park or forward to a hot bath and a couple of aspirin.

Quill climbed up the slope to the top of the hill. Max charged over the top of the rise and plunged down to the lawn below. Quill followed him and stopped before she walked down the slight slope of law to the Inn. She rarely saw the structure from the top of the gorge at night, and she was struck by how beautiful it was. The Christmas lights made a fantastical jeweled web in the dining room windows. At Quill's request, Mike had wound another web of lights around the trunk and branches of the oak tree just outside the front door. The effect was wonderful. The tree glowed with an otherworldly light.

Max dashed to the front door, looked at her, dashed back to her side, and then sat down, tongue lolling, as if to say, "Now what?"

"If I go in the front door, chances are good that someone will see me and shriek like a banshee. And I'm just not up for that, Max. If I go into the kitchen, it's certain I'd run into Meg or worse yet, Lydia and the television shoot, and I'm not up for that, either. So it's the burglar's way for us. As it is, even if I get myself cleaned up so it doesn't look as scary as I think it does, you know what's going to happen as well as I do. Somebody will insist on calling the sheriff's office, and Davy Kiddermeister took Dina to the movies tonight in Syracuse, and it would just wreck her date if he had to come back here and mooch around the dark in the snow. And Meg would drag me to the ER. Nope. I'm sneaking in."

She felt quite noble about her decision. She looked at the fire escape on the east side of the building. Her rooms were on the third floor, directly across from Meg's. And she had the keys to the fire door with her. At the moment, it looked like a long way up.

It took less effort to climb the fire escape stairs than she thought it would, perhaps because Max insisted on coming with her. Quill patted him frequently, grateful for his affection. These particular stairs scared him and it took him forever to decide to leave one landing and take the stairs to the next. She was feeling quite like her old self when she let herself into her rooms. She shrugged off her coat, kicked off her boots, and took a good long look at herself in the bathroom mirror. What had felt like a giant bump to her fingertips looked quite harmless. There was a slight swelling, and there was a faint bluish tint to her skin, but that was it. The scrape was barely visible. And there was hardly any blood.

Quill was conscious of a feeling of disappointment. "I mean," she said to Max, who was listening with every evidence of intense curiosity, "you'd think that being knocked cold by a midnight attacker would be more, I don't know, obvious."

Her feet and toes were quite warm now, too. And although her skirt was soaked from the snow, and clung unpleasantly to her calves, she was actually feeling quite warm in her fisherman's sweater.

She swallowed some aspirin, washed her face, combed her hair, and changed into dry trousers, a lighter-weight sweater, and a pair of knee socks and comfortable shoes. By the time she got downstairs, her headache was gone. To her surprise, the dining room was a quarter full of people still eating dinner. To her further surprise, when she flung the swinging doors into the kitchen open and announced, "I'm back," Meg merely looked up her from her place at the stove and said, "How come you're back so early? It's a good thing that you are, though. I could use a hand here."

Quill looked at the kitchen clock. It was barely eight. It seemed as if a lifetime had passed since she wakened in the woods. Clearly, she'd been unconscious for mere minutes.

Although the area around the new stove and prep sinks was clear, the rear part of the kitchen was filled with stage lights, video monitors, and a large video camera with a stand. Benny fussed with a wreath of spices that hung over the bread hearth. Five elves in costume lounged around in various poses; two were slumped comfortably in portable director's chairs, one sat cross-legged on the floor, and two stood with their backs against the wall in the short hallway that led to the outside door. With the hats, clown white makeup, fake noses, and tights and jerkins, it was impossible to distinguish one from the other.

"Plate!" Meg shouted. Kathleen grabbed the entrée Meg had flung on the countertop and trotted out the door.

"Poached pears!" Mikhail grabbed a strainer, and began to take the pears simmering in wine out of the pot one by one.

"I need someone to prep Steak Quilliam," Meg said, "and that's you, Quill, since Mikhail's busy with the pears."

"But—" Quill gave up. If Meg hadn't noticed she was bravely ignoring a significant head wound by now, she wasn't going to until the food preparation was over.

Quill took a plate from the warming oven, arranged the Potatoes Duchess, sprigs of rosemary and cinnamon-spiced apple rings on it, and stepped back as Meg took a filet from her sauté pan and lifted it carefully into the center of the food. She handed the pan to Quill, who carefully drizzled the sauce over the beef.

"Meg!" Benny called out. "If that's the last of the orders, can we try another run-through?"

"Yes. You can have my kitchen full time, now, Benny.

That was the last entrée. If any dessert orders come in, Quill and I can handle them."

Kathleen returned from delivering the final entrée and took her place in the lineup in front of the bread oven.

"Everyone line up!" Ajit stood behind the camera and put his eye to the lens. "Elf on the left move over three feet to your right. No, no, your other right."

"Is Melissa there?" Quill said. "I can't tell which one of you is which."

"After rehearsal," Ajit said firmly. "Come on now, dear. Ajit wants to get some dancing feet on tape." He sent Quill a brief, comradely grin. "We only use one camera on the live shoot, but we want the production values to look pricier. So we do a lot of cutting with shots we've taken earlier."

Quill nodded as if this made sense to her and sat down in her rocking chair. She sighed rather loudly, put her hand to her forehead, and gently rubbed her bump.

"So how was choir practice?" Meg asked as she briskly swabbed down the stove.

"I didn't stay."

Meg laughed. "The hip-hop version of the 'Hallelujah Chorus' get to you?"

"Harvey seems to have changed his mind about that."

"Thank goodness."

Quill sighed more loudly. "Do you have something I could use as a bandage around here?"

"Of course we do. The first aid kit's under—oh, no, it isn't, we moved it." Meg reached under the sink and brought out the white plastic box. "Did you cut yourself?"

"I got whacked on the head."

Meg looked up, startled. "You what?"

"I walked back through the park and someone hit me on the head. I was out cold," Quill added rather pitifully, "for quite some time."

Meg was at her side in seconds. "Where did you get hit?" she asked anxiously. "There, on your forehead?" She touched the bump lightly with two fingers. The tension ran out of her shoulders and she straightened up. "Well, for heaven's sake. It doesn't seem like too much of a bump. And what happened?" She stiffened. "Were you mugged?"

"Of course not," Quill said, "this is Hemlock Falls."

"What happened?

Quill explained. Meg rubbed her nose and said skeptically, "Are you sure you just didn't slip and fall? I mean, it must have been quite a smack, and that's a shame, but why would anyone hit you on the head?"

"I don't know."

"I think you're just a little disoriented," Meg said kindly. "I'll get you some hot tea. You get a good night's sleep, and you'll have forgotten all about it in the morning."

"I was sure I saw a third set of footprints there." Quill closed her eyes trying to remember. "Well, maybe I did. And maybe I just knocked myself out. Do you think?"

Meg patted her shoulder. "One way or another, sister dear. You always do."


Myles didn't call.

Quill refused to worry. There could be all kinds of reasons why. But when she slept, she dreamed of footprints and moonlight and kept waking in the night, reaching across the mattress to him.

She fell into a heavy, restless sleep just as the dark began to lighten into day.

A loud, imperative banging on her door jerked her awake. Max was curled at the foot of the bed. The knocking jerked him awake, too. He jumped off the bed and began to bark. Quill rolled out of bed. Her head was fuzzy, her unsettled stomach was back, and her muscles ached from the fall she'd taken in the woods. She pulled on a bathrobe and stamped to the door. "This," she snarled as she pulled it open, "had better be good."

"It's not good at all," Meg said. She stepped into the room. Her short dark hair was tangled, as if she'd been trying to pull it off her head altogether. "Mike found Zeke Kingsfield's body at the bottom of the gorge." She stepped inside the door and pulled it shut behind her. "I can't believe it, Quill. He's dead."

"Dead?" Quill stared at her sister in horror. "Zeke Kingsfield's dead? How? Why? Do we know what happened?"

Meg shouldered past her and went into the Quill's little kitchen. "Have you had coffee yet?"

"I haven't even been to the bathroom yet," Quill said indignantly. "Just tell me what's happened, okay?"

"He went out for his cross-country ski run about seven this morning, just as it was getting light. He's usually back by eight thirty to have breakfast with Lydia . . ."

"She didn't go with him this morning?"

"She said they got back too late from Syracuse last night. At any rate, she sent Mike out to look for him in the snowmobile. It looks like he went over the edge of the gorge where we put in that little fence. Dammit! We put that fence there to prevent stuff like this from happening."

"Good grief." Quill sat down on the stool at her kitchen counter. "Poor guy."

Meg dumped coffee beans into the grinder, pushed the button, and waited until the beans had been reduced to a fine powder. She filled the electric teakettle with water and plugged it in. "Mike jumped off the snowmobile and climbed down the slope to the river. He said it looked as if Kingsfield's neck was broken, but, of course, we won't know for sure until the autopsy's done."

"I hope it was quick," Quill said with a shudder. "It's awful. Just awful. How is Lydia taking it?"

Meg didn't answer. She put the filter in the Melitta cone, added the coffee, then the hot water.

"She knows, doesn't she?" Quill said. "Don't tell me no one's told the poor woman."

"Of course she knows. Mike came back and went straight to her after he told me. He wanted to wake you up, but I said I'd take care of it, which is why I'm here." She poured out a cup of coffee and handed it over. "I haven't seen her, so I don't know how she's taking it. Mike called the sheriff's office and the EMTs and then he took Lydia back to the site on his snowmobile."

"So she's down there with the body?"

"Yep."

"One of us should be there."

"Yep."

"And you've got to get breakfast out."

"I should be there right now."

"Okay. Go back to the kitchen. I'll go down myself. It'll take me a few minutes to get dressed." She paused on her way back to her bedroom. "Mike put those fence posts in with concrete, Meg. And the fence was made of chain link. I don't understand how he could have gone through it."

"Kingsfield apparently hit a boulder under the snow and veered into the fence. Mike says he was probably clipping along at a pretty good rate at that point. Anyhow, the freeze-and-thaw cycle we had a few weeks ago must have loosened the posts. One was pulled right out of the hole." Meg spread her hands in a "that's it" gesture. "I'm off. Call me if you need me."

Meg let the door bang closed behind her. Quill showered, then pinned her hair back with a clip. She pulled on a silk turtleneck, a heavy sweater, and wool pants. Her boots were still wet from the night before, and she rummaged in the back of her closet for an old pair of acrylic-lined pull-ons.

She sat on the edge of her bed, put on a heavy pair of socks, and paused with one boot in her hand. She *had* been hit over the head. She was sure of it. Which meant that someone had been in the woods surrounding the gorge the night before Zeke Kingsfield fell to his death in an accident that shouldn't have happened. Somebody who didn't want her to see . . . what?

Quill frowned, visualizing the spot where Zeke had gone off the cliff into the gorge, and its relationship to where she had been last night. The ski path Mike had created fell away from the west side of the Inn, curved around the edge of the gorge, and then circled back to the east side of the Inn. She'd been struck—she was positive she'd been struck—at a point about an eighth of a mile from the curve. If someone had come up to that point from the park, they would have been concealed all the way. If they'd come down from the Inn, they would have been visible the length of a football field before reaching the seclusion of the trees.

And they reach the curve and do what?

Quill shook her head, remembering the advice Nero Wolfe always gave Archie Goodwin: Never theorize ahead of the facts.

Quill left the Inn by the front door several minutes later. A helicopter hovered over the gorge. A cluster of police cars, an ambulance, and a fire truck were parked every which way in the parking lot. Beyond that, at the spot where the ski trail curved around the gorge, she could see yellow-coated firemen, police in dark blue anoraks, and a small crowd of lookers-on.

Quill followed the short trail left by snowmobiles and booted feet across the field to the far lip of the gorge. She looked first for Lydia. The widow stood next to an empty collapsible gurney, about forty feet away from the remains of the chain-link fence. LaToya and Ajit stood a few strides away huddled together as in the middle of a storm.

"Lydia?" Quill asked quietly.

She turned at the sound of Quill's voice. Quill's first reaction was one of slight shock. Lydia's hair was a mess. She wore no makeup. She'd thrown on somebody else's parka, which was too big for her. Her small feet wallowed in a pair of boots at least three sizes too big. Quill recognized those boots; it was an old pair she kept by the back of the kitchen door. "Quill," she said blankly. She turned away again, to stare down the cliff. Quill walked up and stood next to her.

Down below, a group of men had placed the body on a portable stretcher. It had been placed in a black body bag. Artie Guttenwald, the head of the Hemlock Falls Volunteer Ambulance Corps, was carefully zipping the body bag closed. Then Davy Kiddermeister, who had been promoted to sheriff when Myles resigned the position, picked up the front end of the stretcher. Artie and another EMT picked up the rear. They began the slow struggle up the shale rock to the top. Two other figures in jackets marked TOMPKINS COUNTY SHERIFF'S DEPT. crouched at the wrecked remains of the skis.

The helicopter swooped lower and continued circling. Quill looked up; a cameraman leaned out of the passenger-side door, his camera aimed at the action below. Lydia followed her glance. "I can see that offends you, Quill. But Zeke would have loved it." She gave Quill a faint smile. "He wasn't afraid of going broke. Or of any of his businesses going bust. He was mortally afraid that he wouldn't be remembered. He wanted to be able to walk into a McDonald's anywhere in the world and have somebody point and say, 'It's the Hammer!'"

"McDonald's?"

Lydia shrugged. "You get the idea. He always saw himself as the quintessential American entrepreneur. And he believed that this is the age of the businessman, that four hundred years from now, even a thousand years from now, people would remember him the way we remember Julius Caesar."

Or Boss Tweed or Jack Abramoff, Quill wanted to say, but didn't. What she did say was, "I'm sorry."

Lydia sighed. "I'm sorry, too. And I'm afraid you're going to be even sorrier, Quill. This whole area belongs to the Inn, doesn't it? And you directed Mike Santelli to set up this very dangerous ski trail. My lawyers will be in touch with your insurance company."

Davy and the others reached the top of the cliff, struggled

up and over, and set their burden down. Lydia walked up to the stretcher, crouched down, and pulled the body bag open.

Quill looked away. When she looked back, the bag was zipped shut again. Lydia had risen to her feet and was headed toward the ambulance. Davy and the others picked the stretcher up and followed her. Davy looked over his shoulder and nodded. Everyone watched in silence as the awkward parade proceeded the hundred yards across the field to the parking lot. The helicopter increased the circumference of its circle. With an unwelcome intrusion of her imagination, Quill could almost hear the hushed, smarmy excitement of the TV reporter's narration. "And now the widow, head bowed, hands clutching the borrowed coat across her chest, follows the body of her dead husband across the wild expanse of this remote upstate village."

Or something like that. Quill said, "Ugh," to the surprised disapproval of those within earshot. She debated a long moment, then walked over to LaToya and Ajit, who were dry-eyed, but somber. "Is there anything I can do for you two right now?"

Ajit put his arm around LaToya's shoulder. "I think coffee'd be a good thing."

"With maybe a little brandy in it," LaToya said with a shudder. "That's the first dead body I've ever seen. And it's somebody I knew." Suddenly, her eyes filled with tears.

"Now, now," said Ajit. "Now, now."

"Take her on back to the Tavern Lounge," Quill suggested. "Ask Nate to make both of you a hot toddy. I'll be down in a moment." She waited until they'd gotten halfway across the field to the parking lot. Beyond them, the ambulance took off, sirens silenced, red lights flashing. Most of the crowd of gawkers surged forward. Overhead, the helicopter turned and flew off after the emergency vehicle.

Either the Tompkins County Sheriff's Department or Davy himself had strung a yellow police tape around the spot where Zeke's skis had apparently hit a large tree trunk hidden beneath the snow and been thrown into the fence. A police photographer crouched in the snow, taking pictures from every angle. Quill walked down the ski trail, attempting to trace the Zeke's path. A substantial portion of the trail had been obscured by snowmobile treads.

"I didn't think about leaving any evidence for the police to find when I went looking for him this morning," Mike said from behind her. "Until I saw the busted fence. Then I stopped and got right off." He pointed at the snowmobile parked under the trees at the edge of the trail opposite the gorge. "She's still parked there."

"I'm so sorry about all this, Mike."

Mike shoved his orange Arctic hat further down his fore-head. "Yeah, well, I can tell you this, Quill. I was out here to groom this trail yesterday and there's no way that the tree trunk was there."

"Oh?"

"No, sir," he said firmly. "And I told the police that. Somebody put that tree trunk there, and dug up the posts to my fence, and then let the snow last night cover all of it. I swear to God that's what happened. You know what? Some bas . . . that is, some jerk's setting me up." Mike had a pleas-ant, unexceptional face, the kind that got lost in a crowd very easily. He was in his midforties now; he had a wife and two kids who were a junior and senior at Hemlock Falls High School. He was the kind of guy that did his job, did it well, and went home to Monday Night Football and a comfort-able, contented wife.

It was rare—unsettling—to see the anger in his face now.

Quill put her hand on his shoulder for a brief moment. Mike had worked for them for years, ever since they'd brought in enough money to pay for his landscaping skills. Actually, Quill thought, it was before they were making a profit. The beauty of the woods and gardens surrounding the Inn were an inextricable part of their success. A large part of that was due to Mike.

Quill took a deep breath. If Mike was right, this wasn't an accident.

"You get what I'm saying?" Mike said.

"I not only get what you're saying, I believe you," Quill said.

"Then you want to tell that to those bas . . . those cops over there?"

"I will. And I'm going to do my best to find out what happened here, Mike. You can be absolutely certain of that. Right now, I think it'd be a good thing if you took the rest of the day off."

"I'd rather get into culling out that deadwood on that back acreage."

"I can see why," Quill said. "I wouldn't mind working out some of my frustrations with this using a chain saw and an ax. But I think it'd be wise if you were unavailable for the time being, except to the police of course."

Mike's lips worked. Finally he said, jerkily, "Now, if it's that you're going to be wanting to fire me, I guess I can see why. But I'm here to tell you it ain't fair."

"The only way you'll lose this job is if the bank padlocks the doors for debt," Quill said. Then, at his look of horror, she said, "Bad joke. Really bad joke. Now listen to me, you remember when Meg and I arranged to have you and Doreen and Kathleen own a small percentage of the Inn? Because you three were such an important reason for our success?"

"Well, sure."

"I mean, not that being a shareholder has been exactly profitable for you all these days," Quill said wryly. "I'm doing my best to fix that, if I can. But my point is, you're a partner in this business, Mike. A small partner to be sure. But a partner nonetheless. And you don't fire your partners."

He nodded, jerkily. "Yeah. Gotcha. And thanks." He stared at his feet for a long moment. "Look. I'll lay low for a couple of days. But if you and Meg need me"—he put his thumb and forefinger to his mouth and ear in a jaunty imitation of a cell phone—"all you gotta do is call."

They shook hands. Mike got into the snowmobile, gunned it, and took off in a spray of white. Quill waited until she was absolutely sure he was out of earshot and muttered, "Lie low, lie low, *lie* low."

"Excuse me, Quill?" Dave Kiddermeister tapped her gently on the shoulder. "You're talking about somebody laying low?"

"I was relieving my tensions by having a grammar snit. And if *you* don't pay attention to your verb forms, I'm going to rat you out to Dina."

"Ha-ha," Davy said in a bewildered way. "Just wanted to tell you we're about finished here. We're wrapping it up." He shook his head. "Terrible accident. Just terrible. And of all the people to buy the farm on your property. The most famous man in America."

"He was certainly the most notorious man in America," Quill said tartly. "And you took Mike's statement, Davy. You know this wasn't an accident. Mike never would have left that tree trunk directly in the path of the ski trail. Anyone with half a grain of sense can see that a skier would be picking up speed down that slope, and that at the very least, there'd be a nasty fall into the fence."

"It's easy to overlook these things," Davy said. "And I know how upsetting this must be for you. I mean, the most famous man in Amer—"

"Stop," Quill said.

"Yes, ma'am. And there's Mrs. Kingsfield saying already that she's going to sue you—and Kingsfield's life has gotta be worth a mint."

"Kingsfield's life has got to . . . what?!"

"There's no cap on the cost of a wrongful death in New York State," Davy said helpfully. "This Mrs. Kingsfield can sue you for everything your insurance company's got, plus whatever you've got, too."

Quill shoved her hands in the pocket of her parka and looked at him. Davy squirmed uncomfortably. "Now, I'm not so sure why you're getting hot under the collar here."

"I'm getting hot under the collar because I cannot believe that you are going to let this murder go uninvestigated. Unsolved. That you'll let a murderer walk free and clear."

"But, Quill . . ."

"But Quill nothing. You know Mike. You know how honest and reliable he is."

"I've got to have corroboration," Davy said. "He doesn't have anyone who can back him up."

"I can back him up!"

He folded his lips in determination and regarded her sternly. "You inspected this ski trail yesterday and can attest to the fact that the tree trunk wasn't there? You inspected the fence to make sure that the foundations hadn't worked loose because of this last thaw-and-freeze cycle? And you'll swear to that in court?"

Quill glared at him in frustration. Davy had fair skin, bright blond hair and very blue eyes. She remembered the days when Davy was so shy he turned bright pink when talking to anyone but his high school buddies. She remembered when he was so unwilling to give out speeding tickets that an investigator from the county sheriff's office showed up to see if he were taking bribes. And now this . . . this junior G-man had turned into a bully. "At least call out the scene-of-the-crimes unit," Quill said. "I'm positive if you look hard enough, you'll find something incriminating."

"Like what?"

"Did you lift up the tree trunk to see if it had been moved recently?"

"As a matter of fact, we did."

"And?"

"The evidence is inconclusive," he said stiffly.

"What's that's supposed to mean?"

"That any halfway decent lawyer can pull it apart in court."

"And what about the fence posts?"

"That's inconclusive, too."

Quill rubbed her forehead, forgetting her bump. She winced.

"Anything wrong?" Davy asked with concern.

"Just that I was mugged in the woods last night," Quill snapped.

"You're kidding. Are you okay? Did you see the guy? Why didn't you make a report?"

"Yes, I'm okay, and no, I didn't see the guy." Quill bit her lip. "And to be perfectly fair, I may have tripped. But I don't think so. I'll tell you what I think, Davy. The person who smacked me last night was either on his way to, or coming from, putting the tree trunk in the way of Zeke Kingsfield." She looked up at him. "And I intend to find out who it is."

Davy unzipped his official Hemlock Falls Police Department jacket, as if he were suddenly hot. "Quill, please. It's bad enough that somebody like Mr. Kingsfield's croaked on your property without you and Meg interfer—"

"With Meg and me what?"

He shifted his shoulders uncomfortably.

"You have to admit that we've been pretty helpful once or twice in the past."

Davy didn't look as if he were willing to admit this at all. Then he said, "Is the sheriff due back anytime soon?"

"David, *you're* the sheriff. Myles hasn't been sheriff for several years now."

"True enough." He smiled reluctantly. "I can't help thinking he could handle you . . . I mean this situation a lot better than I can. I'm good at traffic tickets and shoplifters. This kind of stuff, especially with somebody this famous, well, I'm not sure what steps I should be taking, to tell you the truth."

"I'll tell you what Myles might suggest," Quill said briskly. "If nothing else, we're going to be plagued with a lot of souvenir hunters and gawkers. You might station a few patrolmen around the scene here for a week or two, just to keep the crowds from forming."

"That's a great idea."

"And you won't mind if I poke around the woods for a bit?"

"I guess not. Are you looking for anything in particular?"

"You bet I am. Evidence that someone set up this murder."

Davy flushed. "Quill, you can't go messing around in the woods."

"And why not? Look, Davy. Either this is a murder or it isn't. If it is, you should get your forensics team in there and check everything out. If it isn't, there's no reason why I can't go back there myself, is there?"

"Dammit!" Davy wore a knitted blue watch cap, standard issue for the winter uniform. He pulled it off and balled it up. "You've got a point. Okay, we'll check the woods out."

"You don't mind if I wait right here, do you?" Quill asked.

"Suit yourself. Just stay well back from the police tape, okay? This will take a while. And it's cold out here. Maybe you ought to go back to the Inn."

"No chance," Quill said. "I just know you're going to find something."

It *was* cold. Davy sent three patrolmen into the woods. She saw them fan out in a semicircle, with the tree trunk as a nexus. They disappeared into the underbrush. Quill walked up and down for a bit to keep her feet warm. Then she jogged in place to keep the rest of herself warm. She was just about to call it quits and return to the Inn when she heard a shout. One of the patrolmen emerged from the woods and waved for the photographer. After a short colloquy with the patrolman, he hurried over to the remains of the chain-link fence. He knelt down, examined the tipped-over fence post, and yelled, "Got it!"

Quill walked a littler closer to the police tape and stared hopefully at Davy.

He did his best to ignore her. He took his watch cap off

and put it on again. He stamped his feet. He walked up and down. Finally, he ducked under the tape and came up to her. "Okay," he said. "We found something. But it's not all that significant. Not by itself."

"What?"

"It's purely circumstantial, mind you."

"Okay. But what is it?"

"You hang any wires across the trail recently?"

"Ah-ha," Quill said. "He was tripped."

"That's a pretty big leap. We did find a scar in the tree trunk behind the boulder, and a similar scar at the same height on the post."

Quill looked from the fence to the woods. "So whoever it was stretched the wire across the trail. But it's behind the boulder. You know what it was, Davy? It was a backup plan. If Zeke didn't hit the tree trunk when he came zipping down the slope, the wire would have tripped him up. He didn't have to hit the tree trunk at all. And," she added with excitement, "whoever it was must have been there this morning. Otherwise you would have found the wire, right?"

"Maybe," Davy said. "I'm putting it all into the report. The rest of it will be up to the ME's office."

"Gosh." Quill shivered. Suddenly, it seemed very cold. "Whoever it was must have stood there and watched Zeke Kingsfield die."


She walked back to the Inn, lost in thought. She came in through the kitchen door, to be greeted by Max, Elizabeth, and Mikhail, and no one else. "Where is everybody?"

"Mrs. Kingsfield's in the Tavern Lounge with Ajit and the rest of them," Mikhail offered.

"The rest of them who? LaToya? Ajit? The Bs?"

"Yes. Ajit thought they should all go back to New York. Mrs. Kingsfield and LaToya want to stay here and finish the Christmas shoot. I guess they're arguing about it."

"What about Meg?"

"She left us in charge of the kitchen," Elizabeth said. "And she went up to her room to get something, and then she stomped outside, got into her car, and drove off."

"I think she went to that special meeting of the Chamber of Commerce," Mikhail said. He was a good-looking kid, with a smooth, caramel-colored complexion and a sweet smile. He looked ill at ease and very unhappy.

Quill looked at her watch. She was astounded to see that it was after eleven o'clock. "I suppose I'd better go down and get her." She looked at each of them in turn. "Are you going to be all right?"

The two of them exchanged glances. "Things are pretty creepy," Elizabeth admitted. "And I don't know if the two of us can handle the kitchen all by ourselves."

"Where's Melissa?"

"She hasn't been in yet in this morning." Mikhail shrugged his shoulders. "So, I don't know."

"Give her a call," Quill suggested, "and tell her you really need that extra pair of hands. Kathleen's out in the dining room, isn't she? Good. I'll ask her to give some of the backup staff a call. I'd be truly grateful if the two of you could carry on, though. Do you think you can manage?"

"I think so," Mikhail said. "But the thing is, Quill. When Meg ran out of here, she was carrying a gun."

# CHAPTER 9

Quill stood in the parking lot of the Village of Hemlock Falls Town Hall. She kept her hand firmly clasped around Meg's right wrist and said, "Give me the gun."

Meg shrugged her off and kept the paintball gun aimed at the Hemlock Falls Fireman's Auxiliary's latest addition to municipal decorations. A twelve-foot inflatable Santa Claus bobbed gently in the middle of a fifteen-foot inflatable toy shop. The Santa was surrounded by a dozen inflatable elves. The exhibit stood smack in the middle of the lawn.

"What in the world set you off like this?" Quill demanded.

"Stress," Meg said promptly. "You get ulcers. I get an irresistible desire to whack helium-filled lawn ornaments. You know the whole thing lights up at night," Meg added accusingly.

Quill sighed. "Yes, I know." Meg cocked the trigger and she added, "If you puncture that Santa Claus, the mayor's going to insist that we pay for it. Those things are expensive."

Meg lowered the paintball gun and looked speculative. "How expensive?"

Quill told her.

Meg shook her head. "Good grief! Well, it isn't worth it, I suppose." She ejected the $CO_2$ cartridge. "Why can't people stick to plain old Christmas lights? What was wrong with last year's decorations? Good old wooden Christmas trees."

"There does seem to be some kind of weird extra enthusiasm for the holidays this year," Quill admitted. "If you're not going to splatter the Santa Claus all over the snow, we'd better get going. It's way after one o'clock. They'll have started the Chamber meeting without us."

Meg slung the paintball gun over her shoulder and trudged down the sidewalk in grumpy silence. Quill followed her. "I'm surprised that the mayor hasn't called off the meeting. Zeke Kingsfield was supposed to give his real estate seminar. And of course, now it's moot, isn't it?"

"Moot." Meg stopped in her tracks, swung the derringer up, aimed at a denuded maple tree, and pulled the trigger. The wad of orange paint hit the trunk and dribbled down to the snow. "This is quite therapeutic, sis. I mean, I'd far rather turn Lydia Kingsfield and her raft of lawyers bright orange, but hey, this isn't a bad substitute."

"Is there a reason why you decided to go to this meeting? You avoid Chamber meetings like the plague."

"I thought I might hear something about this so-called accident that can help us avoid being sued." Meg's face turned pink. She flung her hands up in the air. A few drops of orange paint splattered on her knitted hat. "And I don't want to think about the wreck of all our hopes."

"The wreck of all our hopes?"

"Doesn't this mean that the whole Kingsfield deal is off? Not to mention the fact that Lydia's going to sue us for every nickel we haven't got."

Quill tugged at Meg's jacket. "Hang on a minute."

Meg clutched the little gun to her chest. "It's mine. If you want to shoot something, get your own."

"I can tell you something about the accident."

"What?" Meg asked suspiciously.

"It wasn't one. Zeke Kingsfield was murdered."

Meg's eyes widened. "You're kidding."

"I am not." She told her about Mike. "And he'll swear on a stack of Bibles that the tree trunk wasn't there when he finished grooming the trail just before dark yesterday."

Meg did a jig in the snow. "This is great! This is terrific news!"

"I would like to remind you," Quill said repressively, "that the poor man is dead."

"But it's not our fault!" She stopped in mid-jig. "What about the fence post? Did the murderer loosen the fence post, too?"

"He's less sure about that," Quill admitted. "That thaw we had a few weeks ago might have loosened the dirt around the Sakrete. But he's sure that couldn't account for the post coming all the way out of the hole the way it did. So my guess is that the murderer took advantage of that."

"So we're okay."

"Not totally. They could bring a civil action, Meg. I mean, that's what Nicole Brown Simpson's parents did. But the lawyers would have a much tougher time collecting anything from us above and beyond what our insurance limits are."

"Did you tell Davy? That it's murder?"

"Of course I told Davy."

"And does he have any leads? Is he going to investigate?"

"He did a little more investigation than he would have if it'd just been an accident. I had to goad him into it, but he did. He found some evidence that suggests someone strung a trip wire across the trail."

"Well, there you are, then!"

"It's circumstantial. At best. And even I know enough about the law to know it's too feeble to be called a case. And Davy's not eager to follow it up. I can't say as I blame him. I mean, just think of the tabloids. They're going to have a field day as it is."

"I can see the headlines now," Meg said glumly. "Murder Inn. This is just awful. This is a calamity."

Quill stopped and put her hand on Meg's arm. "It's not the end of the world, surely."

"Lydia's going to pull out of the lease. The whole thing's going down the tubes," Meg said dejectedly.

"Not if we find out who did it."

Meg stuck her forefinger in the pistol's trigger guard and twirled it like a top. "Qulliam and Quilliam, PIs," she said. "I like it. I really like it." She came to a halt, and Quill stopped beside her. They were at the church. "So the deal is, we sort of nose around and ask questions?"

Quill nodded. "Who had a grudge against Kingsfield?"

"I don't know. Who?"

"Will Frazier, for one," Quill said promptly. "And maybe even Charley Comstock, if what Marge says about the Gorgeous Gorges deal is true. We'll just have to devise discreet but pointed questions. You take Charley, I'll take Will. We need to find out what kind of alibis they had last night."

"And if both them have alibis?"

"Zeke Kingsfield," Quill said soberly, "was the kind of man who had lots of enemies. We've barely scratched the surface."

"Well, I'm no quitter. And neither are you. We're going to get to the bottom of this." Meg stamped up the broad steps of the church with a determined air. Quill followed her inside.

The church was almost full. Quill stopped just inside the door, startled at the mob of people. Most of the Chamber members were there. And there was a confused mix of townspeople, reporters, and most of the residents of the Gorgeous Gorges trailer park. But many in the crowd were totally unfamiliar to her. And over the year, she'd met just about everyone who lived in Hemlock Falls.

"I've never seen some of these people before," Meg said. "Where do you suppose they're from?"

Quill shook her head. "They have to be from Syracuse.

Or even Ithaca. I suppose they're here just for the notoriety of it."

"It's the money," Marge said bluntly from behind them. "That forty-three million dollars Zeke claimed he was going to spread around. Go on and sit down, you two. I saved us a couple of seats near Dookie."

Dookie Shuttleworth, the Hemlock Falls Church of the Word of God's gentle, absentminded pastor, turned to wave a welcome as Marge and Quill came up the aisle, although he frowned in a puzzled way at the orange paint on Meg's hat. He made a space for the three of them. Quill sat down next to his wife, Wendy. Marge sat on Quill's other side. Meg sat next to Dookie himself.

The pews in front of them and behind them were filled with Chamber members, like lambs huddling together in a field of wolves. In the pew in front of them, Howie Murchison and Miriam Doncaster sat next to Harland Peterson. In the pew behind them, Charley Comstock sat next to Adela Henry. Esther, Nadine, and the others filled the remaining seats in the pew.

"It *is* nice to see you here, Quill," Wendy said in her gentle voice. "Although I'd hoped to see Myles, too. Will he be home for Christmas?"

"I hope so."

"I heard he was somewhere in the Middle East," Wendy said sympathetically. "Worrisome for you."

Quill nodded. She looked around, a little puzzled. "I thought we'd missed the start of the meeting. The mayor isn't here yet?"

Wendy shrugged. She was a slender woman, with a wispy sort of fragility that reminded Quill of a dandelion after the petals had blown off. "Adela said he was taking an important phone call. He'll be here as best he can. I hope it's sooner rather than later. This is a very odd sort of crowd, don't you think? They seem restless. More like a mob than a congregation."

Quill had to agree with her. Most of the faces she knew looked disturbed, or angry, or a combination of the two. The faces she didn't know looked avid.

"Who *are* all these people?" Adela asked suddenly. She turned around and looked accusingly at Quill. "Where have they all come from?"

"Well, I don't know, exactly." Quill glanced at Marge. "Some of them may be here as a result of the announcement yesterday. The news that that amount of money was to be dropped on a town like ours could attract . . ." Quill wasn't sure how to end the sentence.

Marge did it for her. "Shysters. Crooks. Con artists," she said bluntly. "She jerked her chin at the frail old lady Quill had seen at the trailer park yesterday. Mrs. Huston, the woman who'd been taking care of Melissa's Caleb. A man who was clearly her son, his hard-looking wife, and three sullen teenagers surrounded her. "Jean Huston, for example. Hasn't seen that no-good son of hers for years and surprise, surprise, he got here as fast as his beat-up Toyota could carry him as soon as he heard the news about her million bucks." Marge pointed at a thin, ferrety-looking man slumped inconspicuously in the corner of a pew. "That's Dieter Jacoby. The National Association of Realtors kicked him out of the group last year because he was shafting his clients. And a lot of the rest of these?" Marge's gaze swept the crowd contemptuously. "Gawkers," she said contemptuously.

Adela was dressed in a vivid green pantsuit. A fist-sized pendant of amber and silver rested on her considerable bosom. She fiddled with it nervously. "I wish Elmer would get here," she said fretfully. Her eyes swept past Meg, then back again. "Why does Meg have orange paint all over her hat?" she demanded.

Meg felt the top of her head, then took her hat off and stuck it in her parka pocket.

"Have you been by to see my Christmas decorations lately?" Adela asked in a dangerous tone.

Quill asked, without a blink, "At your house, do you mean? I haven't had a chance to, yet, no. I'm sure they're quite beautiful."

Adela frowned at Meg. "Not any more they aren't. I had an elegant Santa's workshop in the front yard. New this year. It was quite impressive. Somebody shot it."

"Shot it?"

"With orange paint. There was orange paint all over the place."

Quill bit her lip. "Hm."

"That is *such* a shame," Meg said brightly.

Adela leveled a long, thoughtful look at Meg. There was a stamping of feet from the back of the aisle, and she turned her head a little. "The mayor has arrived," she said. "And not a moment too soon. You will excuse me." She huffed her way out of the pew and followed Elmer up the aisle to the front of the church.

Elmer went to the lectern. Adela sat in the deacon's chair, folded her hands in her lap, and glared at Meg. Meg wriggled her fingers in a cheerful salute.

"Will you cut that out?!" Quill hissed at her.

"Friends," Elmer said uncertainly. "I welcome you all to this special meeting of the Hemlock Falls Chamber of Commerce. I know that you were all looking forward to the real estate seminar of the late . . ." He stopped and mopped his brow. "Mr. Kingsfield. But as you know, Mr. Kingsfield met with a trag—"

"Where's the body?" someone shouted.

"They took it on down to the coroner's office, fathead," somebody responded.

A thin, elaborately made-up woman in the front pew sprang up and waved her hand. "Mr. Mayor. Mr. Mayor. I want to know what's going to happen to my uncle's million dollars, now that Zeke's dead. I heard that the money's here in the bank at Hemlock Falls. Is that true?"

"Yeah!" Mrs. Huston's son shouted. "We want our money!"

The crowd began to chant, "Money! Money! Money!"

"Well," Elmer gasped. "I don't know a thing about this. Not a thing." His desperate gaze swept the audience. "There! The guy you want to ask about that is right over there." He pointed at Charley Comstock. "That man Charley Comstock's on the board at the bank. That's a question you want to ask him."

"Elmer, you fathead," Marge said fiercely. "Shut the hell up!"

There was a surge of people toward the pew behind Quill, where Charley Comstock had risen to his feet.

Meg turned and looked at the Chamber members. "Are you all thinking what I'm thinking?"

"That we need to get our little keisters out of here?" Marge said. "You bet. Grab hold of Dookie, Meg. Quill, you take Wendy. As for you, Charley, keep your head down and follow me."

Marge let nothing stand in her way. She shoved, pushed, stamped on a foot or two, and bulled her the way out of the church and onto the relative safety of the lawn, "Like Moses leading the children of Israel," Dookie gasped. "Thank you all, my friends." He drew Wendy apart from the crush flowing down the steps, his arm over her shoulders protectively.

"Didn't help Charley all that much," Marge observed dispassionately.

And, in fact, Charley had been waylaid by a small mob. People pulled at his sleeve, blocked his way, pushed at him, and shouted.

"Do you think we should do something?" Quill said. "Maybe we should give Davy a call?"

"Nah," Marge said. "He's handling it. Look at him."

With little ceremony, and even less courtesy, Charley knocked aside the people in his path. He made his way steadily toward his Buick Park Avenue, elbowed a woman away from the car door, got in, and slammed the door. He gunned the engine three or four times, and the remnants of the crowd fell back.

A few moments later, and it was all over. Groups of two and three people clustered together, their voices loud and indignant, but the violence that had simmered just below the surface was gone. Cars roared out of the church parking lot, one after the other.

A half-empty Coke can sat in the snow piled up by the church steps.

Dookie bent and picked it up; the kindly minister looked infinitely sad. Wendy took his hand and folded her own over it in comfort.

"That's it," Quill said. She was so furious the words came out in a strangled whisper. "I'm calling a council of war."

"The thing about people with red hair," Meg said in an undertone, as they sat around the largest table in the Tavern Lounge, "is that when they lose their temper, they *really* lose their temper."

"I've never seen Quill so mad," Dina said in simple admiration.

"She's been like that since we were little," Meg said proudly. "You can push her pretty far, but one step over that line and foom!" She mimed an explosion.

"That musta bin some meeting," Doreen said. "I'm sorry I missed it. I heard somebody pushed the Rev'rund right into a snowbank."

"Nobody pushed anybody into a snowbank." Quill carried a tray of drinks over from the bar and set them on the table. "A ginger ale for you, Marge. A Coke for Doreen. A Diet Coke for Dina, coffee for Meg," she said as she handed them out, "and I am having a glass of wine, since you guys insisted."

"Keep your blood pressure down," Marge agreed.

"Mellow you out a little," Meg said.

"Settle your stomach."

Quill took a sip. It was a red zinfindel and quite good. "Okay. Here's the deal. The town's gone crazy. The Inn is about to be sued for more money than our insurance policy offers. That's two compelling reasons why we have to solve this murder . . ."

". . . If it is a murder," Dina said. "Davy says . . ."

"Davy can say what he likes, Dina. It's murder. There's a pile of evidence. But it's all circumstantial. But our problem is bigger than that. We have no credible leads. No tangible clues. Nothing to give us the faintest indication of who did this and why."

"The 'why' isn't hard," Meg muttered. "Zeke Kingsfield was a jerk."

"Exactly," Quill said. "And the fact that he was a jerk gives us our first lead."

"It does?" Marge said. "I know a lot of jerks. And nobody's murdering them."

"You're exactly right, too," Quill said. "So let's take a look at his particular brand of obnoxious behavior and see where it takes us. With luck, we're going to end up with a list of questions. If we get those questions answered, we'll be well on our way to finding out who did this.

"First, it's clear that Zeke rode roughshod over the people living at Gorgeous Gorges trailer park. Will Frazier is a man who feels responsible for their welfare. And both Marge and I saw Will Frazier run out of the church about seven o'clock last night, vowing to find Zeke and call him to account. Not twenty minutes later, somebody hit me over the head, when I was walking in an area not five hundred yards from the spot where Zeke went into the gorge. So the first question is: where was Will last night between the hours of seven, when he left the church, and six o'clock this morning, when whoever it was sent Zeke tumbling into the gorge?"

Doreen raised her hand. "I think I might be able to find

out some of that. Will's girlfriend sent me an app to work as a maid last month. I didn't follow up, because we were layin' people off instead of hiring. But I can start with her. And I don't mind walking up to Will and askin' him straight out if he can prove where he was last night."

Quill had her sketchpad in front of her. She made a note. "Good. Next, and this is critical, *what happened to the trip wire?*"

"Do we know for sure it's a wire?" Dina asked. "Did you actually see the cut it made in the tree and the post?"

"Those are two good questions," Quill said. "I suppose it could have been a rope."

"It's easy enough to tell." Dina rummaged in her backpack. "You know what I can do? My cell phone has a camera function." She pulled it out of a side pocket and brandished it. "I'll go down to the murder site and take a couple of pictures. Maybe we can get a better grip on what we're looking for."

"Seems like a long shot to me," Marge said. "Whether it's a wire or a rope, it's probably long gone by now."

"It might not be as easy to dispose of as you think," Quill said. "Zeke went out at first light. Mike found him forty-five minutes later. It takes at least twenty minutes to get to that spot in the trail from the departure point by the vegetable garden. Whoever was hidden in the woods had to gather up the wire and get out fast."

"Maybe they hid in the woods all day," Dina suggested.

"I doubt it. It was twenty degrees out there. And it was risky, once the police and the emergency crew showed up."

"The police searched the area and didn't find anything or anyone," Meg said. "I agree with Quill. The murderer had to take the wire with him." Then she added conscientiously, "Or her. And it had to be at least forty feet long to run from the tree to the fence post. That's a lot of wire. Or rope."

"Dumpsters," Dina said. "I'll check Dumpsters. I'd better make a note of all this." She tapped at her cell phone with one finger. "I'm text messaging myself," she explained.

"Now," Quill said. "Let's take another look at motive."

"I'll give you something interesting for motive," Doreen said. "That Lydia's got a motive. Kingsfield didn't sleep in his own bed."

"Really?" Meg said. "Now *that's* interesting."

"How can you be sure he didn't sleep in his own bed, Doreen?" Marge asked skeptically. "You see him in somebody else's?"

Doreen looked at Marge pityingly. "You don't know much about innkeepin', do ya?"

"It's like this," Dina explained carefully. "When you, like, work at a place like this, you end up knowing a lot more about people than they might want you to know."

"It's inevitable," Quill apologized.

"Comes with the territory," Meg said.

Doreen shrugged. "Only one side of the mattress was laid on. Only one pillow was wrinkled. Only one set of towels used in the bathroom. And before you wonder how I know it was that Lydia that was there and not him, there was makeup all over the towels and Opium perfume all over the pillow. Some kinds of perfume," Doreen added ruminatively, "leave an awful stink."

"Do you know where Kingsfield *did* sleep?" Marge asked.

"That LaToya's," Doreen said. "Both sides of the bed slept in, and as far as the sheets . . ."

Quill cleared her throat. Doreen clamped her mouth shut.

"Hah," Marge said. She looked a bit flummoxed. "I never thought about it before, but if you run a hotel you see a lot. I'll bet you get some kind of divorce lawyers nosing around here."

"Once in a while we do," Quill said. Fred Sims' face flashed into her mind. "Well, I'll be!"

"What?" Meg demanded.

"Nothing. That is, nothing I want to say anything about right now." She made a note to herself in her sketchpad: *Check out Sims!*

"And the last rule of innkeeping is keep your lips zipped," Dina said sunnily. "That's the first thing I learned when I got hired."

"So we got a jealous wife?" Marge said. "And maybe a jealous mistress?"

Quill looked thoughtful. "I don't know, to tell you the truth. I mean—it seemed as if they were a devoted couple. But who really knows? And it didn't seem to me that LaToya was all that fond of Zeke. But you never know, do you? And of course, as his wife, Lydia probably inherits a large chunk of those billions."

"Billions would be a strong motive for a lot of women," Meg agreed. "I think you should tackle that one, Quill. If Lydia's going to talk to anyone, she's going to talk to you."

Quill nodded agreement. "So I'll talk to her and to La-Toya. In an offhand sort of way, of course. We certainly need to know where the two of them were the night of the murder."

"That's easy enough," Meg said. "Ajit was shooting the dancing elves. LaToya was there all the time. As for Lydia— she was in Syracuse with Zeke."

"So LaToya's a good suspect?" Dina said eagerly.

Meg looked doubtful. "Well—she was never out of my sight long enough to zip down the side of the gorge to the ski trail, bash Quill on the head, roll the log into place, and zip back up again. That had to take at least twenty-five minutes."

"Are you sure the log was moved last night?" Marge asked. "Couldn't it have been moved early this morning?"

Quill shook her head. "It was buried under the snow when I saw it. Mike finished grooming the trail about quarter to six last night, and he swears the trail was free of debris. I believe him. And it stopped snowing around ten thirty. So the log had to have been moved into place between those times."

"The incident Quill had in the woods narrows the time still further," Meg added. "And I think the murderer came back down in the early morning and set up the wire just to make sure the plan worked."

"Mike snowmobiled over any tracks the murderer may have made," Quill said. "And of course, the police and the ambulance people stamped around the crime scene, too."

"LaToya and Will are the only suspects so far?" Marge complained. "This case seems pretty skimpy to me."

"Oh, there're more suspects," Quill said. "Marge, do you think you could find out where Charley Comstock was last night?"

"Charley?" Marge seemed taken aback. "Well, now. Come to think of it, he was pretty dam' antsy when I started pushing him on the banking arrangements Kingsfield had with the First National." She grinned. "Oh, yeah. I can check out old Charley."

"And then," Quill said, "there's Mr. Albert McWhirter."

"Old Scrooge?" Marge looked even more startled. "You suspect him?"

"I don't know that I really suspect anyone at this point," Quill said with perfect truth. "But I do have some questions. For example, why did McWhirter ask for this particular assignment?"

Marge shrugged. "Meg's food is famous? He's an art lover and wanted to meet you?"

"He hasn't said a word about art to me. And he won't *eat* Meg's food, so why would he care that it's famous? He says he has stomach trouble and he's had to avoid rich food for years. He's not behaving like any consultant I've ever heard of before. Why do I keep stumbling over him in unlikely places? At the Chamber meetings. At choir practice. What's at either of those places that would interest a restaurant consultant? And there's another mystery I'd like solved. Who is this Fred Sims, and who is he to the other guests here at the Inn?"

"Fred Sims?" Doreen said. "That nosy guy in two-fourteen? You just gimme a hour, I'll get into that cruddy old briefcase he carries and I'll find out for sure."

"We don't want to do anything illegal," Quill said.

"Not too illegal," Meg said. "I think you should check him out the first chance you get, Doreen."

"Let's get back to McWhirter." Quill leaned forward and tapped her forefinger on the table. "I was there when McWhirter and Zeke ran into each other. It was pretty clear that they knew each other. And even clearer that they didn't like each other." Quill turned to Marge. "How much do you know about his background?"

"I can find out more. Make a few calls."

Quill closed her sketchpad and looked at them gravely. "So. There it is. It's a start. How much time should we give ourselves before we meet and see how the case is coming along?"

"I say we get right on it." Meg thumped the table energetically with her fist. "Lydia's lawyers are going to show up any minute and put a lien on my brand-new Garland stove, if we let them. What if we meet in Quill's room tomorrow right about this time?" She looked at her watch. "That's three thirty tomorrow. Gives us twenty-four hours to come up with some results."

"I'm off to look at the crime scene." Dina leaped to her feet. "One for all and all for one!"

Quill sighed. "Or something like that."

"I'm off to nail Charley Comstock," Marge said with relish. "If there's any fast-breaking news, Quill, I'll give you a call." She turned and marched out of the Lounge without wasting any more words.

"And I'm goin' to talk to the housekeeping staff. Tell 'em to keep their eyes peeled." Doreen, too, left the room abruptly.

Dina pushed her glasses up her nose and sat down again, with a thump. "I'll get my parka on and go out to get pictures of that tree before it gets dark. But before you start your detecting, Quill, Elizabeth wants to see you in the kitchen."

"She wants to see *me* in the kitchen," Meg corrected her.

"Nope, she said Quill, specifically."

Ajit, Bernie, and Benny came into the Lounge and waved

at them. Quill decided it was as good an opportunity as any to discover Lydia's plans for the future. "Tell Elizabeth I'll be along directly, would you, Dina?" She made her way amid the sparsely populated tables and greeted the *Good Taste* crew with a warm smile and a conventional expression of sympathy. "You three must be exhausted. I'm so sorry about your loss."

Ajit shrugged, charmingly. "Thank you. It was certainly unexpected."

"Actually," Benny said, "we're better off without him." He jumped. "That's my ankle you just kicked Bernie, thank you very much. And why should I pretend that we're crying in our beer? We're not. Zeke was nothing more or less than a panderer to popular taste, Quill. He was putting a lot of pressure on Lydia to subvert the show."

"He was?" They had selected a table for four. She settled into the unoccupied chair, as Nate came up to them. "Can I ask Nate to bring you all something?"

"Ajit's a club soda man," Benny said. "But Bernie and I will have a Cosmopolitan. Or maybe a margarita, Bernie. What do you think?"

"I think it's far too early in the day for a sweet drink. I'll have a white vermouth."

"You're right, ducky. The same for me, Nate."

Nate, who never needed to write orders down, said, "You got it," and lumbered back to the bar.

"I haven't had a chance to talk to Lydia today," Quill said. "I did see her at the . . . out near the gorge, of course."

"And she was ranting about suing you, I expect," Bernie said. "That's just her way, sweetie. I wouldn't take it to heart."

"You mean she's decided not to sue us?" Quill said hopefully.

"Goodness no. I think the chief wolf in her pack of lawyers is already headed this way. What I meant is that it's nothing personal."

Quill, reflecting that it felt very personal, said merely, "I suppose you'll be heading on back to New York?"

"Oh, no. Not until we've taped all of the establishing shots." Ajit accepted his club soda with a brilliant smile. Quill found herself wondering what it would be like to paint him. It'd be difficult. That kind of beauty always tempted an artist into sentimentality. "Zeke's accident will make little or no difference to the plans for *Good Taste*. The budget for the show comes from the magazine. And although Zeke's name is on the letterhead, so to speak, he actually doesn't own any of the company."

"He doesn't?" Quill was startled. "But I thought he personally bought *L'Aperitif*."

Ajit's smile held an acidic edge. "Sure. If you believe what you read about Zeke. But what you read about Zeke is a lot different from the reality. Magna Publications spun off *L'Aperitif* to Kingsfield Publishing. I think Zeke actually may own some stock in Magna. And he may even own stock in Kingsfield Publishing. But not necessarily. Both are publicly held companies. Both are traded over the stock exchange. For all I know, your investment banker's put some of your savings into KP. The point is, he could just be a figurehead and not wield any real voting power at all."

Quill thought about this. "But, isn't Zeke a millionaire?"

Benny burst into laughter. "Sorry! Oh, shit. The vermouth's up my nose." He sneezed heartily. "That's the sixty-four-thousand-dollar question, isn't it? If I had to make a wild-ass guess, I'd say he's worth about the same amount of money that his daddy left him. Twenty or thirty million. At best."

"Which is nothing to sneeze at," Bernie said. "Unless, like Benny, you've got vermouth up your nose."

"You said that Zeke wanted to subvert *Good Taste*, Ajit? What was that all about?"

Ajit's slender fingers were restless. He rolled his cocktail napkin into a neat tube and smoothed it out again. "What

Zeke is, is a deal maker. One of the best. He was putting together a plan to distribute the show on a global basis."

"Very profitable," Benny said. "Potentially."

Ajit held up an admonitory finger. "But the cable company he was talking to has a strong preference for reality shows."

"Extreme wrestling," Bernie said. "Gross-out reality shows. Horrible stuff."

"Worse, they've got amazingly cheap production values." Ajit sighed. "And, of course, if they bought the show, and agreed to produce however many segments, there was a good chance that it would look like . . ."

"Dog doo-doo!" Bernie drained his vermouth and put the glass on the table with an emphatic thump. "Do you really think the dancing elves were Lydia's idea?" Quill nodded. "You did? Oh, she'd squirm if she heard that. She has a huge respect for your talent, Quill. Huge. No, that was Zeke's little baby."

"She does? Respect my talent?"

"Not that she'd ever admit it," Ajit said with a faint smile. "It's not in our Lydia's character to give credit where credit's due."

"Let me see if I understand this correctly," Quill said. "The only control that Zeke actually has—had—over *Good Taste* was the force of his personality?"

"It's more complex than that," Ajit said. "That personality. His public persona, if you will, was having a large effect on the quality of the show."

"Huge," Benny said.

"Huge," Bernie echoed.

"Quill?"

Quill turned around with a start. She'd been concentrating so hard on the conversation with Ajit that she'd lost track of time. "Elizabeth! I'm so sorry! Dina said that you wanted to talk to me." She stopped herself in midsentence. "You're holding a baby?"

Elizabeth looked down at the blue-blanketed bundle she held in her arms. "It's Caleb." She smiled and stroked the baby's cheek tenderly. "Melissa's little boy."

"Melissa brought Caleb to work with her?" Quill said. "I thought she'd made arrangements with her neighbor at the trailer. Has something happened?"

Elizabeth held the baby out to her. Without thinking about it, Quill accepted the warm little body. "Melissa hasn't shown up for work. Well, she must have shown up at some point, because Caleb was wrapped up next to the fireplace in the kitchen, but she's not here now. And she left a note.

"She's giving the baby to you."

# CHAPTER 10

"Pampers?" Meg's voice over the cell phone was slightly panicked. "I don't see Pampers. I see Huggies. I see some Kmart brand stuff. But I don't see Pampers."

Quill walked up and down the length of her living room. Caleb lay peacefully asleep over her left shoulder. She cradled his bottom with her right arm and had her left hand cupped over the back of his head. Her cell phone was crushed between her left shoulder and her left ear. She thought her neck might be permanently frozen in that position. "I don't suppose it matters whether the diapers are Pampers, Huggies, or made by the Jolly Green Giant. Just buy whatever looks the nicest."

She heard the faint rattle of a shopping cart as Meg went down the aisle.

"Quill?"

"Still here."

"They come in sizes."

"Sizes?!" Quill jiggled Caleb gently up and down. "That twenty-four-pound turkey you made for Thanksgiving? He's about that size."

"The sizes are not listed according to turkey weight," Meg said patiently. "It's umm . . . newborn, three months, six months."

"Six months. Caleb is six months old."

The baby stirred on her shoulder. The note from Melissa had read:

*Dear Quill:*

*This is Caleb. He is six months old. He loves Gerber baby food, and maybe some solid foods, like applesauce. He likes Carnation formula. I know you will take good care of him until I return.*

*Melissa*

"Okay. How many diapers should I get?"

"Well. I don't know. I would think he'd use one or two a day at least."

"The packages are huge."

"Well, one package then."

"Okay. I've a couple of cases of baby food: spinach, squash, applesauce, carrots, strained chicken, etcetera, etcetera. It's quite a balanced diet." Meg's voice faltered, and she said nervously, "I think. It would be for a person, anyway."

"And the baby formula?"

"Check."

"And the wipes and the talcum powder?"

"Check. And the baby shampoo and some cream."

"I wonder if we should get some baby aspirin?"

"Oh, no. Oh, no." Meg's voice threatened to spiral into panic. "If he's running any kind of temperature or anything, we call Andy right away."

Meg's former fiancé, Andy Bishop, was Hemlock Falls' best (and only) pediatrician.

"But I'll get a baby thermometer. Now, don't move. I'll be home in twenty minutes."

Caleb made a small, sleepy sound. Quill dropped the cell phone and laid him gently on the couch. Max nudged her aside and sniffed the blanket with intense interest. Quill sat down and picked the baby up again. There was a tap at the door and a muffled query.

"Come in, Doreen!"

Quill thought she'd never been so glad to see anyone in her entire life. Doreen gave the two of them a sharp glance, then took off her navy wool winter coat and draped it over the kitchen counter. She put her winter boots neatly by the door and asked, "You're doin' all right?" She walked up to the couch. "You want me to take him?"

Quill clutched him a little closer. "No. No. Of course not. I just want to be sure that he's okay. I gave him the bottle that Melissa left and then I put him over my shoulder and patted him until he burped. That's right, isn't it?"

"Exactly right," Doreen said with a gentleness totally foreign to her prickly nature. "D'ja change him?"

"There were a couple of diapers in the basket. Meg and I did it," Quill said proudly. "And then Meg figured we'd need more supplies, so she took off for Kmart."

"She's plannin' on coming back, isn't she?" Doreen said sharply. "Melissa, that is?"

Quill picked up the note. Doreen read it and said, "T'cha."

"Couldn't have said it better myself."

"So what are you going to do now?"

"I've been sitting here thinking about it."

Caleb woke up abruptly, with a wail that rivaled the Hemlock Falls Volunteer Ambulance Corps siren. Quill took him out of the blanket and held him upright on her knee, her hands under his shoulders. "There, there, baby." His wails increased in frequency and volume.

"Put him back over your shoulder," Doreen advised. "He's expecting to see his mamma's face, not yours. And did she leave him any toys?"

"Just a stuffed lamb. It's in the basket by the reading

lamp." Quill put him over her shoulder again and jogged him up and down.

Doreen retrieved the lamb and tucked it under the baby's fists. The crying ebbed, and then stopped.

"How *could* she?" Quill said fiercely. "Just walk off and leave this little guy?"

"Beats me. But the little I talked to her, she din't seem like the kind of mother, like some I read about."

"I didn't talk with her much, either. But she *did* love him. I know she did. This just doesn't make any sense."

There was a sharp rap at the door. "That'll be Meg, Doreen, and she's probably got her hands full. Would you let her in?" Caleb grabbed her hair in one tiny fist and gurgled. His lamb dropped in her lap. Carefully, she settled him in her lap and looked at him. His eyes were blue. They met her own, and for a moment, his downy brows contracted and she thought he'd wail again. She smiled at him. He smiled tentatively back. Then he hit her in the nose and said, "Gaaah."

"Gaah," Quill said. "Did you hear that, Meg? He said 'gah'!"

"It wasn't Meg at the door," Doreen said. "It's these two."

Quill looked up and caught her breath in dismay. "Oh, dear. Mr. McWhirter."

Albert McWhirter stood behind Doreen with his briefcase in his hand and a frown on his face. Fred Sims was with him. Sims lounged against the kitchen counter, a toothpick dangling from his lower lip. "And Mr. Sims?" She made an attempt to get up and sat down again. "This is a very awkward time, as you can see. Could I possibly persuade you to see me tomorrow? And Mr. Sims? I'm afraid these are my private quarters. If you need some assistance, I'd appreciate it if we could take care of it downstairs."

"That's my grandson," Mr. McWhirter said. "That's my grandson you're holding. And I want to know where my daughter is."

Quill stared at him.

"May we sit down?" He glanced at Fred Sims. "This gentleman is a private detective. He found Melissa for me. He discovered she was working here, for you, and reported back to me in Syracuse."

"Which is why you were so insistent that the bank send you out here and nobody else." Quill took a deep breath. "Yes, please do sit down."

"I'll make some coffee," Doreen said. "Or tea. Whatever."

"Nice digs up here." Fred Sims rolled the toothpick to the other side of his mouth and sat gingerly at the edge of Quill's Eames chair. It was where Myles always sat. Quill suppressed the urge to tell Sims to move.

"May I?" McWhirter gestured toward the other end of the couch.

"Of course."

"Gah," Caleb said. *"Gah!"*

Quill kissed his cheek. "Gah. I couldn't agree more." She settled the baby more firmly in her lap. "Now, gentlemen. If you would tell me what's going on?"

It was, Quill told Myles later, a sad and familiar story. McWhirter and his wife divorced. McWhirter had custody of his daughter, Ashley. She rebelled against the discipline—and, Quill suspected—coldness of her home environment and, at the age of sixteen, found herself pregnant.

"Sixteen!" Quill said, in dismay. "She told us she was twenty! Or rather, she told Jinny Peterson. I don't understand how she qualified for the unemployment program."

"The real Melissa Smith's a student at Cornell," Sims said. "The likeliest scenario, see, is that Ashley hooked up with her in one of the local hangouts in Ithaca and got a look at her Social Security card. Once you got that magic number, the rest is easy. Of course, that's also how I was able to track her down."

"The mortgage on her trailer," Quill said suddenly. "You helped her with that, didn't you, Mr. McWhirter?" Caleb squealed and gnawed at his lamb. She smoothed the hair on his head with her cupped hand. "That explains how Good-Jobs! got into the mortgage business."

McWhirter's sallow complexion flushed deep red. "She had to have a place to live. And Ms. Peterson felt that if I confronted Ashley, she'd run and God knows if I'd find her again."

"So there it is, Ms. Quilliam," Sims said briskly. "The cat's out of the bag. So if you could just tell us where we can find Ashley, we'll take the baby with us and be on our way."

"Could somebody *please* give me a hand with these?" Meg shouted from the front door.

Quill got to her feet.

"You sit right there, missy," Doreen ordered. "And as for you two,"—she glared at Sims and McWhirter—"you touch that baby and I'll give you a clout you won't forget."

Meg tumbled into the room, plastic bags dangling from each hand, and a baby car seat slung over her back. She pulled up, shot a glance at McWhirter and Sims, and said rudely, "What are you two doing here?"

Caleb began to shriek. Max started to bark. Meg set the packages down one after the other and dropped the car seat near the French doors to the balcony. This left little place to stand in Quill's small living room. Sims backed up and tripped over the pine chest Quill used as a coffee table. McWhirter backed into the tiny hallway.

"Stop!" Quill ordered. "Stop it right this minute. Meg? Please take Max out into the hallway and send him down-stairs. Doreen? Please take Caleb and do not, I repeat do not, let anyone else have him but Meg or me. Albert? You and Fred follow me downstairs. We're going to settle this in my office."

Quill stamped downstairs battling a combination of worry and rage. By the time McWhirter and Sims reached her office, she had dialed 411, asked for Jinny Peterson's home phone number, and stayed on the line while the call went through. She gestured furiously at the two men to sit.

Jinny answered on the third ring.

"Jinny? It's Sarah Quilliam here. I have Albert McWhirter in my office. He claims that he's Melissa Smith's father. Is that true?"

"Oh, dear," Jinny said uncertainly. "I was afraid this might happen. Has he confronted her? I told him that would be a very bad idea."

"He'll have to tell you that himself. I'm putting you on speakerphone," Quill said. "He's here in my office with this Sims person." She addressed McWhirter, "Jinny wants to know if you've spoken to Melissa, Ashley, whomever." She punched the speaker button.

Jinny's voice flooded the small office in a tinny echo. "Mr. McWhirter? Are you there?"

He cleared his throat. "Yes, Ms. Peterson. And I have to assure you that I haven't seen or spoken to Ashley since I arrived here."

Quill thought about this. Every time McWhirter had come into Meg's kitchen, Melissa had disappeared. "But she knew he was here, Jinny," she said. "And it looks as if she's gone."

"Gone?" The dismay in Jinny's voice was clear.

"Gone," Quill said firmly. "Have you heard from her?"

"I spoke with her yesterday. She was tremendously excited about this business with Kingsfield. She wanted to know if she should give part of the money to the job bank."

"And you haven't heard from her at all today?"

"No. I haven't. You say she's gone?" Anxiety replaced the dismay. "What about Caleb?"

"Caleb's here with me." Quill paused to think. "Look. If you hear from her, will you let me know right away?"

"Of course I will. Quill, this is awful. Do you think something's happened to her?"

"My guess is that once she realized her father was here, she decided to leave Hemlock Falls for good. And then this business with Kingsfield came up and she had to stick around to collect the money. Now that the deal appears to be in jeopardy, I think she just lost it and ran." Quill ran one hand through her hair. "But that's what John Raintree used to call a WAG. A wild-assed guess. If I hear anything, I'll call you. And you'll call me, right?"

"Right!"

Quill hung the phone up. She folded her hands in front of her and made a determined effort to relax. The two men stared at her. "Okay," she said finally, when she felt calmer. "I don't know where Melissa is. She's not here. Mike Santelli went out to Gorgeous Gorges as soon as I read the note she left me, and she isn't at the trailer park, either. He talked to Will Frazier—he's the manager of the park—and Will said Melissa left the park about eleven o'clock this morning. She stowed suitcases and a duffle bag in the back of her car and strapped the baby in the front seat. That's the last he saw of her. She arrived here for work just after twelve noon. The kitchen staff didn't think twice about the fact that the baby was with her; she's brought Caleb to work before." Quill took a breath. She blinked back tears. "Excuse me. I don't know why . . . it's been a long day." She pulled a tissue from the pocket of her skirt and blew her nose. "At any rate, Caleb was asleep in his basket by the fireplace, and no one noticed that Melissa had gone until he woke up and started fussing. Peter Hairston took his bottle to him and found this note attached to his blanket with a safety pin." Quill took the note out of her other pocket and handed it to McWhirter. "I don't know where Caleb's mother is. And until I do know, you aren't getting your hands on this baby. Melissa—Ashley— left her to me."

There was a prolonged silence. Finally, Sims said, "She has a car? Miss McWhirter?"

"She went right down to Peterson's used car lot and bought an old Escort, the day she received the ten-thousand-dollar check from Kingsfield," Quill said. "She was quite proud of the car. And of course, it gave her the chance to leave."

McWhirter sat absolutely upright. His back didn't touch the couch. His hands were on his knees. There was a terrible grief in his eyes. Quill's heart ached for him.

"Albert," she said softly, "I think we should call the police."

"No! No." He shook his head. "She would hate that. She hates me. She doesn't believe me."

"Perhaps. But perhaps it's time for the two of you to sit down together and have an open discussion about what's happened here. You've gone to enormous lengths to see that she's safe and that her child—your grandson—is safe. All without expecting anything from her. She may not believe what you say, Albert. But she certainly can see what you've done for her."

"There's no need to call in the police," McWhirter said. "She's not a criminal." He nodded stiffly at Fred Sims. "I'd like to authorize you to go ahead and see if you can find her."

Sims got to his feet. He tucked his toothpick carefully into his pocket. "If she's got a car, now, it's gonna be rough. I have to agree with Miss Quilliam, here. It'd be smart to get the cops in on this. They can put out an APB for her."

"But she hasn't committed any crime!" McWhirter cried. "The police will refuse to get involved."

"I think I can call in a few favors," Quill said quietly. "And if I can't, well, she has committed a crime, technically. She's abandoned her child. If we have to, we can fall back on that." She put her head in her hands. "I'll make the calls. And if you two will excuse me, I'd like to be alone for a while."

Quill was still awake at midnight. Caleb was peacefully asleep in the portable crib Meg had dragged home from Kmart. Max was curled protectively beside him.

She'd discovered that babies use more than one or two diapers a day. She'd also discovered that they'd need more bibs. Caleb thought it a huge joke to decorate his snuggies, the kitchen floor, and Quill herself with his creamed spinach.

She'd also found out that he fit into her arms as if he'd been born for that specific purpose.

Her phone rang, finally, at a quarter after twelve.

"Myles," she said. "Oh, Myles. Thank goodness. The most amazing thing has happened."

# CHAPTER 11

"I've never been all that fond of babies," Lydia said. She picked up the napkin Quill had used to wipe breakfast applesauce off Caleb's chin with her thumb and forefinger. She dropped it fastidiously to one side. She was wearing a black turtleneck and elegant black slacks. The color may have a concession to her new and sudden widowhood. Quill wasn't sure. "Particularly not before breakfast."

"That's a shame," Quill said. "Babies are great!" She put Caleb over her left shoulder and patted his back with such expertise that she was amazed at herself. "And this is a particularly good baby, you know. He slept almost the whole night through." Babies weren't a usual part of the guest list at the Inn, having, Meg had pointed out, little use for gourmet food and even less for their excellent wine list.

"Is he going to spend the rest of the morning with us?" Lydia asked with a pained look. "If so, I'm going to move to another table."

"Nope, Doreen's coming to take him for the morning. As a matter of fact, here she is now." Doreen walked through the archway into the dining room. Her usual work uniform was a pink version of the black and white uniforms the wait staff wore. Today she had on a warm fleece hoodie, gray sweatpants, and a neat green blouse. Quill waved Caleb's lamb at her. She grinned and waved back, calling, "There's my boy," as she came up to the table.

"Morning, Lydia," she said. Then to Caleb, "Morning, you." She swept him out of Quill's arms and onto her own shoulder.

"Gah!" Caleb said. His little fists grabbed onto Doreen's fleece. Then he spit up the rest of his applesauce.

"Oh, for heaven's sake!" Lydia grimaced. "It's all over your jacket."

"That's babies for ya," Doreen said with an even bigger grin. "It's why I've got my grandma suit on 'stead of the uniform." She bent and picked up the diaper bag Quill had carefully packed. "You put everything I told you in here?"

"And a little bit more than that," Quill confessed. "Meg must have bought out the entire infant's section at Kmart."

"You sure you don't want him to spend the night with me and Stoke? We're all set up for my grandkids."

"No, no."

Lydia drummed her fingers impatiently on the tabletop. Quill bowed to the inevitable and kissed Caleb good-bye.

Kathleen set plates of yogurt and berries in front of them, and Lydia picked restlessly at hers. "I never could picture you as a mother, Quill. Or myself, either, for that matter."

"You and Zeke decided not to have children?"

"You have *got* to be kidding. He and his second wife, that nitwit supermodel, you remember her. April?"

"April what?"

"Just April."

Quill made a noncommittal face. She didn't read fashion magazines and never had time to watch the news.

Lydia swallowed a spoonful of raspberries. "They had the Brat from Hell. You must have heard about *her*. Lexington.

169

Her name is Lexington. Anyway, one spoiled rotten child of Zeke's is—was—enough to inflict on the world."

"You really ought to try and eat something," Quill said gently. "Are you getting any sleep at all?"

Lydia patted her face with her fingertips. "Have I got circles underneath my eyes? I've got sleeping pills. Everyone's got sleeping pills. But they didn't seem to work very well last night at all."

"I'm not surprised."

"And there's no time for a nap today. I've got the first set of lawyers coming in. There's a lot to see to."

Quill wasn't sure how to phrase her next question, but Lydia saved her the trouble. "Zeke wasn't worth as much as people thought he was. And he set up a trust for the brat, so at most, I'll clear maybe five, ten million. We'll have to see. But he had a whacking big life insurance policy. And it has a double indemnity clause for accidental death. So that's twenty million for me right there. Although of course we'll have to see how the lawsuit against the Inn at Hemlock Falls, Inc., goes. There could be more."

" 'I used to be nice,' " Quill said wryly.

"Eh? What? You're nice enough now, Quill."

"That's what you said to me the day before yesterday. When you checked in."

Lydia's eyes narrowed to slits. "If you think whining is going to talk me out of a civil suit, you can think again. If it weren't for that damned cross-country ski trail, Zeke would be alive today."

Quill finished her raspberries and started on the yogurt. She was famished. "Did I sound as if I were whining? I wasn't. I was making an observation. And you didn't use to be all that nice," she added reflectively. "But you certainly weren't as mercenary as you are now."

A slight flush streaked Lydia's cheekbones.

"And you're *smart*. The changes you've made in *L'Aperitif* are good ones. The magazine was getting stale. The same

170

articles about the same out-of-the-way boutique restaurants in Kuala Lumpur were recycled once a year. You've stopped all that. You brought a fresh look to the magazine. And—dancing elves notwithstanding—the ideas for *Good Taste* are wonderful. I've talked to Ajit and LaToya about the scripts."

"Do you think so?" Lydia looked away. She looked pleased. And to Quill's amaze, there was a shine of tears in her eyes. "The magazine means a lot to me. What you've just said means a lot, too." She clasped Quill's hands with her own, and then let them go. "We had some great times in high school together. Didn't we? I thought it might be just like old times when I came up here to shoot the show. Of course, with all this fuss about Zeke, that's not going to happen." She sighed. "So, no cozy glasses of wine and looking at the yearbook for us, Quill. At least, not until the funeral arrangements have been taken care of."

Quill resisted the impulse to bang her head against the table in frustration. There didn't seem to be any way to get Lydia off her planet. "So you'll remain editor of *L'Aperitif*. And the show itself is going to go on."

"And the line of foodstuffs, too. We'll be spending quite a lot of time together after all this is settled. I'm so glad neither of those things were affected by Zeke's death. I'm sure you are, too."

Kathleen came back to the table with a fresh pot of hot water for Lydia's tea and a basket of fresh brioche from the kitchen. "Dina says there's a couple of calls for you, Quill. And she's got something to tell you."

"Thanks, Kathleen, I'll be with her in a minute." Quill was sitting with her back to the archway to the foyer. She looked over her shoulder. "Is she having any trouble keeping the reporters out?"

"Not so far. Mike's out there with a whacking big snow shovel and he says he'll stay out there as long as I keep the coffee coming."

"I told Dina to let me know right away if there was any news about Melissa. I take it the police haven't found her yet?"

"Nope. But it's early days yet. Davy's not a quitter, Quill. He'll keep at it."

"Kathleen's younger brother is our sheriff," Quill said to Lydia. "Thank you, Kathleen. Please tell Dina I'll be with her in a minute."

"Exciting times you have here," Lydia murmured. "Babies dropped on doorsteps. Missing pot girls."

"Murders," Quill added bluntly.

Lydia suddenly looked very tired. "You aren't beating that dead horse again, are you? It was an accident. Give it a rest."

"I'm truly sorry, Lydia. But there's every reason to suppose that Zeke's death wasn't an accident. And if he was murdered, wouldn't capturing the murderer mean more to you than . . ." Quill stopped herself from finishing the sentence.

Lydia finished it for her. "Than collecting a couple of million dollars from your insurance company." Lydia's smile was wry. "Of course it would." She slumped a little. "I know it may not seem like it, but I had a real respect for Zeke. And a real affection, too. I know that a marriage like ours, to someone like you, may seem arid. More of a business arrangement than a love match. You know, of course, that I knew about Zeke and LaToya."

"You did?" Quill said. She was startled. Then, as she thought about it, she said, "I guess that doesn't surprise me as much as it should."

"I think you're beginning to see how it was for us. People like you marry for love, Quill. People like me marry for position, for money, for power. But it's enough. Don't you see? It's more than enough. It's a huge part of why I loved Zeke. And because all that's gone now, I am genuinely sorry. And if you want my help in looking into this accident, you have it." Tears spilled down her cheeks. Quill silently handed her

172

a tissue. Lydia carefully dabbed it under her eyes. "I don't understand the look on your face," she snapped.

"I'm feeling just . . . tremendously sorry," Quill said. What she didn't add was, *for your incredibly awful sense of what relationships are all about*. But she wanted to. Instead, she said aloud, "You and Zeke *did* confide in each other?"

"Of course." Lydia folded the tissue into a neat square. "Zeke said I had an excellent brain for business. He trusted me with a lot of information. Bounced a lot of ideas off me. He didn't have many close friends, you know. And he always had a lot of—contempt, I suppose you could call it—for his business advisors. He was sure he knew most of the answers himself. And," Lydia said with simple directness, "he usually did."

"So if you were to make a list of people with a reason to harm him, who would be at the top?"

"A list like that would stretch from here to Kenosha, Wisconsin. As many people hated Zeke as admired him. Or envied him."

"We can narrow the list down quite a bit," Quill said with a faint smile. "We're fairly sure that the log was moved into position before the snow stopped falling at ten thirty. And Mike left the site just before dark, about five forty-five. And then the murderer showed up again, very early in the morning, to run a wire across the ski trail. No one thought to check the area surrounding that site for footprints until after he fell. But that morning—other than those left by Mike's snowmobile—the EMTs and the police vehicles and I made the only visible tracks. And those all came from the Inn."

"So you're saying it had to be someone staying here?"

"It's highly probable, don't you think?"

Lydia made a flippant gesture with her hand. "Maybe your guy Mike sabotaged the trail?"

"If he had a grudge against Zeke, I suppose so. He certainly had the most opportunity. But what kind of motive would he have?"

"True. I doubt Zeke noticed his existence. Well, Ajit, the Bs, and LaToya can all alibi each other. Your little Melissa, too. They were shooting the dancing elves all evening, while I was in Syracuse with Zeke."

"But the shoot started at six. What about the hour or so before that?"

Lydia rubbed her forehead thoughtfully. "LaToya and I were piddling around the kitchen getting the lighting angles straight. I think the Bs and Ajit were in the Tavern Lounge."

"Ajit was," Quill said. "He was drinking vodka with my sister."

"Well, Benny and Bernie were around somewhere. You'll have to ask them."

"Can you think of any grudges any of them might be carrying?"

"Not the *Good Taste* crew, no. But there's one person at the Inn you should take a good hard look at if you think it's murder." Lydia dropped her voice and leaned forward. "Zeke got involved with a big condo project in Syracuse two years ago. The funding fell apart, and a few of the investors were left holding the bag." She shrugged indifferently. "It happens. Zeke was always too smart to put his own cash into those things—you know the rule—the producer never puts money in the show—but there was one fellow who was pretty upset."

"And he lives here in Hemlock Falls?"

"You hired him as a consultant. It's Bert McWhirter."

Quill remembered the hostile exchange between the two men the day that Zeke checked in. McWhirter had claimed to be working in her office yesterday afternoon. What if Melissa had seen him crossing the fields just after dark? Was that why she'd run? So that she didn't have to identify her father as a murderer?

Or was there a more sinister reason Melissa had fled?

Quill touched the bump on her forehead.

"Was that any help?"

"I think so." Out of the corner of her eye, Quill saw Dina in the archway. She gestured frantically. Quill signaled "one minute" with her forefinger and got up from the table. "Thank you for that lead. And you'll let me know if there's anything I can do for you? Will you be all right for the rest of the day?"

"I'm taking the troupe down to the Resort for massages and facials. You really ought to think about adding that service to the Inn, you know. Anyhow, we're at a temporary standstill and it seemed the least I could do for LaToya and the others. Little Melissa's defection's caused a bit of upset. We're short an elf, which puts the kibosh on laying down more tape until we find someone else." She ran an eye over Quill's figure. "I don't suppose that you'd be willing to lend us a hand? Or a foot, as it were?"

"Sorry. But I'll see what I can do. If you'll excuse me, I've work piled up."

Quill crossed the short distance from the dining room to the reception area. Dina clutched at her arm as she came through the archway and whispered, "You're not going to believe what Marge has found out! And I've got something to show you, too." She peered over Quill's shoulder at Lydia. "How's she holding up?"

Quill rubbed the bump on her forehead and sighed. "Who knows? She's this weird mixture of self-awareness and self-ishness. I don't know what I think about her. But she's given me some important information about McWhirter. Come into the office and I'll tell you what I've found out."

Dina settled excitedly at the little Queen Anne–style conference table in the office. "First, let me show you the pictures I took of the tree and the post." She reached over and pulled a stack of sheets from the color printer. "I downloaded them onto my laptop. Blew them up and printed them out. Look at the edges of the cut in the tree."

Quill picked up the photograph of the tree trunk. "It's wire for certain." The enlarged image showed that the thin scar across the trunk of the mountain ash was saw-toothed.

"I think so, too. And I measured the diameter; the width of

the cut is three millimeters. The depth, of course, doesn't matter. Although you can see here that the wire cut more deeply into the tree trunk on the west side. The vic was headed east, you see, and when he hit the wire, blam! The force of the blow drove the wire deeper into the tree."

"The vic?" Quill said in a bemused way.

"Cop talk," Dina said tersely. "But that's not all. I talked to Mike. And I said, have we got any wire that's three millimeters across with spiral twist to it, and look at this!" Dina laid a one-quart zippered plastic bag on the tabletop. It contained a short piece of cable.

"Oh my gosh," Quill said. "Did you find that at the site?"

"No. We keep a roll of this cable in the toolshed. Mike cut a piece off for me so I could see if it fit into the groove of the tree and the post. And, Quill. It does!" Dina laid another picture down. The cable fit the groove in the tree precisely. "It looks as if the murderer got what he needed right from us!"

"Oh, my." Quill sat back. "Dina, this is excellent work."

"Thank you," she said modestly.

"We really need to turn this over to the police."

"I did," Dina admitted. "Well, in a way. I showed all of this to Davy before I came into work."

"Let me guess. He said it was all circumstantial."

"Yes."

"And that the wire could have been wrapped around the tree at any time in the past couple of days, for any reason."

"No."

"No?"

"It's a fresh cut," Dina said. "I put a call into a friend of a friend who's an arborist at Cornell. I've got him coming out this afternoon to see if he can tell us when the cut was made. He's pretty sure he can help."

"I am really impressed," Quill said, and she was. "Will he be able to give us a narrow span of time, as you can with bodies?"

Dina's face fell a little. "Well, no. But he can give expert evidence that the cut occurred within the last few days or so."

"It's still a terrific boost to the investigation." Quill traced the line of the scar with her thumb. "Do you suppose we can find the wire itself? If you think that it actually struck Kingsfield and spun him into the fence, there might be trace evidence on it. From his ski pants, perhaps."

"I bet you're right. The cut measures three and a half feet from the floor of the forest. How tall do you think Kingsfield was?"

"Golly. Six-four, at least. He was a big man."

"Then this would have snagged him right in the shins, about here." Dina wore a pair of wool trousers; she grasped her leg just below the knee. "I'll tell you what. I'll bet you a dollar to a doughnut there's some bruising on the body. Even if it's really really faint. He wore this superexpensive ski suit, didn't he?"

"Bright red and silver, yes."

"It would be so cool if we found the wire. The impact had to drive those fibers into the twisted part."

"Dumpsters," Quill said. "You said you were going to check the town Dumpsters."

"Davy's doing that, at least. Sort of officially unofficial, if you know what I mean. He says the ME's office is going for the accident angle so his hands are kind of tied."

"Figures." Quill yawned. "Sorry. I can't believe I'm going to fall asleep in the middle of a murder investigation. Some detective I am."

"I can't think of any other detectives who have a baby to worry about," Dina said. "The little guy is so cute. You must have had a lot of fun last night."

"Yes," Quill said with some surprise. "I did. You said Davy's checked the Dumpsters?"

"Not personally. He called the guys at P and P Waste and Disposal and asked them to keep an eye out. I told him he needs to find a coil of wire cable with a radius of about four feet and a weight of about thirty pounds."

"You figured all that out from that little piece of wire?"

"It's just basic algebra. What? What's so funny?"

"Sometimes I forget that you're a doctoral candidate at one of the most prestigious schools in the country."

Dina wriggled her eyebrows. "I engage in a lot of protective coloration."

Somebody rapped on the office door and pushed it open.

"Marge!" Quill said. "Come in."

"Glad to see you two whooping it up." Marge sat down on the couch with a grunt. Quill knew this morning's pair of chinos were different from the ones she'd worn yesterday because the transparent plastic strip reading "size 14s 14s 14s 14s 14s" was still on the right leg. She leaned forward and pulled it free.

"D'ja get my message?" she demanded.

"I was just about to call you. Marge, look what Dina's discovered about the trip wire." Quill passed the photographs over. Marge went through them slowly. Then she turned the plastic bag over and over in her fingers as Dina explained the meaning of the evidence. "I'll be. Tell you what, Dina. When I get my insurance agency back from Charley Comstock, I want to hire you as an adjuster. This is damn good work."

"Thank you, Marge," Dina said demurely.

Marge tossed the package onto the tabletop. "Kind of wire you can pick up at any good hardware store in the county," she said. "That's a kick in the knee. On the other hand, it's a pretty good-sized reel to just toss in the nearest Dumpster."

"Davy's on the lookout for it," Dina said.

"It's the only piece of real evidence we've got," Quill said in frustration. "Or rather, that we haven't got." Something Marge said struck her, and she said, "Hey! You're going to buy your insurance agency back from Charley Comstock?"

"I'm not going to buy it back," Marge said with a certain

grim satisfaction. "I'm going to get it back for free when he defaults on his payments to me."

Dina and Quill both leaned forward. "And he's going to default because?" Dina prompted.

"Because we're going to get him arrested for the murder of Zeke Kingsfield," Marge smacked her knees with both hands. "I did a little digging after I left our case conference yesterday . . ."

"Case conference?" Quill said.

"That's PI talk," Dina said.

"As opposed to cop talk," Quill said. "Got it. And what did you dig up, Marge?"

"It looks like our Charley is the front man for BFD. And danged if he wasn't going to be the one left holding the bag if the whole thing went and collapsed."

"You're kidding!" Quill said.

"Am I not?" Marge said. "He's the one that put up the four hundred grand."

"You mean *he's* the mysterious depositor?"

Marge looked blank.

"Well, you were the one that told me how odd it was of Charley to betray bank confidentiality. He didn't really break it. Just sort of bent it a little." She sat back. "Wow. Yesterday we were fishing around for one good motive. Now we've got three. I haven't had a chance to tell you what Lydia said." She briefed the other two on Lydia's revelation about Albert McWhirter.

"I'll tell you what we have to do now," Marge said. "We've got to find out where each one of those buggers was last night. And they've got to be able to prove it!"

"What if they can't?" Dina asked. "We still won't be able to pin the murder on them. We don't have any hard evidence."

"She's right, Marge. We still don't have anything that connects a perpetrator—any perpetrator—to the scene of the crime."

"Let's worry about that when we've narrowed the suspect pool down to one." Marge got up with the air of General Patton about to pay a duty visit to the MASH unit. "First one we tackle is my favorite. We're going to track down Charley Comstock and hang him up by his heels to find out where he was last night."

Dina looked somber. "Good luck, Quill. And you, too, Marge."

It wasn't hard to track Charley Comstock down at all. Unlike Marge, who relied on her cell phone and her answering machines for customer service, Charley had a live and chatty secretary.

"You walked right past him when you came in here," Arlene said. Charley had moved the offices of Marge Schmidt Casualty and Surety to a one-room office directly opposite Nickerson's Hardware. "He's over to the Croh Bar." Arlene took her eyeglasses off, breathed on them, and wiped the lenses clean with a tissue. "I know it's your place and all, Marge, but I wish you'd drag him on out of there. It's barely eleven in the morning and he's probably drunk as a skunk."

"Does he make a habit of going in to drink this early?" Quill asked.

Marge shook her head. "I would have heard about it by now. My guess is this started right about the time Zeke Kingsfield swanked into town." She darted a shrewd look at Arlene.

"You'd be right," Arlene agreed.

"If he's at the Croh Bar, at least it that makes it easy to find him," Quill said. "Thanks, Arlene. We'll walk right over."

As unprepossessing as it was, the Croh Bar was extremely profitable for Marge and her restaurant partner, Betty Hall. They'd picked it up when the original owner, Orville Croh, packed up and moved to a trailer park in north Florida. Although the place was now scrupulously clean, Marge had wisely left the original furnishings in place. A scarred and battered pine bar occupied the front third and met patrons as soon as they walked in. The remainder of the space consisted of booths with peeling red Naugahyde and a few battered tables and an odd assortment of chairs. Marge had replaced the red Mediterranean-style indoor-outdoor carpeting with a pattern as much like the old one as possible.

Charley wasn't hard to find. He sat on a barstool at the darkest end of the bar. He had a highball glass in front of him. As Marge and Quill walked in, he rapped the glass on the counter. The sound brought Betty Hall bustling in from the kitchen in the back. She was as gaunt as Marge was round, and as silent as Marge was loquacious. She was also the best diner-style cook in the whole of New York, or so Meg claimed. She raised her hand in greeting and poured Charley a good three inches from the bottle of bar Scotch. He didn't look up. Quill was certain he hadn't even registered their presence.

Betty screwed the cap back on the Scotch and replaced it beneath the bar. "I got my chili on for the lunch special," she said to Quill. "You want a cup?"

"Are you having some, Marge?"

"I've been up since five," Marge said. "And it's been a long time since breakfast. You bring us a coupla bowls, Bet."

Quill lingered a moment by the front door, waiting for her eyes to adjust to the dim light. "I've got a plan," she whispered. "We'll sit on either side of him, and then I'll sort of ease into asking Charley how well he knew Kingsfield, what a loss this will be to the real estate community, etcetera, etcetera."

"Mm-hm." Marge stamped to the end of the bar, hoisted herself onto the barstool to Charlie's right, and said, "Hey, Charley. I understand you got in way over your head with Zeke Kingsfield." She tapped his glass of Scotch. "Doesn't seem to me to be the best way to settle the problems you've got."

Charley lifted his head and regarded her with a listless eye. "Suits me down to the ground."

Quill took a seat on Charlie's other side.

"How are you, Quill?"

"Fine, thank you. And how is, is . . ." For a moment, Quill couldn't recall his wife's name. "Linda?" she said triumphantly.

"Put a lid on it, Quill," Marge said. "So how much are you in for, Comstock?"

"Me, personally? Four hundred grand. I pledged my 401k."

Marge said, unsympathetically, "That was stupid."

"No kidding."

"What about the rest of the investors?"

"Zeke brought in a group from New York. King's Key. They owned forty-nine percent." Charley lifted the glass to his mouth. Marge took it out of his hand and placed it out of reach.

"King's Key filed for bankruptcy under Chapter Seven yesterday afternoon," Marge said. "You're six kinds of an idiot, Charley. So tell me what happened after you discovered the folks at Gorgeous Gorges cashed their checks and there was nothing left in the BFD account except a bankrupt partner and you."

"I didn't believe it when Mark told me," Charley said with heat. "I mean, Zeke Kingsfield! Who would have thought it? Bastard left me holding the bag."

"It's not like he hasn't done it before," Marge said. "All you had to do was Google him. The newspapers are filled with stories like yours. They just don't make the headlines. So, did you decide to knock him off? Get a little of your own back?"

"Me?"

To Quill's ear, Charley sounded genuinely astounded.

"You," Marge said flatly. "I want to know where you were yesterday from five thirty until seven this morning."

Betty Hall emerged from the kitchen with three bowls of

chili balanced on one arm. She set the bowls, three spoons, and a pile of napkins in front of them. Quill discovered that her breakfast of yogurt and berries had left her feeling famished. "Try some of this, Charley," she said kindly. "You'll feel better."

"Kingsfield fell off a cliff," Charley said. "What are you talking about, me knocking him off?"

"This is the way I see it," Marge said. "You're in a world of hurt right now, pally. And you owe me a tidy sum of money for my agency. So you can expect a little bit of slack from me these next few months while you figure out how you're going to get back on your feet. Or you can lie to me about where you've been for the past eighteen hours. If you do that, I'll come down on you like a load of bricks."

Charley swallowed a spoonful of chili. "A big transfer of funds was supposed to come into the BFD account yesterday morning. Mark gave me a call about one o'clock. The money hadn't shown up, and by this time," he said bitterly, "every piece of trailer trash in Gorgeous Gorges had cashed their ten-thousand-dollar checks and the BFD account was headed toward a negative balance."

"All the funds were covered though, weren't they?" Quill asked.

"Yeah. Unless there are a couple of checks out there I haven't heard about. Anyhow, Mark wanted to know when we could expect the transfer. I called Zeke on his cell phone. He spun me some bullshit and hung up on me. Then Mark called me back." He eyed Marge with dislike. "I guess you'd been poking your nose in, Marge Schmidt. Asking questions. Getting everybody all churned up. Mark really started bearing down on me. Who were these guys with King's Key, blah blah blah. He found out about the bankruptcy filing around seven thirty, I guess. I was at choir practice. You saw me there. I went straight from choir practice to the bank. Mark had called this guy the OCC had recommended, what's his name? McWhirter. Anyhow, McWhirter's had some experience with Kingsfield before." Charley pushed the bowl of chili away. "He said it was no use crying over spilt milk. That I had to take steps to keep the trailer park people from coming after me and that I'd better get a lawyer. Once that jerkola Frazier figured out that I could be on the hook for the money, he started spouting off, too. It was one helluva mess."

"Will Frazier was with you?" Quill said.

"Yeah. Mark told McWhirter he should be hearing about all of this from the git-go. So McWhirter showed up with him." Charley shook his head. He half rose from the barstool and reached for his drink. Neither Marge nor Quill made an effort to stop him.

"And what time did the three of you get to the bank?"

"About eight fifteen. We broke up around one. Frazier dropped McWhirter off at the Inn. Me? I stopped in here until Betty kicked me out about two. She called the wife and the wife came and got me. Didn't figure I was fit to drive home."

Marge glowered at him. Then she glowered at Quill. "I can't believe this. Last night we had no motives and three suspects. Today we've got three motives and no suspects. What the hell?"

Quill started to laugh. "You have to admit, we're pretty lousy detectives, Marge. Oh, dear." She used a cocktail napkin to dry her eyes. "We have got to find that wire. Otherwise you're right. We're in the soup."

"We haven't got a snowball's chance in hell of finding that wire," Marge grumbled. "Hang on. Is that your cell phone ringing?"

Quill patted her skirt pocket, extracted her cell phone, and squinted at the teeny little screen. "It's Dina. Maybe she has some good news for us!" She flipped the phone open and put it to her ear. She closed it and put it back in her pocket without a word.

"What?" Marge demanded.

"It's Meg. She's been arrested."

Marge was temporarily stumped. "Arrested? Who arrested her?"

"Davy. Dina said he had to." Quill took two large swallows of chili and got off the barstool. "I've got to go bail her out. You want to come with me? Davy took her straight to the courthouse."

"It's Thursday," Marge said. "Howie's sitting in Justice Court. But what the heck did she get arrested for?"

Quill put five dollars on the counter for her chili. "She's claiming, Dina says, that it's a trumped-up charge."


"I want a lawyer," Meg demanded. "This is a totally trumped-up charge." She stood defiantly in front of the judge's bench in the small—but highly functional—village courthouse. Other than Howie Murchison, who was sitting on the bench, the room held four other people. Dina looked a little flustered. Davy Kiddermeister accompanied Meg. He was in full uniform with his sheriff's hat in his hand.

The fourth was a triumphant Carol Ann Spinoza.

Quill took a seat in the guest gallery, which was immediately behind the action.

She herself was not unfamiliar with the venue. It was a beautiful old room. The ceilings soared to the height of a diminutive cathedral. The walls were wainscoted in hickory. The finish on the wainscoting and the wide-planked oak floor had seen better days. The prosecutor's table on the right exactly matched the pine defense table on the right. The jury box was reminiscent of the choir pews in the Hemlock Falls Church of the Word of God, except that the seat covers were worn green corduroy instead of worn red velvet.

Howie Murchison was dressed in the unadorned black robe that had been the town justice's attire for more than 200 years. He looked down from the bench at Quill's sister. Howie was a kindly man in his midfifties, with a comfortable paunch, balding gray hair, and steel-rimmed spectacles that had a tendency to slip down his nose.

"You're certainly entitled to a lawyer, Meg," he said, "and the court will appoint one for you if you are unable to afford one yourself, as you know already from watching all those episodes of *Law and Order*. But let's see if we can't set the legal window dressing aside for a moment and see if we can settle this ex parte."

"That's outside the system, bozo," Meg said to Carol Ann. "Sure, that's fine with me."

"Does this mean she can get out of going to jail?" Carol Ann asked suspiciously.

"We can pursue that course if it's necessary," Howie said. He smacked the gavel on its rest and announced, "Court is adjourned." He took off his robe, moved from the bench to the witness stand, and said, "Now what seems to be the problem?"

"Vandalism and malicious mischief," Davy said.

Carol Ann shrieked triumphantly. "All this time it's been her! This person has been slaughtering Christmas lawn ornaments all over town. And I caught her red-handed!"

"Is this true, Meg?" Howie asked.

"Nope," Meg said. "It's a big, fat lie. And I want to countersue this person"—she jerked her thumb at Carol Ann—"for malicious mischief to my reputation."

Howie took his glasses off, pinched the bridge of his nose between his thumb and forefinger, and put his glasses back on again. "Okay. Let's start from the beginning."

"There have been several complaints about the destruction of inflatable lawn ornaments in the past three days," Davy said. "Mrs. Elmer Henry. Mr. Francis Findlay. And the principal of Hemlock Falls High School, Norm Pasquale. And Ms. Spinoza, here. All of these complaints have suffered losses in the amount of . . ." Davy paged through his notebook. "Approximately two hundred and twenty dollars each, give or take some change."

"Shot right through the heart, all of them!" Carol Ann said. "My Santa and his reindeer had died in a blaze of disgusting orange paint. And she's responsible!" She pointed her finger straight at Meg. Meg folded her arms underneath her slight bosom and said, "Baloney."

"What evidence do you have that Ms. Quilliam's behind this, Ms. Spinoza?"

"That!" Carol Anne shrieked. She grabbed the evidence bag from Davy and held Meg's paintball pistol up to view.

"That," Meg said, "was obtained illegally. Without a search warrant."

Howie sighed deeply.

Carol Ann scowled shrewishly. "I was up at the Inn this morning to inspect that very dangerous fence where poor Mr. Kingsfield met his death . . ."

". . . You're adding fence inspection to your general all-around nosiness, Carol Ann?" Meg said sweetly.

"And I stopped into the kitchen and there it was. Right in plain sight. I've been looking all over town for the paintball gun. And it was just like that story by Edgar Allan Poe. Right out there in plain sight."

"'The Purloined Letter'?" Howie said with interest. "Hm."

Quill sat upright, as if stung. She grabbed Marge's arm.

"Ow! What the heck, Quill?"

"The wire!" she whispered. "The wire, Marge! It's right in the shed!"

# CHAPTER 12

"I can't believe that *you* believed that little stinkpot Carol Ann," Meg fumed. "And I can't believe you paid her off."

"Did you shoot those Santa Clauses?" Quill demanded. She, Marge, Dina, and Meg had all piled into Quill's Honda the minute after Howie had the vandalism charges dismissed. Quill gunned the little car up the hill, fishtailing a little in the slush.

"Of course I did. In any other civilized country there'd be a fine for *owning* the ugly things. In this country I have to pay for getting rid of them. Not to mention the community service. Phooey."

"I always thought they were kind of cute," Dina said. "I like the ones with the big huge ball and the skaters. I wonder how they get it to snow inside."

Meg rolled her eyes. "I believe that they're actually banned in Canada."

"Count yourself lucky Carol Ann didn't press charges," Marge said. "You'd find yourself with a nice little criminal record."

Quill pulled the Honda to a stop in front of the Inn's tool-shed. "And we didn't pay her off. We made restitution." She and the others got out of the car. Quill looked down the driveway for Davy's squad car. "He said he'd be right up. What do you suppose is keeping him?"

"Carol Ann," Dina said darkly, "that cradle robber. You should have seen the way she was sucking up to him at the police station."

"Here he is." Marge stepped back as Davy came up the drive. He had one of the uniforms with him, Norm Pasquale's oldest son, Tony. Davy rolled down the driver's window and considered the toolshed.

"Took your time," Marge said. "And you're takin' your time now."

Davy looked up at her. "You think the wire that was stretched across the ski trail's in here?"

"It has to be," Quill said. "How much time did the murderer have to dispose of it before Mike found the body? Zeke went out to ski as soon as it got light, around seven. Lydia tried to raise him on the cell phone at seven thirty. Mike found him fifteen minutes later. It takes twenty to forty minutes to reach that point in the ski trail from the Inn. Your men have searched the grounds and the woods. And Davy, the thing is large. Dina calculated the size. It's a hard thing to get rid of."

Quill threw open the shed door. The coil of cable stood against the wall, just inside the door. As Dina had predicted, it was at least four feet high.

"There's a light," Quill said. She turned it on.

"Just step back, please," Davy said a little testily. "Tony? You have that garbage bag?"

The two of them pulled on latex gloves, then carefully maneuvered the coil of cable into the garbage bag. They stowed it in the trunk of the squad car. "Okay," Davy said, "that's it. Tony will drop this off at the forensics lab in Syracuse. We'll take it from here."

"You'll let us know if there's anything unusual about it?" Quill said hopefully.

"I can't make any promises." Davy got back into the squad car and rolled the window partway up again. "Quill?" he said. "Even if nothing comes of this, I appreciate the fact that you called me in rather than taking things into your own hands." He put the car into gear. "Ladies? We'll be in touch."

Quill waved farewell to them. She waited until the car disappeared around the bend before she stepped into the shed.

"It'll be days before we hear anything," Dina said fretfully, following her. "What if we're wrong? What if it doesn't have a thing to do with the murder?"

"It has to do with the murder," Quill said. "Look at this."

Meg crowded against her shoulder. Quill was on her knees at the spot where the coil had rested against the shed wall. "That's glitter!" Meg exclaimed. "That's the same kind of glitter Benny used in the elf costumes!"

"Yes,' Quill said soberly. "It's one of Zeke's inner circle after all." She got to her feet and brushed her skirt free of the dirt from the floor. She stood still for a long moment, trying to get her thoughts in order. "But which one?"

"But everyone of Zeke's inner circle, as you call it, was in the kitchen on that shoot from five until well after the snow stopped falling," Meg said. "I would have noticed if someone had slipped out."

"Would you? With five people dressed exactly alike roaming around the kitchen with no particular place to go? It happened right under our noses. One of the elves slipped out during the shoot last night, passed me in the woods coming up the slope and socked me in the head, moved the six-by-six piece of lumber in place, and loosened the fence post. It couldn't have taken more than twenty minutes, at best. And they were all in costume, so pinning down who was where with eyewitness testimony is absolutely impossible. You were in the kitchen the whole time, Meg. Do you remember anyone going missing?"

"I was cooking!" Meg said indignantly.

"Pretty ingenious," Marge said. "You had the murderer in plain sight all along."

"There's a slim chance that Ajit noticed the missing person. And the other three might have seen something and not put it together until Zeke was found dead. Melissa was the likeliest one to say something, but she'd run away from Hemlock Falls by then. She may not know that Zeke is dead."

"Or if she does, she may be afraid to come back," Dina said soberly.

"Perhaps," Quill said. "And there's no good reason for any one of the *Good Taste* crew to turn the murderer in. Each one of them had an excellent reason for wanting Zeke gone. He was about to destroy the quality of the show. Benny's very ill, as you can see just by looking at him. His chances of getting a new job if the show folds are nonexistent. And Benny's the bright light in that relationship. If the show is a disaster, and Benny unemployable, what sort of job will Bernie be qualified for?"

"What about LaToya? She was Zeke's girlfriend," Marge said. "Although she may have slept with him without liking him much. I've heard of stuff like that happening before."

"Or maybe she's just loyal to the others," Dina said. "I think I might be."

Quill shook her head. "We may never know for sure. La-Toya's been embarrassed on national television. She was promised a responsible job in one of Zeke's companies, and here she is working as an assistant on a cable food show. I doubt there's any love lost between her and Zeke. That's a pretty tight group."

"You'd think one of them might have told Lydia, though," Marge said.

Quill looked at her. Marge was a pretty shrewd judge of human nature. "That's more than possible. But Lydia stands to lose a pile of insurance money if Zeke's death is ruled a murder and not an accident. If she does know anything, don't you think she would have come forward by now? I don't think we can count on anyone giving evidence. Unless we put on the right kind of pressure."

"So what do we do now?" Dina asked.

Quill tugged at the curl over her left ear. "There has to be some proof. Some evidence of who was where."

"The tape?" Dina guessed. "The tape of the dancing elves?"

"Fat chance," Meg said. "It's just feet. We've all peeked at Ajit's monitor while the show's being taped. I know I have. Quill has, too. I watched her watch it."

"Feet!" Quill said. "Oh my. Oh my. Feet!"

So that was it.

"What?!" Meg said.

"She knows who did it!" Dina shrieked.

"You're kidding me," Marge said. "You know who did it because of feet?"

Quill took a deep breath. She looked at her watch. "It's noon. Everybody's at the Resort getting massages. There might be a way. But we need Doreen and the housemaids to do it. And it's really, really risky. And I need to talk to Howie Murchison before I do anything at all."

"Fabulous dinner, sweetie." Benny drained the last of the cappuccino. "You're a genius with lamb, Meg. A positive genius."

"We should consider it for the spring show," Lydia said. "I mean, lamb, asparagus, new peas, young lettuce. Classic. Simple. Brilliant." She tapped a few notes into her Black-Berry. "The mint chutney in particular, Meg. It's wonderful. I think it should be part of the product debut. And we certainly want to spotlight it on the spring show."

Meg had prepared the first of ten menus she'd selected as candidates for the *Good Taste* program. It was for the debut program, in the spring, and she'd gone to a great deal of trouble to get fresh ingredients shipped in and taken her time over the meal itself.

Quill hadn't said much during dinner—which had been spectacular. She was preoccupied with the very risky chance she was going to take.

Did she have a choice? There was no way to bring Davy and the sheriff's department in on this, not legally. And Howie had been very clear about the scarcity of evidence. It was almost certain that the murderer would go free even if what Quill was about to do actually worked.

Doreen had grasped the problem immediately. She'd turned Caleb over to Quill for the afternoon and gone to work. Quill looked at her watch. Past nine o'clock, and the dining room was almost empty except for the *Good Taste* party. Caleb was asleep in his crib upstairs, under Dina's watchful eye. And Doreen still hadn't signaled her yet.

"We've been neglecting meringue," Lydia said. She poked her spoon delicately into the remains of the dessert. "I have to admit, Meg. This is a work of near genius, just like the chutney. Do you have a name for it?"

"Christmas Angel," Meg said a little doubtfully. "I'm not very good at that part of menu planning. Names, I mean. But it's a meringue whipped with peppermint. I was afraid the peppermint chocolate mousse in the middle might overwhelm it."

"The only thing it overwhelms is me," Bernie said blissfully. "It's perfect."

"I have to agree," LaToya said. "Although if you ditched the mousse, it'd be a terrific dessert for anybody with an eye on the scale. Like me."

"Exactly," Benny said enthusiastically. "Now, if you'd given me much more than a demitasse-full, it would have been too much, given the delicate nature of my digestive system. And think of the changes we can ring on this. I love the idea of flavored meringue. I can see a whole show designed around flavored meringues.

"Is there any reason why the meringues have to be sweet?" Ajit asked. "Eggs whites are neutral. Why not curry-flavored meringues? Or dill?"

Lydia's eyes glowed. "Now *this*," she said with excitement, "is exactly what I was hoping would happen with the show. Innovation. Creativity. Food used in ways it hasn't been used before. Isn't this wonderful, Meg?"

Meg glanced at Quill. "Yes," she said dryly. "It is."

"Are we boring you, Quill?" Lydia asked somewhat acidly. "You keep staring off in the distance." She turned around and followed Quill's gaze. "Your foyer is just as overdecorated as it was the day before yesterday. Oh. There's your whosis. Your housekeeper. She's waving at you like mad."

Doreen gave Quill an abrupt nod.

Quill took a deep, shaky breath. It was now or never. "Everybody? I've arranged for liqueurs in the conference room. Would you all come along with me?" She rose from the table. Except for Lydia, the others got automatically to their feet. Quill waited. With a snort of exasperation, Lydia pushed herself away from the table and got up. "Lay on, Macduff."

"The conference room?" LaToya said. "What about the Tavern Lounge? It's so cozy there. So Christmassy with that big tree in the corner and the pine scent in the air and the fire burning cheerily away. I love it."

"Have you noticed," Benny whispered to Quill as they trooped down the hall, "how cheerful everyone is now that you-know-who is out of the picture?"

"Yes," Quill said. As she passed Doreen, she gave her hand a brief squeeze. "I have."

A few moments later, she opened the door to the conference room and stepped aside so that they all could file in.

"You have our monitor in here," Ajit said with displeasure.

"Yes," Quill said. "I have to apologize for taking it without telling you. But I discovered that your tape wouldn't work in our machine. The commercial equipment is quite different."

"I would really prefer that you not borrow my equipment," he said testily. "And what tape are you talking about?"

Kathleen and Nate had set up an array of brandies and liqueurs on a trolley under the whiteboard and set out crystal and napkins at seven chairs. Quill waited until everyone was seated, then wheeled the trolley around to let everyone serve themselves.

She turned the video monitor on, and then faced them all. "Zeke Kingsfield was murdered this morning. This was a clever murder, committed by an organized person with a great deal of daring. But it was a murder."

No one else noticed Davy and Nate slip into the back of the room.

"Sometime just before seven thirty last night, this person left the kitchen by the back door and went outside to set a trap on the ski trail. The Christmas lights illuminate the field that lies between the Inn and the drop over the gorge, so this person went over the rise and into the woods that lead down to the gorge; it was here that this person ran into me. I was stunned. The killer continued on to the drop. The six-by-six log was rolled into place. The fence post was rocked back and forth to loosen it still further, and Zeke's killer returned to the Inn undetected.

"Except for one important clue."

Quill looked into a sea of staring faces. At the door to the conference room, Nate and Davy stood with their arms folded.

Dina's photographs lay on the trolley in a manila envelope. Quill took them out one by one and held them up. "The next morning, the killer returned to the drop, strung a cable between the loosened fence post and this tree, and waited for Zeke to come around the bend at a pretty good clip. He tripped on the tree trunk and fell into the wire. The impact was enough to tear the post out of the ground completely and he fell heavily into the chain-link fence.

"Did Zeke fall to his death as he spun out of control? Or did the killer push him over the edge as he lay stunned in the snow? We'll never know for certain. I'd lay odds, however, that the killer provided the last bit of assistance needed to assure Zeke's death. The killer returned to the Inn, leaving the wire in the same place it'd been found. It was a perfect crime.

"Except for another important clue."

Quill flipped the video monitor on. "This is the tape of the dancing elves Ajit laid down yesterday morning. It's hard to tell who is who, isn't it? All we know is that the feet belong to LaToya, Bernie, and Melissa Smith."

Quill fast-forwarded. "And this is the tape Ajit laid down after dinner. Look at the feet. See the shoes on the left? They don't fit. This elf has unusually tiny feet. Now, Melissa Smith left the Inn late yesterday afternoon taking everything with her but her elf costume and her baby."

Quill switched the tape recorder off. "Shall we check to see who among us has a size-five shoe? It's you, Lydia. You didn't go to Syracuse with Zeke last night. You stayed here."

"That's absurd," Lydia said hoarsely.

"And here is the ski tag that was caught in the cable as the murderer detached it from the tree and wound it up. It's from your jacket, Lydia." Quill held it up. "It's only half of the tag. The other half is on your silver jacket." Quill looked at the other faces around the table. "It's absurd to think that none of you suspected that it was Lydia under that clown makeup and belled hat and not Melissa Smith. It was a safe bet that no one in Meg's kitchen would mark the difference. It was too chaotic. The costumes were exactly alike. The gentleman behind you," Quill continued in a conversational way, "is Sheriff Kiddermeister. Sheriff, what's the penalty for an accessory to premeditated murder in New York State?"

"Lethal injection," Davy said tonelessly.

"No!" Ajit exploded. "That's too much to ask of anyone, Lydia. I will not keep quiet anymore. Of course I knew that Lydia had taken Melissa's place."

Lydia leaped to her feet, her lips drawn back over her teeth. She hissed like a cat at bay. Ajit stood up slowly, both hands held out, palms up, as if in supplication. "It's too much to ask of me," he repeated quietly.

Quill looked from Ajit's handsome, perfectly proportioned face to Lydia and back again. "The two of you aren't having an affair," she said. "It isn't that. So what is it?"

"To tell you the truth," Benny said. "I knew it was Lydia, too." He raised an eyebrow in Bernie's direction. His partner ran his hands over his face, then nodded, resignedly.

"You *all* knew about this?!" Davy asked. "You were going to let her get away with murder?"

"Zeke'd been getting away with murder for years," Bernie said wryly. "It only seemed fair."

Davy looked revolted. Quill felt revolted, too.

"He was disgusting," Lydia said.

Quill, looking at her, was struck with a sudden hallucination. It wasn't Lydia standing there. It was a huge snake. Coiled, head drawn back to strike.

"Disgusting," Lydia said, her voice sibilant. "He was a blot. That cocky smugness. That arrogance. That oily self-regard. You only had to look at him to want to smash his head like a rotten pumpkin. He polluted everything. Ruined everything. All he had to do was touch it, and it was tainted, destroyed. That hundred-pound thumb of his on my magazine was the last straw. I did the world a goddam service."

It was, Quill thought, the first time she'd come across that particular motive for murder: Zeke Kingsfield just didn't fit into Lydia's elegant design.


"You don't think I've done enough community service by tracking down and capturing a murderer?"

Meg looked so pathetic Quill's heart was wrung. She patted her sister consolingly. "It could be worse. Howie could have sentenced you to salting municipal parking lots instead

197

of a couple of hours out with the Hemlock Falls Chamber of Commerce caroling group."

"At least Harvey dropped the Angel-ettes idea," Meg muttered. "I suppose I should be thankful for small mercies."

"You should be just as thankful that I'm going to be noble and spare your feelings. I am *not* going to remind you that I'm the one that tracked down and captured the murderer."

"And I'm going to be equally noble and *not* say that getting Lydia Kingsfield hauled off to the pokey means we're going to go bankrupt for sure."

"No, we won't. There's a bit of a hitch in our proceedings that's true. But the leasing agreement is still in place, and we're still going to get a check every month from Kingsfield Publishing, so we'll manage."

"What about him?" Meg rolled her eyes in Albert McWhirter's direction. He stood gravely next to Mark Anthony Jefferson, his knitted hat placed precisely on top of his head. His gaze met Quill's. He looked very tired. It had been four days since Melissa's disappearance. Caleb's fate was hanging over them all.

"I don't know," Quill said truthfully. She looked down at Caleb, who was tucked safely next to her in the pew. Her beautiful borrowed baby. "It's Christmas Eve, Meg, and Albert's let Caleb stay with us for now. I'm just going to trust that this all turns out for the best." Quill adjusted the knitted cap on Meg's head. The cap was one of twenty knitted by the Hemlock Falls Ladies Auxiliary. The wool was a sprightly combination of red and green and stitched across the front of each one was the legend: H. F. CAROLERS. Meg's hat was missing an L.

"Are you ready, Meg?"

"I suppose so. You know that I sing off-key. Harvey thinks I'm doing it on purpose."

Quill gestured at the rest of the singers. "It's the spirit that counts."

It was Christmas Eve, and twenty of the twenty-four members of the Chamber of Commerce were assembled at the Hemlock Falls Church of the Word of God. Adela Henry was passing out the rest of the knitted hats (and accepting the compliments on them as her due). Dookie and his wife, Wendy, each held flutes. Howie Murchison carried a guitar, and Miriam, with one hand on his coat sleeve in a proprietary way, carried a tambourine. Outside, the snow had started to fall in big, fat flakes.

Harvey clapped his hands together and said, "Carolers! Are you ready?! Let's all line up at the door. The bus is warmed up and ready!"

Quill tucked Caleb in the baby carryall at her breast, and checked that he was well wrapped up against the cold. His lamb was clutched in one tiny fist. Quill had tied a red-and-green plaid ribbon around its neck. He waved the lamb with a chortle, then gummed the ribbon with a contented squeal.

Marge, Dina, and Doreen edged their way through the crowd toward them. Dina bent and stroked Caleb's cheek, "And how's Mr. Cutie this evening?"

"Gah!" Caleb said.

It took some time for the hopeful carolers to sort themselves out, get into line, and trickle onto the bus. Quill and Meg were near the back, Caleb between them. Albert took the seat ahead of them and sat alone, staring out the window. Marge and Harland sat across the aisle, and Dina sat shoulder to shoulder with Doreen.

"Well, at least you didn't end up with the flu," Meg said philosophically. "And Ajit's going to run the *Good Taste* show past the new editor of *L'Aperitif*, who, as it turns out, is the old editor, Lally Preston, so there's a chance she'll at least consider it. So I suppose it's not such a terrible Christmas after all."

"Really?" Quill said. The snow on the window blurred the Christmas lights of Hemlock Falls to a celestial blur of color. Beside her, Caleb crooned to himself. "It seems a little sad to me."

Harvey, his knitted cap rakishly askew over his ear, strode up the aisle, a pitch pipe in his hand. "People! Our first stop is the Gorgeous Gorges trailer park. We're going to bring some Christmas cheer to those poor souls."

"Wonderful," Meg muttered. "What are the chances that if they recognize Marge and the two of us; they'll dump eggnog all over our heads? I mean, we're the ones that put the kibosh on their million-dollar jackpot finally and forever."

Quill made a small movement of protest.

Harvey skidded to a halt beside their seat. "Meg!" he said accusingly.

"The very same," she said agreeably.

"I've changed my mind about you humming instead of singing. You go right ahead and sing."

"Thank you, Harvey." She smiled impishly at him. "Merry Christmas!"

"And Merry Christmas to you." He clapped his hands. "People! Let's limber those voices up!" He blew into the pitch pipe. "Let's have a nice, upbeat version of 'Jingle Bells.'"

"Gah," Caleb said.

This was followed by "Santa Claus Is Comin' to Town." On the second verse of "Frosty the Snowman," the bus bumped down the end of the path to the Gorgeous Gorges trailer park and came to a halt, and the choristers, for the most part, were in a merry mood. They all filed out of the bus and lined up in front of the single-wide trailer marked OFFICE. Caleb waved a delighted fist at the inflatable Santa's workshop.

"I see these ornaments escaped the Christmas massacre," Adela said as she passed by them. "Huh!" She stopped at the sight of the baby in Quill's arms. "Well," she said. "And who's this then? Who's the nicest little baby?" She patted his head.

"Would you mind if I held him a bit?" Albert said shyly at Quill's elbow.

"Of course not," Quill said. "You're his grandfather, after

all." She extricated Caleb from the carryall. "Here, cup your right hand under his head and your left under his bottom."

Albert held him, but the expression on his face was so terrified, that Quill laughed despite herself. "Just think of how warm and solid he is," she suggested. "Think of how safe you want him to be."

Albert relaxed a little. He looked down at the baby tenderly.

"You seem an old hand at this, Quill," Adela said with heavy jocularity. "You sure you don't have another one of these at home?"

Quill blinked at her. "What?"

"I said, are you sure you don't have another one of these . . ."

"Yes," Quill said. "Yes, I heard you." She clutched at Meg's arm. "Meg? Meg!"

"Not now, Quill. We're getting ready to sing."

"People!" Harvey shouted. "I want you all to line up in three rows now. Shortest singers in front. Tallest singers in back! First carol is: 'We Wish You a Merry Christmas!' "

As the voices rang out, twenty strong and accompanied by guitar, flute, and tambourine, the doors to the trailers of Gorgeous Gorges opened up and the residents came out to listen. Will Frazier stamped down the path to the circle of lawn where the singers stood and joined in. The large blonde with the curlers and the pink bunny slippers came out with a tin of cookies in her hand. The Mexican family from number 43 came out with mariachis, a stack of paper cups, and a large pitcher that sent steam into the air.

And from number 36, Mrs. Huston came out. She was well wrapped in a down coat.

There was a slight, brown-haired figure at her side.

Meg saw her before Quill did. "Oh, my," she whispered. "Oh, gosh." She took her sister's hand and held it.

"Melissa," Quill said. She closed her eyes against the sudden tears and bit her lip, hard. "She was with Mrs. Huston all the time. Some detectives we are. We should have guessed."

Meg didn't say a word, just held Quill's hand all the tighter. And she was the one who tugged at Albert McWhirter's sleeve and pushed him toward his daughter.

"Well, that wasn't too bad, as community service stints go," Meg said cheerfully. She swung her feet up on the oak chest that Quill used as a coffee table. "And Myles said he'll be home when?"

"A couple of hours," Quill's voice was muffled by the bathroom door. "Maybe you could give me a hand picking up?"

"Sure thing." Meg set her glass of eggnog down and began to pick up the scattered toys, stuffed animals, and baby bottles. "That stuff you picked up at the drugstore make your stomach feel any better?"

"Nope." Quill emerged from the bedroom.

"Oh, that's a shame. What do you want to do with all this baby stuff? Do you think Melissa and her dad can use it?"

"Nope."

Meg turned to look at her. She set a box of Pampers down. "My goodness, Quill. You look ecstatic."

"All this baby stuff?" Quill opened her arms. "I should have known I'm too young to have an ulcer. We can't give away that baby stuff. We're going to need it."

# QUILL
# CHRISTMAS PI

Meg and Quill are exceptionally fond of the h———but the decorations present a challenge. The smallest ——e at the Inn is fifteen feet high, and the ornaments need to be as impressive if they aren't to be lost in the greenery. This year, Quill purchased foam blocks to create a hanging village. You can do it, too.

At a craft store, purchase foam blocks in graduated sizes: eight inches, six inches, and four inches. Purchase cones in twelve-inch, eight-inch, and six-inch sizes.

Stack the blocks to form two-story houses, with the smaller blocks on top. To create a church, place a six-inch cone on top of a stack of blocks. Use cones with a small glass ornament on top to create the three kings. If you are adept with an X-Acto knife, purchase the heavy green foam that is used by florists and carve angels, animals, and other figures. Let your imagination run free.

Wrap the blocks and cones in luxurious fabric, such as satin, velvet, or taffeta, just as you would wrap a Christmas package. Cut the fabric to size first, do a trial run to see that the blocks are covered, then glue in place with a glue gun. If you are covering animal or angel ornaments, wrap the entire figure in ribbon, and glue in place with a glue gun.

Let the ornaments dry overnight. Then trim the ornaments with fanciful and elegant ribbons, fake jewels, gold lace doilies, fur trim, sequins, and gold wire.

Using short lengths of picture wire, affix hooks to the tops of the ornaments.

# MEG'S CHRISTMAS DELIGHTS

## JOY ON A CLOUD

### MERINGUES

> 6 egg whites
> Pinch cream of tartar
> 1 tablespoon sugar

Whip the egg whites until they stand up in peaks. Add sugar and cream of tartar as the egg whites begin to stiffen. Drop a large spoonful of egg white onto an ungreased cookie sheet. Shape into flat clouds with a spatula. Put a depression in the middle with the bowl of a large spoon. Bake in a 250-degree oven for about an hour. Meringues should be dry and hollow to the touch.

### CHOCOLATE MOUSSE

> 8 egg whites
> 1½ pounds semisweet chocolate
> 4 egg yolks, beaten
> ½ cup sugar
> ½ cup very strong coffee
> ¼ cup Grand Marnier
> 1 cup heavy whipping cream

Melt chocolate over low heat on stove. Add warmed coffee, stirring carefully until chocolate is glossy. Add beaten egg yolks, stirring carefully until chocolate is glossy. Remove chocolate from heat, and stir in brandy until chocolate is glossy. Let mixture stand until tepid.

Whip egg whites to a glossy peak.

Whip heavy cream to peaks and add sugar.

By this time, the chocolate should be tepid to the touch. Using a very large bowl, fold all three mixtures together. Using a wide rubber spatula, turn the mixtures over and over carefully until blended. Chill for four hours.

Spoon mousse into the centers of the meringues.

# THE ANGEL'S KISS COOKIE

*1 cup butter at room temperature*
*1 cup ground almonds*
*2 cups powdered (confectioner's) sugar*

Blend with hands until very well mixed. Shape into plump pillows and place on an ungreased baking sheet. Bake in a 350-degree oven for ten minutes. While warm, sprinkle with confectioner's sugar and add a small slice of maraschino cherry to the top. Let cool. Cookies will be crisp and chewy.

# MEG'S MINT CHUTNEY

*1 cup red wine vinegar*
*6 firm pears, peeled and sliced*
*½ cup raisins*
*1 cup sugar*
*Handful of green peppercorns*
*2 tablespoons cardamom*
*1 handful chopped fresh mint*

Boil the vinegar and sugar. Reduce heat to medium. Add the pears. Add the peppercorns, raisins, and cardamom. Cook until thickened, about twenty minutes. Stir in the mint leaves. Let cool. Refrigerate for at least twenty-four hours to let the mint infuse the chutney.

**CLAUDIA BISHOP** is the author of fourteen previous novels in the Hemlock Falls Mystery series. She is at work on the third mystery novel in her new series, The Casebooks of Dr. McKenzie. She is the senior editor of three well-received mystery anthologies, including the musical mystery collection *A Merry Band of Murderers.*

As Mary Stanton, she is the author of eleven books for middle-grade readers and two well-regarded fantasy novels for adults. She will debut an exciting new classic fantasy in 2008, currently titled *The Beaufort Files.*

Claudia divides her time between a small home in West Palm Beach, Florida, and a goat farm in upstate New York. She can be reached through her website, claudiabishop.com.